THE
Prospector's
ONLY
PROSPECT

THE
Prospector's
ONLY
PROSPECT

USA TODAY BESTSELLING AUTHOR
DANI COLLINS

Entangled Publishing, LLC
644 Shrewsbury Commons Ave., STE 181
Shrewsbury, PA 17361
Visit our website at www.entangledpublishing.com.

Amara is an imprint of Entangled Publishing, LLC.

Edited by Lydia Sharp and Liz Pelletier
Cover design and art by Bree Archer
Stock art by The Killion Group and
ImagineGolf/Gettyimages
Interior design by Toni Kerr

Print ISBN 978-1-64937-341-0
ebook ISBN 978-1-64937-342-7

Manufactured in the United States of America

First Edition April 2023

AMARA

To the L's who made this happen—Liz, Louise, and especially Lydia for her brilliant editing. Also to my daughter, Lainey, who is an amazing critique partner. Honorable mention to DougLas and SamueL for their patience and cheerleading. It takes a village to create a fictional mining camp. My biggest, warmest thanks to each and every one of you!

CHAPTER ONE

DENVER CITY, TERRITORY OF KANSAS, JULY 13, 1859

After eight days of steady travel, every bone in Marigold Davis's body creaked when she stepped down from the stagecoach. She was rattled and rumpled and no doubt smelled of her fellow travelers' cigars, which at least disguised her lack of a recent bath.

The Leavenworth City & Pike's Peak Express Company had touted itself as "tremendously comfortable," but that was a gross overstatement. Perhaps it wasn't their fault that any carriage ride longer than an hour made her sick, but the drunken mule driver, the windstorm that had left her blowing into her gloves to warm her hands, and the mosquito swarms that had pocked her face with bites hadn't helped.

The few hours she'd been offered a bed, she hadn't dared fall asleep, not with only a muslin wall to protect her from the soldiers and waystation handlers who'd never taken their eyes off her. And the little food she'd managed to eat at those places had been difficult to choke down and *keep* down.

She was unfit for a coffin, let alone an introduction to her prospective bridegroom.

For a time, she had thought she might be dead. The first days of limitless nothing had had her edging toward prairie fever. She'd been saved by her glimpse of bison, but soon the land had begun to roll even more than her stomach. She had finally arrived in Denver, and a fresh knot of anxiety formed in her belly over what might await her. Based on recent experience, resounding disappointment, most likely.

As men hurried to help with unloading, she stepped out of the way, hugging her carpetbag as much for comfort as from fear of losing it. It was third-hand and threadbare, but all she possessed.

Her only family, her sister and uncle, had been left behind. The sheer isolation of this new place hit like a kick to the face.

Marigold pressed her back to the exterior wall of the Express office while she got her bearings.

Dear Pearl, she mentally composed to her sister. *The frontier optimism continues unabated in Denver "City."*

What a joke that word was. She couldn't see one cobbled street or painted storefront or even a single cherry tree, despite her research telling her Denver had been founded on the banks of Cherry Creek. All she saw was chaos and wagons and a sawmill at the river that seemed to have started more structures than it had finished. If roads were laid out, the buildings were placed too sparsely on the trampled, muddy ground to tell.

Across the creek lay the slightly more robust settlement of Auraria, but it was also a hodgepodge of shops, shanty shacks, sod huts, tents, wagons, and teepees. Like this side, some of the homes were in proper rows with fences marking the borders of the homestead. One had several lines of denim trousers and gray shirts, so she supposed it was a laundry

service. She could hear the faint ring of a black-
smith's hammer and the bark of a dog, but otherwise,
she was surrounded by men and horses and the funk
of manure.

She didn't see women of any description.

And there, beyond the South Platte that Cherry
Creek flowed into, rose the muscled peaks of the
Rocky Mountains. They were so imposing, they
seemed to compress the breath out of her.

She had longed to see mountains again. It had
been the one glimmer of anticipation that had kept
her spirits up while she'd endured this journey. The
Rockies weren't like the Appalachians, though.
There were no soft green wrinkles and folds that had
bunched around her like a comforting blanket when
she'd been a child in Bedford, Pennsylvania.

These were sharp, broken teeth, craggy and hewn
and forbidding as they shot upward above the tree
line and attempted to tear holes in the silk-blue sky.

I should have stayed in Topeka.

She'd had nowhere to stay there, though. No
place that was safe. No place that wanted her. It was
the story of her life to hear the words, *You can't stay
here.*

"Lady, are you waiting for mail? If not, move
away from the window."

She glanced at the wiry man wearing filthy
clothes and muddy boots. His eyes were bright beads
in a face of scraggly gray whiskers and brows. Men
who looked equally disreputable were gathering
behind him.

She moved to enter the Express office, but an
employee barred her.

"We close while we sort the mail," he told her.

"I only want to—"

He closed the door in her face.

"—wait for my party out of the wind." Marigold bit back a huff. She wasn't a timid woman, but after four years of her uncle's politics getting them into confrontations of ever more serious natures, she'd learned that even the battles worth fighting could leave you standing in the rain at midnight while your home went up in flames.

Turning from the door, she looked for a place to sit. Not here. Danger scented the air. The line of men continued to grow, and she knew it was only a matter of time before—

"Hey, lady. Are you married? You want a husband?"

"Looking for the cathouse? I'll show you where it is."

"What's that you're wearing?"

Oh, these infernal bloomers.

Marigold sent a dismissive smile toward the men. "I'm waiting for someone."

"Who?"

"Mr. Virgil Gardner." She didn't know what she would do if she had missed catching him. She didn't have money for a boarding house.

"You're his bride?" A series of grimaces and skeptical brows rippled across their faces. It was a collective *Yeesh* that wasn't the least bit encouraging.

Before she could say, *Not exactly*, she heard her status as his bride being relayed over one shoulder to another, down the line. Men even stepped out to look.

"*Her*?" More brows wrinkled as they stared unabashedly. "Huh."

The man closest to the mail window rapped on the glass and called through it, pointing. "That's her. That's Gardner's bride."

The mail window screeched open. The clerk who'd closed the door on her poked his head out.

"*You're* Pearl Martin?" He frowned at her bedraggled appearance. "He said you'd send a letter to tell him when you would arrive." He snapped his fingers at the men. "A dollar to fetch Gardner. His wagon's at Pollock's, but try the saloons."

"I'll do it." A less-than-spry man of sixty-odd years took off in a hitching trot.

Marigold opened her mouth to correct their assumption that she was Pearl but shut it again, saving her breath for the man who had written, *I enclose a prepaid ticket on the Express. You'll find me to be a fair, respectful man to all but liars, cheats, and thieves.*

• • •

"Do you drink out of your own barrels?" Virgil Gardner asked Cecil Dudley, keeper of the Dudley Saloon.

"It's not what your men are drinking. It's how much," Cecil insisted, mustache quivering uncertainly.

"The hell it is." Virgil leaned his arm on the bar top. Like the floor, the surface was gummy as a sugar birch in spring, but he ignored it and dipped his chin to level Cecil one of his most intimidating stares. "I know the difference between a hangover from too much whiskey and gut rot from moonshine. I don't care how you turn a profit, Ceese, unless it interferes with how *I* turn a profit. If you poison my men again, you and I will talk further." Virgil found it best to be vague with his threats. It kept him from having to follow through on things he didn't really want to do.

As perspiration broke out on Cecil's brow, someone burst into the saloon, calling out, "Is Virgil Gardner here?"

Virgil slowly turned his head, keeping one eye on Cecil. Fear had its uses, but it made men do stupid things.

"I'm here, Skip." He recognized the old-timer as one of the men who had worked for them in Quail's Creek between prospecting his own claims.

"*She's* here." Skip took a few limping paces toward him.

She? There could only be one *she* looking for him.

"Miss Martin?"

Skip nodded proudly, as if he'd been the one to arrange her arrival himself.

Well, wasn't that as convenient as rain after planting? Virgil had written that he came to Denver City every second Wednesday for supplies, but he had thought she would write to tell him when to expect her, not just show up. It would seem that Pearl Martin was as "cheerfully accommodating" as she'd promised. That boded well for their future.

Virgil sniffed the whiskey Cecil had poured him from the bottle labeled Real Kentucky Bourbon before he knocked it back. He hissed out the burn.

"That's what I want you to serve my men when

they come in, not whatever you and the missus cook up in the shed."

"We're still getting the hang of it," Cecil muttered, sniffing the bottle.

Virgil dropped his foot off the rail and shifted to see his reflection in the cloudy glass behind the bar. He smoothed his hair and resettled his hat on his head. There wasn't anything he could do about the puckered scar down the left side of his face. It put some people off, but it came in handy when he wanted to make a saloonkeeper shit his britches, so he didn't mind living with it.

He'd warned his future wife about it in his letter so she wouldn't be too shocked by the sight of him, but he wished he had a fresh haircut to make a better impression.

Cecil had the sense to keep his hands where Virgil could see them, but he sounded constipated when he said, "How do I know if a man is working for you?"

"If he's paying with our promissory notes, that's a good indication, isn't it? Anyone who lies about working for me will have me to tangle with. Do *you* think anyone is stupid enough to do that?"

"No," Cecil said glumly.

Exactly. The few who did lived to regret it. Or died before he could settle with them, which was why Virgil preferred to threaten consequences rather than have to live with them—in some cases literally.

"S'pose you should have one on the house," Cecil said in a conciliatory tone as he topped up Virgil's glass. "Seein' as you're gettin' hitched. Best wishes to you. May your love be true."

The handful of men in the saloon tapped their glasses, then raised them in a cheer.

Virgil winced. Toasting to his *love* made him feel self-conscious and foolish.

"She's here to mother my children. We're not in love." He glowered at the group of them until they shrank in their seats.

"What's wrong with being in love?" a young man asked his companion in an undertone. "I want a sweetie to love me. Don't you?"

"That is nineteen talking, knucklehead." Virgil shouldn't have given the kid any mind, but he'd been that young and stupid once. He wished someone had warned him how it would turn out. "What you think is love is that snake between your legs, looking for a burrow. Keep your heart to yourself, or the woman you give it to will stomp all over it."

Virgil shot his whiskey, buttoned his coat, and walked out to meet his bride.

CHAPTER TWO

Marigold couldn't walk away. Mr. Gardner had been sent for.

She would have loved to be left alone, but the men waiting in line for their letters kept asking her for news from the east.

"You bring any papers with you?"

"What's Mr. Lincoln saying these days?"

Given how her uncle's political views had landed her where she stood, feet whimpering and bites itching, Marigold refused to discuss anything from the recent Topeka papers. Out of desperation, purely so they'd quit badgering her, she began to tell a tale from a recent issue of the *Emporia*.

"Speak up!" someone called out.

She gritted her teeth and shifted so she faced more of them, then continued in a louder voice. "After exchanging blows with his father, the young man ran away from home. He wound up shucking oysters in Chicago. A few weeks in, he met a girl selling cherries. Her mother didn't approve of him, but he assured her that he came from a well-to-do family."

"But he didn't," one of the men argued. "Not anymore. His father wouldn't have him back. I struck my father, and I'm not welcome home again. That's what happens."

"He was his father's only son," Marigold said. "Once they married, he and his wife were welcomed back with open arms." *Try reconciling*, she encouraged with a small smile. "Her mother forgave the young woman after she wrote a letter to express her remorse on marrying without her permission. Perhaps you could try the same."

"I can't write," he admitted.

She almost opened her mouth to offer to teach him, but someone else called out, "What kind of cherries? Red or yellow?"

"No such thing as yellow cherries," another man scoffed.

"Are too."

A shoving match ensued.

Dear Pearl, Marigold continued in her imaginary letter to her sister. *I'm starting to wish I didn't make it out of the house that grim night.*

"Red cherries!" Marigold stated firmly. "The young lady's lips were stained by the juice when he kissed her. That's how her mother discovered their affair."

That settled them down. Dare she finish the story and tell how the new bride ran off with another man, leaving the shucking hero in a fever of angst?

Her neck prickled. She realized her words weren't the cause of the men's sudden quiet. Their gazes had shifted past her. They all stood taller, and their expressions grew attentive. Wary. The boardwalk creaked under a heavy step that came up behind her.

"Miss Martin." His deep, authoritative voice sent a tingle into her lower back.

She *had* been Miss Martin, once upon a time, so she turned with a smile of greeting, but it immediately fell off her face, all the way to her suffering feet.

He was bigger than she expected. Tall and broad-shouldered, wearing an ill-fitting jacket that wasn't brushed. He had owned up to thirty-five years in his letter to Pearl, which accounted for the threads of silver at the temples of his dark brown hair. He had also warned Pearl his cheek bore a scar, but Marigold hadn't expected a puckered red line that cut from his brow down his cheekbone into a runnel that left a part in his untrimmed beard.

"Mr. Gardner?" She bravely pressed on, pretending his ne'er-do-well appearance wasn't alarming the life out of her.

Whatever welcome might have been in his rugged features evaporated. His gray eyes became as hard as granite while he frowned in confusion at her appearance.

Pearl had included a self-portrait when she'd responded to Mr. Gardner's advertisement. Marigold had neither Pearl's talent with watercolors, her pleasing round face, her bright red hair, nor her ample bosom. She did have her sister's honey-brown eyes, a deeper sense of responsibility, and a sharper wit—none of which had impressed any man thus far.

Mr. Gardner's brows bunched together even more when his gaze reached the bloomers poking from beneath her shortened skirt. "You're a suffragist?"

Might as well admit to being a witch and light the fire herself.

"I wonder if we could speak somewhere more private?" she suggested.

He snorted. His gaze flickered to the men who were watching them avidly. "You've come to the wrong place for that."

He had her there. She had thought the farmers in Topeka had been starved for entertainment. These miners were nosier than a barnful of kittens.

Marigold slipped around the corner into the alley between the Express office and the building that was being erected next to it. The putrid smell from a nearby outhouse almost knocked her over, but she turned to see Mr. Gardner had followed her.

"The truth is, Mr. Gardner..." She forced herself to lift her chin and not cower before his intimidating presence. "Pearl was unable to make it. I'm her sister, Marigold Davis."

He ignored her offered hand. His narrowed eyes squinted even harder.

Her heart gave a thud of alarm, but she forced herself to continue speaking.

"A man of our acquaintance learned of Pearl's plan to marry here and professed his feelings for her. They're likely engaged by now. Since I also need a husband, I took it upon myself..."

Was he physically growing larger as she spoke, like an anvil head preparing to send tornadoes whipping across the land?

"You did describe your situation as urgent," she reminded him. So was hers. His letter with the ticket for Pearl had arrived while they'd been picking through the ashes of their farmhouse. Marigold had had to decide within a matter of hours whether she would take a chance on meeting him here today or return the ticket unused. She'd had plenty of time to regret this leap into the unknown while she was bouncing around in the stagecoach, but it was too late to go back now. She had nowhere to go back to anyway.

"Why didn't you write to me when your sister did?" he demanded. "So I could make the choice between you myself?"

Because she had thought her sister weak in the head for replying to such an outrageous ad. Which likely said something about her own faculties, now that she stood before him.

"My circumstance changed very suddenly." She gave her arms a rest and set her carpetbag on the dusty ground by her feet. "I wasn't planning to marry...again," she mumbled while she was bent. She warily peered upward as she straightened.

"You're widowed?" His brows lifted.

"Divorced?" She didn't mean to sound so uncertain. There was no doubt about it. She definitely was divorced.

Crash went those dark brows, exactly like thunderheads.

"Whatever you're selling, lady, I ain't buying. You owe me a ticket on the Express and fifty cents postage."

"Mr. Gardner, I'm not— Wait!" She grabbed his arm as he started to turn away, earning a glare that Medusa herself would have found petrifying.

Marigold had had plenty of time while she'd been rolling like a loose marble in the carriage to formulate Plans B and C, anticipating that Plan A might not work out. Plying her wares at a brothel was down around W, and posting a "husband wanted" ad in a saloon was a solid F.

None of those plans offered what he had, though. If Mr. Gardner didn't accept her, she had no real options. No home to go back to, no money to go anywhere else, no family or friends to help her. No *food*. She would have to throw herself on some other man's mercy, and this one, at least, had made what had seemed like an honorable offer. The scar made him seem dangerous, but there was something in his air of command that was also reassuring.

"You don't have to marry me," she blurted. "I like children. I'm good with them, and I'm one of the most educated women you'll find this side of the Missouri River. Two years more than my sister. I've been cooking and keeping house for my uncle. I know how to grow a garden and put up preserves. I can sew. Do you really wish to start over with your search when I'm right here?"

"I already hired a Ute woman to dry meat and make my children's clothes. I want a wife, *Mrs. Davis*." He said her name like it was an accusation. "Having been married before, you should understand a man needs more than a hot meal and a mended shirt."

The way his gaze raked over her seemed to strip her bare and score into her skin, but the underlying contemplation made her blood sing in her veins.

All sorts of affronted words jumbled together in the back of her mouth. Part of her wanted to say, *Women have needs, too*. She had found a certain comfort in snuggling close to a man in the night, but whatever she'd found in her marriage bed had been a lie. Ben had sought his comforts elsewhere, and things had gone horribly wrong.

The injustice of her divorce still made her chest ache and her throat close. It was doubly unbearable when Virgil Gardner stared at her as if he knew all of that and judged her as harshly as everyone else had.

She hadn't let herself dwell on the conjugal aspects of marrying a stranger, though.

Which left her holding this man's lengthy, challenging stare while blushing—because she found herself...*speculating*. What would it be like to lie with him?

An honorable woman would feel intimidated or repulsed by his open talk of marital relations, but Marigold was involuntarily reassessing Mr. Gardner's broad shoulders and thick thighs and wide hands. Something in her found them intriguing. She wondered how his beard might feel in the crook of her neck and whether he knew how to kiss in a way that would scatter her thoughts.

As her face heated and the silence drew out, the colors around her grew sharper. Noises seemed both louder and more distant, as if she were under water. The walls of the alley seemed to close in.

His eyes turned black with a faint halo of silver. He licked his lips and set a hand on the mud-spattered wall. His gaze strolled down the buttons of her short coat again, this time more slowly. He took in the flare of her hips all the way down to the bloomers he had disparaged.

If there'd been any room in her shoes, she would have curled her toes, so visceral was the tickling touch of his attention as it lingered on her ankles.

He took his time coming back to meeting her eyes, and her skin grew tighter while strange yearnings twisted inside her. She resisted acknowledging or labeling the sensations because they were embarrassing. Telling. *Unseemly*.

The haze of interest in his gray eyes held remnants of suspicion as he asked gruffly, "Why are you divorced?"

She dampened her lips, heart seesawing in her chest. "Do you want the reason it was granted or the reason it happened?"

"Both."

She looked down to her wringing hands. "My husband wandered, but he convinced the court I was the one who lacked virtue."

"Do you?"

She straightened her arms at her sides, hands clenching into fighting fists. "I'm being honest with you right now, aren't I?"

"I have no way of knowing whether anything you've said is true." He crossed his arms. "Why do you want a husband? What are you expecting?"

She opened her mouth, then exhaled as she frowned. She *didn't* want a husband. She wanted...

"A roof. A sense of permanence. Protection," she admitted with a pang of despair at not being the resourceful, independent woman she had always aspired to be. It had been lowering to discover how little power she really had. Her dignity and basic necessities and rights had all been casually disregarded.

"Protection from what?" His voice became so charged it sent a shock through her that stung to her heels.

"My, um, uncle moved us to Topeka to support the free-state movement. I'm not sure if you've heard about the disputes there—"

He waved a hand. "I know enough. Is he dead?"

"My uncle? No." Not yet. "But our home was burned to the ground two weeks ago. That's why…" She plucked at her skirt to indicate the bloomers. "These clothes belonged to a friend." They'd been a bold fashion statement, worn proudly at first, but now women were afraid to wear them. "I still support women's rights. I won't pretend I don't." Marigold folded her arms and lifted her chin, but she had to admit, "It's hard to stand on principle when you no longer own shoes, though. These aren't mine, either." She nodded at her feet.

He shrugged. "Why take your sister's place? Does no man in Topeka want you because you're a troublemaker? And divorced?"

Take what little pride she had left, why didn't he?

"No. They don't. I'm curious, Mr. Gardner. Did many women reply to your ad? I ask because when my sister saw it, the paper was several weeks old. She was surprised to hear back that you were still looking. Are you having poor luck finding a bride?"

His shoulders hardened and his face set. "I'm being selective."

"Right. 'An educated woman willing to homestead and care for three children' isn't panned out of any old stream, is she?" A woman with the scantest degree of education would hesitate to jump on an express ticket to Hell, hoping for the best with a stranger. Only someone as idealistic as Pearl would think it was a good idea.

Or someone who had no other choices.

Marigold lifted her brows in a silent *check*. "May I be frank?"

"Use whatever name you like. It seems to be your habit."

"Ha ha. My sister is not the hardy, frontier type, Mr. Gardner. She struggles in Topeka, and we have amenities, and steamboats, and large trains of wagons coming through half the year. She's warm and lovely but far too soft for the life you offer. She answered your ad because she was worried for your motherless children."

"And you're not? I'm shocked."

"Pearl and I both suffered when we were orphaned," she assured him coldly.

He visibly swallowed, but he didn't apologize.

"As the elder, I've always done my best to protect her. I lobbied for her to refuse the Express ticket before you went to the trouble of sending it, but Pearl imagined this as a romantic adventure. She was convinced you two would fall in love."

His lip curled as he said mockingly, "You've come all this way to save me from her fanciful notions? How charitable."

"I'm saving myself. If you don't want me, I'll take myself around the corner and ask if any of those men want a practical woman who is currently in debt one hundred twenty-five dollars and fifty cents."

"I'll do it! I'll marry you!" The muted voice came from behind her and was accompanied by a number of knocks and thumps on wood.

Marigold turned to see the outhouse door burst

open. A heavyset man stumbled out, buttoning his baggy trousers.

"Ain't no women here to marry, but I want a wife," the stranger said with a bobbling nod. "I'll be good to you. Swear. I can make payments on the debt, too," he added to Mr. Gardner. "I got a claim up on—"

"You were in there the *whole time*? Listening?" Marigold cried with disbelief.

"It sounded personal." The man finished pulling his suspenders into place. "I didn't want to interrupt."

"Hell." Mr. Gardner grabbed her carpetbag. "This is going to be all over town before dusk."

CHAPTER THREE

Virgil didn't have many options. Three children were a lot to handle.

He'd bribed the cousin of one of his partners to stay the summer but hadn't found anyone willing to live with him and his children in a half-built cabin through the winter. Even the women at the cathouse said it was easier to look after fully grown men, one at a time, than marry into a ready-made family.

Levi, his son, was old enough to watch the little ones for an hour here and there, but Virgil couldn't leave him all day with his little sister and the baby. Nor could Virgil spend all day with them himself. He needed to work. Grubbing for gold gave him the means to provide for his children. It wasn't a matter of putting his back into farming to do so, either. His partners were depending on him, looking to their company and the claim they'd staked as the means to a future that wasn't as hard as all their pasts had been.

No, damn it, he needed a mother for his children, or at the very least, a motherly minder.

Blast this one for seeming to know that. The few women who had answered his ad hadn't been suitable. Most had barely been literate. Two had had children of their own. And none had been in the hurry he was. They had wanted to exchange multiple letters and ask a lot of uncomfortable questions before they committed. Only Pearl had sounded eager, educated, and earnest. He should have known she was too good to be true.

Could he trust Mrs. Davis, dee-vor-say? A woman who had traveled here under false pretenses? He'd been crossed by a wife once already.

As they returned to the front of the Express office, the men quit jabbering and gave Mrs. Davis a mixture of hopeful, hungry looks, like dogs waiting for a chance to snap a cut of meat from a butcher's block. Prospectors and claim jumpers, every last one of them.

Mrs. Davis might be an opportunist, too, but Virgil didn't want to let her go until he knew for sure.

"You'll work off your debt as my housekeeper," he told her loud enough to dampen enthusiasm in every face around him, including hers.

He paid a man at the front of the line so he could get his mail without waiting.

As the bundled stack was handed to him, Virgil asked her, "Which trunk is yours?" He nodded at the ones stacked near the door. "I'll have it loaded on my wagon."

"I don't have a trunk. Just that." She pointed at the carpetbag he still held.

"This is all you have?"

"I told you there was a fire," she said with threadbare dignity.

He shook it—it wasn't even full. And that backed up her story of being destitute. He heard again the hopeless way she'd said she wanted protection, and it punched a fresh hole in his gut. He wordlessly started down the street to the creek bridge.

It sounded like her uncle had dragged her and her sister from some finishing school out east to scratch potatoes from the dirt while being stoned to death by slavery-supporters. Her sister hadn't mentioned *that* was how she came to be in Topeka.

Virgil couldn't help feeling he was doing something worse. If Marigold Davis was the lady she claimed to be, he'd inadvertently pulled her even farther from civilization to an even harder life. The conflicts over Kansas becoming a state were nothing compared to miners disputing rights to a gulch. He'd heard three gunshots just in the time he'd been arguing with her in the alley.

"Virgil Gardner!" she shouted. "Are you stealing the only things I have left?"

Her voice sounded so far behind him, he halted and pivoted to see she hadn't even crossed the creek yet.

"Keep up," he ordered.

"My *feet* hurt." Her hands were in fists as she stalked across. When she got close enough, he saw her eyes were shiny with frustration. "These shoes are too small and your legs are too long."

"My legs are exactly as long as they need to be to get me where I want to go." He looked at her shoes, which were square-toed slippers, once a bright green silk with a curly-cue bow on top, now caked in mud and stressing their seams. "Those are completely useless. We only have boots for men here, you know. Your feet are too small for them."

She raised a brow. "My feet are exactly—"

"Save it." He bit the inside of his cheek. How could one woman make him so irritated and so amused at the same time? "It's already going to take us longer than it should to get to the trading post." He jerked his head in a new direction and shortened his stride.

"Is that a mercantile?" She fell into a hurried step beside him. "Because I don't have any money."

He had already deduced that from her crushed blue jacket and limp green skirt over those silly bloomers. Her straw hat was dented, and her hair was falling down from beneath it. Her cheeks were pocked with pink bites, and her pointed chin was an indication of her personality.

She wasn't as pretty as her sister's portrait, but he could see the resemblance. And she wasn't plain, either. There was elegance to her fine bone structure and curiosity in her whiskey-colored eyes.

Each time he met her gaze, he felt a little drunk. The effect had been especially powerful when he'd mentioned sex. What had even happened then? He wasn't happy that she'd taken advantage of his sincere offer to Pearl. He had meant his remark about marital relations to be dismissive. Like a wordless shove that let her know who she was playing with.

But something had happened while they'd been glaring at one another. The air in his lungs had thinned and lust had rung his cock like a bell. Not the regular horniness that clung to him like a plague, either. He didn't trust the cathouse not to give him the clap and had grown used to fucking his hand while he'd been married and separated from his wife. He wished for a woman every time. Any woman. But the desire prickling in him now was more personal than that nameless itch, which irked the hell out of him.

"It's a literal post," she said with bemusement as they arrived at the dead tree in a clearing where people had been rendezvousing since long before furs and gold fever had drawn white men to the area. Virgil meandered through the groups of trappers, tribal families, and wagon traders until he found an Arapahoe woman with rawhide and leather at hand.

"Moccasins?" he requested, nodding at Marigold.

Every tribe had their own word for their particular style of shoe, but fur traders had been using that one since they had first mapped this land, and it was the only one Virgil knew. He showed her one of his company's promissory notes, and she nodded that she would accept it.

"It won't take long." Virgil left Marigold for her fitting and wandered to shoot the shit with a handful of local businessmen picking over a wagonful of tools and pans abandoned by prospectors who'd lost heart and gone home.

"Ed, Woodrow, P.J." Virgil nodded in greeting but ignored the tools. He had more in Quail's Creek than hands that could use them.

"Virgil. You'll want this." Ed offered him a printed notice about a convention to be held August first regarding the formation of local government.

Ed loved his pamphlets and bureaucracy. He had led the charge this spring on talking the Auraria Town Company into joining the City of Denver— which was still called St. Charles on its charter papers.

"What's news from your camp? P.J. says we won't have anyone left to stand for election, let alone a population to govern if this keeps up." Ed cocked his dismayed brow at the tools.

"Newspapers back east are writing that Pike's Peak is a bust." P.J. threw exasperated hands in the air. "Everyone's leaving. No one will come back."

"Are *you* leaving?" Virgil asked.

"No," P.J. said dourly. "But I'm losing my customers."

"For liquor and tobacco?" Virgil doubted it. "The ones who think mining gold is like picking daisies don't stick around." He deliberately sidestepped reporting on his company's yields. "But there are plenty of us hardheaded enough to stay and break our backs. We don't want anyone coming along and stealing what we manage to chip out for ourselves, either. We need law."

"We have laws. We're part of Kansas Territory. If we become a state, we'll have more taxes," Woodrow argued. He was a judge appointed by the governor, so he had a vested interest in maintaining the status quo.

"That's why I say we're better off as Jefferson Territory." Ed tapped the paper Virgil still held. "My editorial explains why we should let the feds pay for us to govern ourselves. I'd appreciate your vote on that, Virgil."

Every time Virgil came to town, the two sides of this "state versus territory" argument seemed to have dug in deeper. At least in January, they'd all been on the same page. A delegate had even been sent to Washington, but the slavery debate had forced a delay on any legislation regarding new territories.

Now they were fighting over whether to become a coat or a jacket, and Virgil just wanted to keep the peace without using his pistol.

"Who is *that*?" P.J. stood taller, sucking in his gut. *Ah, shit.*

"My housekeeper," Virgil admitted reluctantly, turning to follow the men's gazes.

"You have a house?" Woodrow scoffed. "I thought you had a pile of felled trees and a carpenter who spends more time with a pan in his hand than a hammer."

"I thought you ordered a bride?" Ed said. "Because if you're not marrying her—"

"I'm still thinking on it," Virgil cut in. "She owes me money and has to work it off. Not that way," he added with a glower when all their brows went up. "She's a proper lady from back east."

"If you say so." That was spoken around the pipe stem Ed stuffed into his smirk.

Virgil glanced over and saw Marigold had opened her bag and was showing its contents to the Arapahoe woman. She had already set out a packet of writing paper with a pen tucked under its binding twine and a small bottle of ink. There were three books, a hairbrush, and an apron. Now came a shawl, a housedress, a *nightgown*, a pair of *stockings*…her Goddamned *underwear*.

He strode over double-time. "What the hell are you doing?"

"Having a conversation." Marigold sent a guileless look up at him. "I mean, she doesn't speak English, and I don't speak her language, either, but she laughed at my shoes, so I thought I'd show her what else we wear back east. This is my corset cover, which goes over the corset, obviously." She demonstrated by placing the corded corset against her chest, then layering the entirely too suggestive, translucent, and lace-edged underthing atop it. "I took mine off because travel was unbearable enough without suffocating."

Virgil was back to pressing a tent into the heavy denim of his work trousers, especially as he noticed she was endowed exactly enough in the bosom department to make his blood heat. She'd removed her hat, and her hair was falling in wavy chestnut ribbons that were approximately seven miles long, and since when did he have fantasies of a woman tickling his skin with her hair?

"Put it away," he said through his teeth.

"I'm almost finished. This is a fresh pair of drawers. These ones button in the slit. You can imagine what a nuisance that is, so I only wear them on laundry day. Another pair of stockings, and this is my menstrual belt—"

"*Nope.*"

• • •

Virgil jerked open her carpetbag and began stuffing everything in willy-nilly.

"If women's talk makes you uncomfortable, move along," Marigold said. "Or take a lesson, because if more people shared information and a new perspective instead of—"

Virgil leveled a ferocious glower at her. It was so close to the contemptuous looks worn by the slavery-supporters who had spit on her in Topeka, she had to turn her face away to hide sudden tears.

"Almost finished?" Virgil asked the Arapahoe woman.

She wasn't bothering to hide her amusement. She offered the leather slippers moments later.

"I enjoyed meeting you. I hope we'll meet again," Marigold said politely, pretending she wasn't still stung by Virgil taking her to task in public. She pulled the slippers onto her feet and rose to take a few testing steps. The firm soles protected her from the poke of rough, sunbaked grass, while the upper was soft enough to hug her foot without squishing it. "Very comfortable." She smiled with genuine plea-sure at how nice they felt.

"I feel like I could run on the wind in these." Marigold fairly skipped as Virgil led her away from the trading post. "I swear women's fashion is de-signed by men to constrict us so you can tell us how useless we are."

No response. His long strides ate up the ground, but at least she could keep up with him now that her feet weren't weeping.

"What was I supposed to do?" she asked when his oppressive silence continued. "Invite myself into her lodging so I could show her my things? Maybe men should quit acting like a piece of cotton is an invitation to congress."

"Do you understand how few women there are here?" He stopped abruptly, and his voice was harder than a scold. It was grave. "A lot of these men haven't seen a white woman in years. They're the kind of men who take what they want without asking permission. That's what the frontier *is*. You're all kinds of right about what men should be, but I'm telling you what they are. When I say don't draw attention to yourself, I'm not trying to constrict you. I'm protecting you. Which is what you asked for."

He walked on, nodding at a man he passed but not stopping to speak to him. The man stared at Marigold.

After a beat, she hurried to keep up, not finding a retort. She was too disgruntled by how he'd turned her own words on her. And by the fact he said he was trying to protect her when she was pretty sure he hated her.

"I only thought she'd be interested," Marigold muttered as she fell into step beside him. "I'd certainly like to know how women in the wild manage...certain things."

"Really? That's your priority?"

"Shouldn't it be? Since that's where I am now?"

He shook his head in perplexity. "You're something else, Marigold. You really are. What sort of name is that, anyway?"

"It's a flower."

"Yes, I know that. What sort of person names their child after a flower?"

"A perfectly lovely English woman whose husband brought her a bouquet of them when she'd gone to the trouble of birthing his daughter."

He smirked. "Does that mean he brought her pearls when your sister was born?"

"Yes. He was a doctor. He had finished school and begun his practice by then, so he could afford something nicer than stolen flowers. Why? What did you give your wife?"

His expression twisted with discomfort. Regret, maybe. "I was working the steamboats when Levi was born. I sent her gold dust from California soon as I could after Nettie."

"And your third? You have three children, don't you?"

"Look." He stopped to confront her again. "If you and I were marrying, I'd put up with you asking me personal questions about my first wife, but we're not. I'm hiring you to mind and school my children. You want to ask me something, ask about that." He started walking again, catching her by the elbow to steer her around some road apples.

When he released her, she felt untethered and had to work to gather her thoughts.

"I suppose I should ask how much you'll pay me?"

"Nothing. You're working off a debt."

"That could go on forever." She scowled, thinking it was too much like her arrangement with her uncle, which had been a similar quid pro quo for his giving her a home after she lost hers in the divorce. "I'd like you to pay me, and I'll pay you back in reasonable installments."

"I'll be providing room and board," he reminded. "I wasn't going to pay my wife."

"And therein lies the reason I told Pearl this was a bad idea. How much are you paying the Ute woman?"

"That was arranged through her cousin and none of your business."

"Fine. Three dollars a day. A dollar per child.

That way I can buy a few things I'm likely to need and can still pay you back by the end of the year."

He snorted.

"What? I'll be doing your laundry along with theirs *and* cooking for you."

"My laborers get two dollars a day plus meals, and they're *making* me money. I'll have to stake you for fabrics and sewing needles and what-not to make winter clothes for yourself. Your debt will grow before it shrinks."

"Those are things I need to do my job. I'm not doing this for less than fifty cents a child. Is the youngest still in diapers? If so, he'll be seventy-five."

"He mostly uses the pot." He scratched under his beard. "Levi minds the livestock and runs errands, so you'll only have him for lessons. Nettie will help you with Harley. You'll be teaching her how to cook and sew and keep house, so she'll help with that, too. A dollar a day and at least fifty cents of that comes back to me every day."

A letter to her sister was twenty-five cents. She could make her own soap and toothpowder, but she would need the ingredients. She'd lost her home remedy book in the fire as well as all her seeds and needed to replace them.

"A dollar twenty-five." She saw a sign in a shop that prompted her to add, "And I can cut hair and keep that money for myself or apply it to my debt as I see fit."

"You can cut hair?"

She'd only ever trimmed her sister's and would need to buy scissors, but… "Yes."

"A dollar twenty-five and my cuts are free." He

held out his hand.

What a procedure! But she was thrilled to have her first paid employment. She thrust her hand into the grasp of his. He waited until her eyes met his, then gave her hand a squeeze and a pump. It felt profound enough to be a blood oath and made her extremities tingle.

An echo of that sexual awareness from a little while ago seemed to creep into the moment, bringing heat into her face so she pulled her hand away a little too abruptly.

She tried to hide her disconcertion by looking around. They were on a main street of sorts, outside a shop that advertised itself as Pollock's Stoves and Metalwork.

"Where, um… I understand you live in Quail's Creek? Where is that?"

"Forty miles that way." He pointed at the mountains. "It's a mining camp. I didn't expect you today. I thought this was my regular supply run, so I brought the oxen and had the wagon filled." He motioned to where men at a mercantile were securing barrels and crates on an uncovered wagon. "We'll leave in an hour."

"More travel. Yay," she said weakly.

"You want to add a night at the hotel and a day of my wages to your bill, we can arrange that."

"You're a very tough sort of man, aren't you, Mr. Gardner?"

"Most people call me a hard-ass."

"I was going to ask if I could call you Virgil, but if you prefer hard-ass…"

He ran his tongue over his teeth, perhaps hiding

amusement, because his eyes held a hint of sparkle within the frost. "You can call me Virgil."

"Well, Virgil, I wonder if you'd be willing to stake me a small cushion?"

• • •

She fell asleep on the ferry.

Virgil had noticed her bruised eyes but hadn't realized how exhausted she really was until her head was nodding as they got underway. He stepped down from the wagon after driving it onto the ferry and helped the ferryman guide the raft across. When he climbed back up, she had stretched across the bench with the cushion he'd bought her tucked under her cheek.

"Marigold." He nudged her shoulder, then again more firmly.

She was so deeply asleep, he grew concerned something was wrong, but she didn't have a fever and had eaten the same stew he'd tucked into before they left. Her breathing was deep and regular, her skin pale, not flushed. She was just...dead asleep.

She didn't stir when he shifted her so her bottom was against his hip and her bent legs were across his lap. He didn't know how else to arrange her so she wasn't falling out of the wagon. It was comfortable enough but also not, leaving him a little too conscious of the fact she was a woman. At least she was quiet.

He drove the wagon off the ferry and carried on up the rutted track into the foothills.

The oxen made it a ponderous journey, but it was

peaceful, and this was a particularly heavy load with the stove and woodworking tools.

Despite the days still being warm, the mountain shadows closed in quickly and dropped the temperature. He dug into Marigold's carpetbag for her shawl and draped it over her. She still didn't move, even when he waved away a mosquito that was trying to add to the bumps on her cheeks.

She had some bite herself, didn't she? He should have found that irritating, but it was heartening. This life was hard.

He was already losing men who'd only arrived a few weeks ago with dreams as bright and misguided as the ones that had lured Virgil to California eight years ago. Like him, those young men had had their spirits crushed very quickly and wound up in the back-breaking position of working for someone else. Sore and disillusioned, they were limping home.

Little Miss Marigold could very well do the same, and he wouldn't begrudge her for it. He didn't know what he'd do if that happened, though. He couldn't take his kids back to St. Louis. He'd only wind up killing his brother-in-law for the way he'd treated them after Clara died. They'd be orphaned all over again.

With a sudden inhale, Marigold jerked upright. She was so disoriented with her legs tangled over his lap that she nearly fell off the bench.

"You're all right." He caught her arm to steady her. Spirited she might be, but she wasn't very sturdy.

"I'm going to be sick."

He pulled on the reins, and she scrambled down to the ground, then stepped off the track and stood with one hand against the torn-paper trunk of an aspen. Their yellow leaves quaked above her as she took several deep breaths.

While he waited for her to lose her guts, he began to feel ill himself.

"Are you pregnant?" he asked with such dread the words left a pall in his throat.

"What? *No*. I get sick when I travel too long."

"You've been sick for days?"

"Yes."

Add it up, lady. He didn't say it, but she must have heard it, because she trudged back to give him a pale, affronted scowl.

"I have only ever been with my husband, and I haven't seen him in five years."

Uh huh. Virgil had been on the other side of that, and Harley proved babies could come with or without a husband around.

"Oh, don't spare my feelings, *Mr.* Gardner." She was not using the title out of respect. "I've been accused of worse by—" She pinched her mouth shut. "I was going to say 'better' men, but honestly? The solicitor who spoke for my husband proved both of them to be putrid as pond scum. They said horrible things about me in front of people I cared about. Friends from school. The wives of Ben's colleagues. *My sister*."

She looked backward on the track that had brought them this far. Her profile was polished white ash.

"I'm tired of being accused of something I didn't do, Mr. Gardner. If that's what you think of me, we'll part ways here. I'll find the cathouse and properly earn the title of strumpet, but right now I do not deserve it."

He opened his mouth to tell her there was no need for dramatics, but the solemn way she met his gaze, and the lingering hurt in her eyes, made his chest itch.

"I didn't call you a strumpet." Maybe he had hinted at it. "If you're not pregnant, good. Fine." Damn, he hoped she was being truthful. "We'll press on while we still have light. Get back in the wagon."

She shook her head. "I'll walk until my stomach settles."

"Suit yourself." He hitched the reins, and the oxen leaned into their yoke. The wagon creaked and rocked and began to jostle in the ruts.

She walked behind, since the trail was narrow enough the brush snapped and scraped the walls of the wagon bed. He tried not to look back at her. She wasn't a child, but he felt as though she was mad at him, and he didn't know why that dug under his skin like a tick. They barely knew each other.

She was awfully quiet back there, though.

He glanced over his shoulder to ensure she was keeping up.

She wasn't there.

With his blood running cold, he yanked on the reins, snatched his gun from beneath the bench, and stood up, shouting, "Marigold!"

CHAPTER FOUR

Virgil's bellow was so alarming, Marigold called, "What?" and hurried to finish her business.

"Where the hell are you?" He sounded furious.

She brushed her skirt down over her bloomers as she came back onto the path. "Nature called."

He was standing in the wagon, a shotgun in his hands, his demeanor tense with readiness. It was such a manly show of strength and concern, she experienced an involuntary flutter of feminine response. A mix of shy pleasure and admiration bloomed inside her.

He promptly ruined it, though, railing at her like a doomsayer warning a sinner against eternal damnation. "Have you heard of mountain lions? Bears? Wolves? When we're on the trail, you tell me when you have to go. I'll say when it's safe."

"For heaven's sake! What a fuss." She caught up to the wagon. "I'm sure all those predators are far more interested in deer than me, and I haven't seen any of *those*."

"Because deer are smart enough to know that predators hunt at dusk."

"At which time they hunker down into the bush? Because that's what I was doing. Safe as a baby fawn."

He swiped a hand down his face. "Christ, you're a nuisance. Get back up here. We're almost at the clearing where we'll stop for the night."

She climbed aboard, accepting his hand to yank her up the final tall step.

He was sitting on her cushion, she noted, but he removed it from under his backside to push it toward her.

As they rambled along, he asked, "Why did your husband say all of those things if they weren't true?"

She was tempted to tell him that if he wasn't marrying her, he didn't have a right to ask, but very few people in Topeka had ever asked for her side of it, let alone believed her when she told them.

"Someone has to be at fault in order for the court to grant a divorce." She spread her shawl over her knees; the air had grown chilly. "I came home from visiting Pearl at my uncle's home. I found Ben with another woman in our bed. I wasn't about to stay married to him after that, but his father is a congressman. Ben aspires to go into politics as well. He didn't want a stain on his reputation, so he put it on me."

"It was your word against his? What did the other woman have to say?"

"That I was sullying her name for my own purposes. Humiliating as the court proceedings were, the worst part was realizing how willing Ben was to ruin me for his own gain. He even took our townhouse. I was left with nothing despite the fact we bought it with money my uncle had saved for me all those years after my parents passed. I thought Ben and I were in love, that I was making a good home for us and our future family, but he strayed after only a few months of marriage. Then to be so cruel on top of that? Frankly, Virgil, your lecture on how selfish men can be was unnecessary. I am well acquainted with what snakes some are. That's why—"

She cut herself off, aware of the precarious position she was in.

He gave her a prompting look to continue.

"Why I'm glad we're not marrying," she finished. If he took offense, she couldn't help it. She was being as honest as she knew how and lifted her chin with what self-respect she had left. "I don't want a man making false promises and leaving me to suffer for his mistakes."

He snorted, and she raised her brows at him.

"That's also the reason I'm glad we're not marrying."

A fresh stab of rejection went into her, but she ignored it.

"Gosh, it's almost as though we were made for each other." She spoke lightly, trying to disguise the catch of hurt in her voice. "That's funny."

"Sure is."

About as funny as a dropped ice cream at a rained-out picnic.

• • •

Virgil fed and watered the oxen, then returned to the small fire, where Marigold was warming the last of her stew. They ate while watching the sliver of a moon rise over the white peaks above them.

"It's pretty here," she said softly. "I've always felt very vulnerable with only the prairie sky around me. But with mountains... They're like guardians watching over us."

He wondered how much of her vulnerability and desire for protection came from leaving a failed marriage and moving into the unrest of Kansas Territory.

She brought her gaze down from the sky and looked at him, her face a little flushed from the fire. "That must sound strange when you can at least see what's coming out on the prairie. Should I really look out for all those predators you mentioned?"

"Yes. And bobcat, lynx, coyotes. Hell, if you come face-to-face with a moose, you head the other way, pronto. Mountain goats can be territorial, but they're pretty shy."

"I was hoping you were teasing me," she said on a sigh.

"Let's not make a habit of lying to one another."

"Deal." She scraped up the last bite of her stew. "We had a rattlesnake in the woodshed one spring. That's the most dangerous animal I've ever encountered."

"You might see one of those here, too," he said.

"For heaven's sake! I'm starting to think I'll be lucky if I'm only attacked by a *man*."

And *he* was starting to think her sense of humor was morbid enough to fit in around here. He bit the inside of his cheek to keep from showing his amusement.

"Where, um, will we sleep?" she asked with a glance around. "That will be safe, I mean?"

"About that." He scratched under his beard. "I usually sleep on the ground by the fire."

"Can I sleep in the wagon?"

"Sure," he said, "if you want to empty it, then

freeze to death. I only have the one bedroll."

Her spine straightened and her mouth soured up.

"Like I said, I wasn't expecting you. If I wanted to attack you, I'd have done it already. We're going to lie back-to-back, same as I've done with men. Fart if you want to. Nothing you do is going to affect me in any way." That's what he kept telling himself, anyway, since he'd realized how ill-prepared he was for company.

She was still looking as though she'd sat on a pin.

"Wash these in the stream." He thrust his emptied plate at her. "You can tinkle on the other side of the wagon if you need to. Then we'll turn in. It'll be a long day tomorrow. I want an early start."

She rose with a small huff and took his plate with a tetchy look. "Well, I'm not so forgiving as you. Keep your gas to yourself."

He watched her sashay away in her billowy trousers and new moccasins, then realized that he was *watching her* and made himself fetch the bedroll from the wagon. He heard metal clank against rocks as he took a final check of the area.

When he returned to bank the fire, he found Marigold had aligned herself on the very edge of the narrow bedroll. She had her shawl wrapped around her head and shoulders and had left the lion's share of the bed and blanket for him.

He set his gun to hand and lifted the blanket, stretching out with his back to hers.

She wasn't as wide and sturdy as the average man, though. When he leaned onto her, she sagged beneath his weight, and her breath rushed out in an "*oof.*"

It would have been laughable if it hadn't fully awakened him to the fact he was lying next to a woman for the first time in years.

He tried rolling onto his stomach, but that put half his body on the cold, rough ground. When he shifted more fully onto the mat, his side was pressed right up against her back and ass. Not unpleasant, but it was inappropriate.

Marigold stiffened and tried to inch away, but he was lying on her skirt.

"Um…" She pulled at her skirt, but even after he lifted himself off her clothes, she said, "I'm on the gravel."

With a grunt of dismay, he rolled onto his back, aware of his body brushing hers as he did. Tension gathered in his belly and blood rushed to his groin. He had the same issue as he'd had on his stomach. The bedroll wasn't wide enough. His shoulder and leg were on the pebbles. The rocks were worn smooth, but they were cold and hard.

"Perhaps top to toe?" She sounded anxious and stubbornly kept her back to him.

"Then I'd have to take off my boots." He didn't want to accidentally kick her in the face, and he wanted to be able to hotfoot it if he needed to.

Oh, screw it. He rolled to face her and scooped her close. At least they would both be warm.

She went stiff as a board, and so did his cock. He didn't mean it to, and he sure as hell wasn't wanting it to, but she'd scrubbed herself in the stream and her hair smelled like mountain air, and it had been a really, really long time since he'd held a woman this close.

"Virgil—"

"Ignore it," he ordered into the hair that tickled his lips.

If only he could take his own advice. She was so *soft*. It took everything in him not to knead his touch against the give of her tense stomach and explore the roundness of her hips and the pliancy of her thighs.

"Breathe," he ordered.

She exhaled raggedly and gasped another one in, like she was drowning and only surfaced for a moment.

"Marigold, I was faithful to my wife even though I didn't see her for years. Even when women in saloons sat in my lap and pushed their…" *Don't say tits. Don't think about hers.* "Their bosom in my face, I kept my vows. I can control myself for one night. Go to sleep."

"Get off my hair, then."

He shifted, and she dragged her tail of plaited hair free, still tense.

"Give me the cushion," he said. "You can rest your head on my arm."

"You should have bought two if you wanted one." She gave it up anyway, then grumbled, "The ground is cold." She snuggled deeper into the curve of his body.

His eyes popped open. This was such torture, his eyes prit-near crossed into the other's socket. Despite the layers of skirt and bloomers and drawers, he could all too well detect the warm, smooth curve of her ass. The heavenly crevice. Damn, that was nice.

"What if something attacks us in the night?" she asked.

"Then I'll shoot you so you don't suffer too long."

"Very funny. Where were you when I was getting a divorce? I could have used that chivalry." She yawned. "Good night, hard-ass."

"Good night, *lady*."

"Hmph." It was a tiny noise of amusement, but for some reason it pleased him.

• • •

The angry chatter of a squirrel woke Marigold.

It had been a restless night. Each time she or Virgil stirred, they rearranged themselves and fell back asleep, but now he was on his back, taking up most of the bedroll, and she was half sprawled across him, her head in the hollow of his shoulder, her leg thrown over one of his. Her arm was on his chest, and the weight of his arm was around her back. His fingers had found a pocket of warmth under the edge of her jacket and were tucked there. His chest rose in the slow, steady breaths of deep sleep.

It was surprisingly comfortable, so she didn't move, only blinked a couple of times, noting the glow of dawn was beginning to reveal the shadowed world around them. The stream continued its steady trickle, but otherwise the world was silent. The squirrel had gone back to sleep, so she tried to do the same.

She was very aware of Virgil, though. Of his solidness and the way their legs were intertwined so her sex was pressed to his hard thigh.

A flush engulfed her. It was embarrassment, but one caused by the fact a different sort of heat was billowing to life within her. Something she had felt a few times in her marriage while kissing Ben, when her naked skin had rubbed against his and he'd fondled her in the dark. It was an internal furnace that made her sex feel damp and her breasts feel hard and made her *yearn*.

Against her better judgment, she imagined Virgil's hands roaming beneath her clothing, finding her skin, shaping and stroking and teasing. She imagined his mouth devouring hers.

Don't.

But the fantasy persisted. She wondered how it would feel for his callused thumbs to rub her nipples. How would his weight feel upon her... With Ben, it had always started out uncomfortable, but sometimes, when he took his time, she had begun to feel strummed into madness by his body's movements within her.

That's how she felt right now, she realized guiltily. As if they had made love and she was in the inflamed afterglow, waiting for her excitement to subside so she could sleep.

After Ben's horrible betrayal, these fleshly, intriguing sensations had tangled in her mind as proof that she was the whore she'd been branded. After all, how could she claim to be virtuous if she was capable of lust? How could she argue she possessed exemplary morals when she wanted Virgil to roll atop her and thrust inside her?

She hadn't moved, but her aroused, uneven heartbeat must have transmitted a message to him.

He drew in a deep inhale and stretched at the same time. His arm around her tightened to hold her in place while his other hand reached to roam up her arm to her shoulder, pulling her closer as he rolled to face her.

She tilted her head and watched his eyes open to glittering slits.

Whatever he read in her expression had him sliding his hand upward and cupping the back of her head. His other arm dragged her higher against him, and he started to settle his mouth over hers.

"Virgil," she whispered, startled, but also thinking, *Yes? Maybe?*

He jerked his head up.

"Fuck." He flattened his palm into the dirt beside her head, levering himself up to walk away into the morning gloom. Seconds later, she heard him splashing in the stream.

Marigold grabbed the cushion and shoved her face into it, moaning with agony and an undeniable frustration. She had *wanted* him to kiss her.

When she heard him coming back, she sat up and brushed her skirt down. Her skin felt so thin she thought he must be able to detect how her heart batted and fluttered with discombobulation.

His expression was cold and grim.

"Let's go. We'll eat when the sun comes up." He plucked the blanket from her weak fingers and balled it, walking away to throw it into the wagon.

Why did he have to sound so disgusted? Was she that repulsive? Did he *blame* her? A searing flame of injustice came to life behind her heart, but it was smothered by the knowledge she hadn't rolled away from him the moment she woke. She had stayed in his arms and wondered how it would feel for him to kiss her.

She shifted to kneel on the unforgiving rocks while she rolled the bedroll, then shakily got to her feet and stowed it in the wagon.

A short time later, they crossed the stream and crept along the track, moving from one shadowed gulch into another. The birds were making every type of racket, but the silence between her and Virgil was tense and uncomfortable.

She tried to distract herself with another imagined letter to her sister.

Dear Pearl, the land is so serrated, it is impossible to see beyond the next hillock or around a bend to what comes next. I don't know where I'm going, and all I can think is that I want to come back to you. I don't know how I can survive here. I'm as unwanted as I was there.

Why was that eating her up? She didn't *want* him to want her. Not in that way, but his rejection had been unequivocal and had stabbed into a place that was already very tender, leaving her filled with embarrassment and regret.

Quite unexpectedly, they broke from the trees and arrived at the shore of a large lake.

The still water perfectly reflected the trees growing in bands on the sloped shoreline. Some were evergreen, and others were beginning to fade toward yellow and orange and red, even though it was still mid-summer. The peaks behind them were chipped like clay crockery, porcelain snow embedded in their cracks. The rising sun set one side of the valley aglow while the other remained in pensive shadow. Above it all was a sky that was bluer than any blue Marigold had ever seen.

Virgil stopped the wagon, and they sat for a long, communing moment.

"Thank you," she murmured. "This is the most beautiful place I've ever seen. I appreciate you letting me take it in."

"I was looking for game."

"To shoot? For heaven's sake, Virgil. Tell me you're joking."

He sent her a look of pity. "Toughen up, Marigold, or you won't last out here."

His remark hit her like a slap. For a long time, she'd been as thick-skinned as she'd thought a woman should ever have to become, but here he was making her feel as though she was still not hardened enough to withstand everyday life. Maybe even as though she deserved the crushing blows life kept dealing her.

She turned her head so he wouldn't see that her eyes filled with tears, not wanting him to know how dejected she was.

"You're proving my point," he muttered.

"I'm *looking* for something you could brain to death with that blunt manner of yours," she lied. "It would save you a bullet." She turned and blinked at him.

His mouth pursed briefly as he considered her.

"Squirrels I can get with a hard look." He sent a glower toward a low-hanging branch.

His unforgiving profile nearly stopped *her* heart, let alone a tiny rodent's, but levity fluttered within her at how absurd he was being. *Was* he mad at her for their almost-kiss? Or merely as confused by it as she was? Because this felt as though he was joking so they could move past it.

"If you get something with fur, I can skin it with my wit." She brushed at her skirt and sat taller. "It's very well-honed."

"That so?" There was a twitch at the corner of his mouth she was entirely too pleased to provoke. "It's good you packed your sense of humor. It doesn't do a damned thing to keep you alive out here, but it stops you from wanting to kill yourself."

"Don't make it easy for me, Virgil. You know a statement like that begs me to ask, 'How have *you* managed to survive this long without one?'" She dipped her chin to admonish him.

"Stubborn works, too," he said drily. "I always carry plenty of that."

He hitched the reins, and they began their plodding journey again, but now the birdsong sounded sweeter and the air felt softer and lighter.

CHAPTER FIVE

She really did become sick from travel. As the morning wore on, Virgil watched her color leech and didn't think it was because the tension between them had dissipated.

He had come really close to kissing her. He kept telling himself he'd been half asleep, but he'd known as he opened his eyes that it wasn't a dream. He'd only wanted to pretend it was. After an agitated night, he'd finally fallen deeply asleep and was awakened by the hardest, most intensively aching cock of his life. Having a woman in bed with him had been *like* a dream, perfectly matching the fantasy he played out for himself when he polished his banister.

Marigold had worn a lovely expression of wonder and invitation. Her lips had parted, her eyes had been heavy-lidded. He nearly groaned aloud recalling how badly he'd wanted to press his mouth over hers. Her lips had looked soft and supple. The warmth of her curves against him had called out for him to kiss and caress her. How would she have reacted?

Clara, his deceased wife, had enjoyed lovemaking well enough, he'd made sure of it, but she'd been shy about touching him or letting herself get carried away. Marigold had the experience of marriage and had seemed receptive.

Ah, hell. He had to stop thinking about it.

He tried to read her profile from the corner of his

eye, wondering if she realized what was in his thoughts or that his cock was thick behind his fly buttons.

"I have to walk," she blurted. Her lips were white, her eyes gleaming with distress.

He stopped the wagon, saying with regret, "I can't let you walk here. Animals are moving down for a drink." He nodded at the lake they'd been circling. The wagon made enough rattles and groans that animals tended to give them a wide berth, but he let her step down and catch her bearings while he fetched a few supplies from the back. "Eat something. Nothing can come up if it's going down, right?"

"Thank you." She took the circle of hardtack and frowned at the effort it took to break off a piece.

"It's sheet iron, I know. I usually soak it with pickle juice or canned peaches. Those cases are under everything else. We'll have to make do with water." He used his pocket knife to carve off a chunk of cheese and gave it to her. "We can make oatmeal when we stop."

They got underway again, moving in and out of the trees, catching slants of sunshine as it rose over the mountain. The track climbed as it paralleled a creek bed that had been reduced to a trickle this time of year.

Virgil stopped where the stream flooded in the spring, leaving shifting pools that allowed the oxen to drink. He liked to pan here while he waited for the water to boil.

Marigold came back from doing her business in the bush and showed him some berries with a sprig of leaves. "Are these safe to eat?"

"The kids call them bear berries. Leyohna lets them eat them." Virgil couldn't be bothered with fiddly work like picking berries, but he took one from the branch she'd brought to remind himself what they tasted like. Palatable enough, he supposed. Pulpy and mildly sweet with a faint flavor of almond in the seeds.

Marigold fetched the bowl she'd used to eat her portion of last night's stew and continued picking while Virgil made the coffee and oatmeal. When he called out that it was ready, she brought her bowl of berries, and they each threw a handful into their porridge.

Next thing, he'd be putting molasses and milk into it, like the children, but he had to admit it made a nice change from plain.

After she rinsed the dishes, she went back to picking while he nudged the oxen to pull the wagon across the rocky bed of the stream and up a steep incline. When he looked back, she was already catching up to him.

She set her filled bowl behind the buckboard and braced it with her bag so it wouldn't spill as they got underway again.

"Did you find any gold in the stream?" she asked.

"Nah. Never."

"You said yesterday that you sent your wife gold dust from California. Did you strike it rich there? Is that how you come to have your own company here?"

He bristled at the mention of Clara, mostly because he felt like such a fool for leaving her and going to California at all.

"No one strikes it rich," he said flatly. "That's a lie to sell newspapers and pickaxes. Owen—you'll meet him, he's one of my partners." He pointed up the track. "He swallowed that tale whole. All he thinks about is making a fortune, so he was determined to go. We were friends since childhood and were in the army together. Since I had mouths to feed, I agreed to go with him."

Virgil had told Clara he was only keeping an eye out for Owen, but the fanciful dreams of riches had sunk under his skin. He'd talked himself into believing he would come back triumphant and show her their marriage hadn't been a mistake. He would prove to himself and his likely dead father that he had made something of himself.

"The dust I sent Clara was a pittance, but it was all I had to show for our first season. We damned near starved to death that winter. Come spring, we got on with a mining company, but wages were already dropping. Eventually, we heard whispers of gold in these mountains, so we made our way here."

"You gambled on coming all this way because of a whisper?"

"That's what mining is. Gambling." It had taken him three decades to understand that nearly everything in life was. "The first men into California won the biggest pots because they got a jump on the best claims, then hired the men who came later. We were the ones who did the real work while they opened the shops that fed and clothed us."

"Is that what you want to do?" She blinked at him as though seeing past the scruffy beard and shaggy hair and dusty clothes to the man with ambition and determination.

Twinges of inadequacy arose in him. Old doubts and echoes of accusations that he would never amount to anything.

"I don't want to be the man who could have done those things and watched someone else do it *again*," he said gruffly. "I started out thinking those men I worked for had something I didn't, but they weren't any smarter than me. God knows they didn't have the skill or muscle to do the work themselves."

"But you do, so you started your own company."

"We did." With only four horses between them and whatever tools and supplies they could scrape together. Not a morning had gone by when they hadn't all woken and looked at each other, wondering if they'd lost their collective minds.

"All my wages were going home to Clara, so I reckoned I'd be halfway back to her if I came this far, but if there *was* gold here, I didn't want a repeat of what had happened in California. *I* would be the one hiring the boys with the stars in their eyes."

"And you did find gold. You must have been dancing in the—well, I guess there was no street." Her ale-colored eyes were bright with amusement, her smile expectant. She was enjoying his story. Everyone loved a happy ending.

"A bust would have been kinder," he said flatly. "We found gold, and all I could think was how much work there was to be done. We knew the rush was only a matter of time. At least supplies are closer now." He jerked his head back toward Denver.

"How did you settle on calling it the Venturous Mining Company?"

"'Misery Loves' didn't win the popular vote."

"Ha." Her smile broadened. She was cute with her one crooked tooth and small overbite. "My uncle says that's the engine of democracy."

"That misery loves company?"

"That people will rally to a common adversity and collectively try to resolve it."

"He's not wrong." He made himself drag his eyes off her and look to where they were going. "They'll also drag you into poor solutions. That's why I hand-picked our partners." And pissed off several opportunists who had thought they ought to be included. "I didn't want to be voted into actions by men I don't trust." Virgil had been in that situation too often in the army and the steamboats and the California goldfields.

"How many men make up your company?"

"We started as six. Tom joined us on the trail, so now we're seven. He's Ute, but he has relationships with the Arapahoe and helps us keep things friendly with them."

She nodded. "And the rest?"

"Owen. He's our talker, so he's our foreman. Emmett builds our sluice boxes and rockers and will get our mill up and running. Stoney works the quartz crush, and Ira cooks the mercury. Wu Bing Sun is our connection to Chinese laborers. They've worked rice paddies and understand irrigation and water diversion."

Suddenly, the bridge came into view, and Marigold gasped, "Oh! I've never been so glad for a sign of civilization."

Virgil realized how companionable the journey

had become, making it pass more quickly. He hadn't meant to yammer on about himself and was embarrassed that he had.

"You get out and walk across first," he said.

"You don't trust it?" She glanced back as she climbed down.

"I built it, so yeah, I trust it. But we won't test it more than we have to." He dropped to the ground on the other side of the wagon and moved to the head of the oxen, waiting for Marigold to reach the other side before he led them across.

The bridge was made of two stalwart logs pounded into the dirt track on either side of the gully. He'd secured sapling rounds across them with lengths of hide, then nailed rough-hewn planks atop that, spaced to form a smooth surface for the wagon's wheels. The whole thing creaked and groaned as the heavy wagon rolled across, but it held fine.

"Where did you learn to build bridges?" Marigold asked.

"Army."

"I should have asked what you bring to the company? Engineering?"

"Charm," he said flatly, and she rolled her eyes. "I'm done cackling like hens. You can walk now." He chucked his chin at the track. "Next patch is bumpy, and I have to pay attention. I can't be looking behind, so walk in front."

• • •

What a shock that Virgil Gardner wasn't inundated with women wanting to marry him.

Marigold strode ahead, but she imagined she could feel his gaze comparing her backside to those of the oxen. At least she wasn't eating the dust of the wagon.

It was pretty here, despite being a rough stretch of loose rocks and potholes that zigzagged back and forth through thinning trees. Eventually the walls of the mountains pushed themselves farther apart and the ground evened out. More sky appeared above the canopy of trees.

She was breathing heavily, even though the climb hadn't been that steep, and climbed back into the wagon to rest. Virgil took them around a final rocky outcrop, and a wide valley opened dramatically below them.

It was both glorious and...disappointing.

The river meandered back and forth across a grassy plain, but the edges were torn up. Water was diverted into wooden wheels and other contraptions. Men worked in small, muddy groups. Trees had been logged and their stumps left between the drying piles of branches. The late summer sun was turning much of the valley a dull brown.

As they ambled down the hill and rolled between a pair of tall posts set on either side of the track, she noted a painted sign that read:

Venturous Mining Company
Report to Owen or you will be shot

"You'll introduce me to Owen?" she said, nodding toward the sign.

Virgil's mouth twitched. "It's a warning to claim jumpers."

"You don't *really* shoot people, do you?"

He gave her the look that called her soft.

"Be serious. Don't you report them and have them arrested? How does one even know if you're jumping a claim? Where do you register?"

"You ask a lot of questions."

"You advertised for an educated woman. How do you think I gained my education? By waiting for someone to decide what I need to know? The only thing you learn that way is that women are thought to have inferior minds to men." She was taking in the approaching cobble of a camp with appalled astonishment. Where were the signs of society and order? She grew more and more nervous as she failed to find any.

This was worse than Denver! It was nothing but tents and huddled, scruffy men.

"There is no law, and there's no one to do the arresting even if there was." Virgil answered the question she'd forgotten she had asked.

She snapped him a look. "What exactly do you mean, 'there is no law'?"

"Thousands of men—fifty, maybe a hundred thousand—have poured through these mountains since we arrived a year and a half ago. That's not counting the Cheyenne and Arapahoe and Ute, who've all been squeezed into these parts by settlers pushing from all sides. You think a handful of politicians five hundred miles away have any control over what goes on here? Hell, they can barely keep from killing each other over where to put the capitol, let alone worrying about what we're doing."

Marigold gripped the edge of her seat while fighting back a hysterical laugh. "No wonder everyone is so worried which way the miners would vote on statehood." These men were outlaws and transients with no stake in what happened at the border with Missouri.

As if to prove her right, a shrill whistle pierced the air. It came from one of the miners down in a trench. Most of them wore heavy hobnail boots and filthy denim trousers. Some had removed their shirts, exposing their tanned, hairy chests crisscrossed by suspenders. They held pickaxes and wide, flat shovels and seemed to be moving gravel from the stream bed into a long wooden box.

"Blow us a kiss, sweetheart!" one of them cajoled. He sent her one with a touch of his fingertips to his lips and an expansive wave of his arm.

Virgil was on his feet so fast, the wagon rocked under the stamp of his weight. "Get back to work!" he snarled.

All the men jolted and turned away. One cuffed the catcaller on the back of his head.

Marigold blinked, stunned. The man had been fresh, but back in Topeka she'd had spittle land on her from men who had stuck their face into hers while they berated and shoved her. She had been called "whore" and "harlot" by her husband and his lawyer.

Through it all, no one had defended her like that. Her sister had said *ignore it,* and her uncle had said *we can't let that stop us.*

A hot ball of mixed emotions formed in her throat. She kept her eyes down to hide it.

"If anything happens with any of the men here, *anything*, you let them know they'll have me to deal with." Virgil planted his butt on the bench again. "Then you *tell me*. That's not just for your safety, but for the children and the rest of the worksite. One step out of line by any of these lunkheads can be a fuse on a powder keg. Understand?"

"Yes." She bit her lips to keep them from quivering.

She knew she was being stared at as they continued along. Men went quiet as their wagon rolled past, stopping work, but Virgil's mood seemed to have traveled ahead. No one else called out until a booming voice shouted, "Boss!"

Virgil drew hard on the reins to stop the wagon in front of the biggest of the few buildings she could see. A wiry man stood in the open door. He had a small chin and a sunken chest and an angelic halo of silver-black curls.

"Marigold, this is Yeller."

"Because I yell, not because I'm yellah," Yeller informed her. "I ain't afraid of nothin'." He didn't so much shout as possess a deep voice that carried like the ring of a church bell.

"Yeller runs the storehouse and will keep an account of anything you take. You and I will settle up at home."

"You must be Miss Martin. Or Mrs. Gardner, should I say?" He tipped an imaginary hat. "Pleasure to meet you."

"Wouldn't it be nice if things worked out the way they were supposed to?" Virgil spoke with a facetious congeniality as he climbed from the wagon. "This is Mrs. Davis, Miss Martin's sister. She's here to mind my children and keep house for me. Do me the favor of telling all and sundry so I don't have to repeat myself."

"Tell 'em what? That you're calling it a house now? Pah. I guess it's better than what I sleep in, huh, Mrs. Davis? You're widowed? My condolences."

"Divorced," she corrected as she climbed from the wagon, not taking her usual care in relaying that information because she was falling into a state of shock, heart sinking faster than a stone in a river, chest growing tight.

"Dee-vorced," Yeller repeated loud enough to turn heads down the way. "You want a husband, you come see me first, hear me? I'm offering myself, o' course. I don't keep a stock o' husbands. Although most days maybe I do."

She supposed these were jokes and she was expected to laugh, but... "Am I to, um, understand that, um..."

Dear Pearl. If you can picture rows of unwashed sheets on a line, you have the substance of Quail's Creek. A town it is not.

Tents. That's all there were. Rows of gray, muddy tents set out the way she'd once seen an army troop encamped on a field.

"Have we, um, *arrived*?" She might as well be called Squeak, her voice had dwindled to such a pale version of itself.

Virgil nodded, making no apologies or excuses. "I'll walk you up to the *cabin*—" He threw a sour look at Yeller. "So you can get settled."

He reached into the wagon for her carpetbag and cushion and started up what seemed to pass for a main street, but it was really only a pair of ruts worn into the grass.

She never should have come, never should have interfered in Pearl's life. She should have turned a blind eye to her husband's adultery and become one of those long-suffering, stuck-up society matrons she had always pitied and judged as lacking a spine. At least those women lived in real towns with bakeries and book shops and gas-powered streetlamps.

What did she have? Not even a change of clothes or the berries she'd picked. They'd eaten them along the way.

As she hurried to keep up with Virgil, a drumbeat sounded in her head.

What have I done? What have I done?

CHAPTER SIX

"That's the office." Virgil nodded at the only other wooden structure besides the storehouse and the outhouses built at convenient locations near the tents and worksites. Last year, he and his partners had wintered in that small cabin across from the storehouse.

"One of us is always in there, so if you need to find me, start there." Four of the men slept there, but he didn't tell her why they kept it manned. She would find out soon enough that the gold was stored there between payday and trips to Denver.

They passed what would be the cookhouse if anyone found time to put walls around it. For now, it was four posts and a roof with a pair of long tables, benches, and a cast-iron stove. The camp cook, Gristle, served army rations with a surly resentment of critics.

Next to that was a laundry run by one of Bing Sun's men, then a poor attempt on Ira and Stoney's part to grow cabbage and onions. A withered patch of tomato plants clung to life nearby.

On the hillside, their original four horses had expanded to twelve and had since been joined by four mules, six burrows, three dairy cows, two goats, and the oxen. Stoney had an order in for two dozen chicks come spring while Bing Sun had mentioned acquiring ducks when he wintered in San Francisco. Levi and Chaveno, the son of Tom's cousin, were armed with slingshots and charged with keeping an eye out for predators along with bringing the animals in at night.

Across the river, the Utes had made a small camp of wickiups and a communal fire. Some of their men worked under Tom while others hunted. The women had been gathering plants, drying meat, and tanning hides all summer. Virgil reckoned they would close up shop right quick if Leyohna was free to travel. They wanted to be well south and meeting up with other family and associated bands before the first flakes of snow began to fall.

Virgil had his eye on a plateau above their camp for his permanent home. It was high enough to avoid spring floods, had a long view of the valley and a glimpse of peaks in the distance. It was close to the hot spring tucked up in the forest and caught more sun than the valley floor, but it wasn't practical to build up there when he had to run back and forth all day between work and—

"Pa!" Levi came sprinting toward them. He stopped abruptly about eight feet away, chest heaving to catch his breath. "You came back."

Those words cut him to the bone every time. It made his voice gruff as he said, "Same as I do every time I run to Denver. This is Mrs. Davis. She's our housekeeper. My son, Levi."

"I thought you said you would get us a mother." Levi frowned.

"Things change," Virgil grumbled, instantly annoyed with himself for putting that shadow of distrust into Levi's eyes.

"It's nice to meet you, Levi." Marigold smiled

and held out a hand to the shirtless, barefoot eleven-year-old. "Please call me Marigold."

Levi was tanned brown by weeks of running around half dressed. His arm was limp as he briefly shook her hand. His, "Nice to meet you, ma'am," was unconvinced.

Virgil shifted uncomfortably. He was a skinflint sort of man. He'd spent too many years scraping and scrabbling to throw away a penny unnecessarily, but he was suddenly embarrassed that Levi was dressed like a beggar.

It was summer, and the children were growing like weeds. He'd ordered fabrics into the storehouse two months ago, but there was no such thing as church here. What did they need fancy clothes for? When they had grown out of the clothes they had arrived in, he'd given Leyohna some of his work-worn things and asked her to do what she could. She'd butchered a pair of his dungarees, cutting out the patched seat to take them in, and made short pants. Levi kept them on his lanky hips by cinching a length of twine around the suspender buttons.

Seeing him through Marigold's eyes, however, it looked like Virgil didn't care. He did, though. It bothered the hell out of him that Levi kept his distance and acted surprised that Virgil came back and that he watched Virgil with wary, storm-gray eyes.

Virgil had been afraid of his own father for good reason, but he wouldn't lift a finger against his own children. He wished they knew that.

"Did you get your work done while I was gone?" Virgil immediately knew it was the wrong thing to say, because Marigold shot him a look of dismay.

"Yes, sir." Levi fell into step beside them, head ducking shyly, but his eyes came up hopeful as a puppy seeking a pat. "Emmett checked my measures and let me saw the boards. He said you would get the nails and rope from Yeller."

"I will." He didn't break it to the kid that the bed Levi had been working so hard to build for himself would have to go to Marigold.

They passed a pile of logs, and the cabin came into view. Marigold made a noise like someone had knifed her.

Okay, it was a shack. It was the best he had been able to throw together given the children had turned up with the spring melt. There had been sluice boxes and rockers to build, channels to dig and gold to recover. Four walls of uncaulked split logs, a shake roof, and a bed to hold the bunch of them had meant shirking his paying work. His partners had been understanding and pitched in to get him this far, but the season was short. The pressure to work the gold was enormous.

Even so, after Virgil put in his twelve hours with the company, he sometimes took Levi up the hill to fell trees. They used the horses to drag the logs down here, but they still needed peeling and planing. Window glass was on order along with frames and lumber for a floor. Somehow, Virgil would have to get all of that carried in and nailed together before the frost.

Marigold didn't know any of that, of course. Her steps halted and her jaw hung slack while her shoulders sagged.

A pound of river gravel seemed to drop into the

pit of Virgil's stomach.

Nettie burst out of the shack with an excited, "Papa!"

She was also dressed like a street orphan in one of his old shirts. The sleeves were chopped off at her elbows and strips sewn onto the bottom to make it a dress that fell to her knees. She was all tangled hair and filthy feet and front teeth that were too big for her face. Marigold would have to squint real hard to see that Nettie cleaned up pretty as her mama.

Like Levi, Nettie jerked to a stop a few feet out of his reach. Her smile faltered between hope and apprehension.

Every time they ran out to greet him this way, Virgil had a thought to open his arms, but they were skittish as feral cats. Big gestures might scare them away for good, but here came another askance glare from Marigold. One that suggested he could do better. What the hell did she know about any of it?

Then again, what did he?

While he bit back a sigh, Marigold moved to crouch in front of his daughter.

"You must be Nettie." She threw a smile toward Levi to include him. "I've been excited to meet you and your brothers."

Nettie's eyes were like Clara's, more blue than gray. They grew turbulent and anxious as she asked, "Are you our new mother?"

"Marigold," Levi provided with a complete lack of enthusiasm, as though she was the fool's gold of mothers. "She's a housekeeper."

"But you said Leyohna is a housekeeper. That's why she can't stay forever." Nettie's mouth trembled with betrayal.

All of Virgil set like wind-baked clay, making his throat dry and the rest of him feel brittle. The children needed a mother. He'd known that from the moment they turned up. Leyohna had been a stopgap, one who Nettie had taken to with immediate and deep affection.

He gave the back of his head a scratch, ready to blurt out that he ought to check on the day's yield when Harley's high-pitched squeal sounded.

The two-year-old staggered out on his fat legs, toddling like a drunken sailor. He wore only a cotton shirt that had shrunk so small on him, it rode above his belly button. His worm and cork bobbled in the breeze as he came at Virgil swift as a whiskey jack looking to steal his lunch.

Could Virgil keep himself from wanting to smile? He had tried. Once. It was a losing battle. Harley's round cheeks and kissy lips and black, curly hair were straight from a picture book of baby angels. Only a monster could resent him.

The boy's eyes were brown but held the shape of Clara's. They were wide and appealing as he hugged Virgil's leg and looked up at him. His smile was Clara's, too. Hell, the dimples on that little brown ass were exactly as Virgil remembered, just like the shape of those ears.

But there was nothing of himself in this kid because Virgil hadn't made him.

• • •

"This is Harley." Virgil set his giant paw of a hand on

the boy's tightly curled hair.

The boy shone a grin way up at his father, but Virgil wasn't looking at the baby. He was glowering at Marigold, daring her to say something about that boy's brown skin. *Daring* her.

It was none of her business, though.

"Hello, Harley." Marigold tried to catch the boy's attention, but the baby was focused on trying to reach into Virgil's pant pocket.

"Peas?"

"Yes, I've brought you all a treat," Virgil said in the closest thing to an indulgent tone he was probably capable of. He dug into his pocket and came up with three lemon drops wrapped in paper.

The older children each darted closer to take one.

"Thanks, Pa."

"Thank you, Papa."

"Peas?" Harley's little hand was flexing urgently as Virgil unwrapped one.

Marigold was about to say he couldn't give such a large, hard candy to a baby when Virgil popped it into his own mouth and gave it a crunch, wincing as though he'd broken all his teeth. He dabbed his fingertip to his mouth to collect a piece and fed it to the baby.

Harley closed his lips over it, and he smiled. "Hmmm."

"Your hands are filthy," Marigold protested.

"It's a bit of rein oil. Hasn't killed anyone yet." He brushed his hand on the seat of his pants and looked toward the cabin. "Leyohna, this is Mrs. Davis."

Marigold pulled herself from wondering why

Virgil had to coax his children like wild dogs to come near him and turned to see a pregnant woman standing on the stoop of what Marigold fearfully suspected was her new home. Leyohna looked younger than Marigold's twenty-six. She had glossy black braids and clothing made of buff-colored hide and what looked to be hand-woven wool.

"Hello." Marigold smiled, and Leyohna smiled back, but with caution. She was studying Marigold's clothes and taking her measure before she glanced over the children, gaze lingering on Harley with conflicted regret.

It was easy enough to sum up that the other woman felt genuine affection for the children but had her own responsibilities bearing down on her. Leyohna and Virgil exchanged words in what Marigold presumed was the Ute language. They ended with him giving a decisive nod.

"Papa, no," Nettie said in a pitifully anguished tone, indicating she had followed their conversation. Her sadness wrenched at Marigold's heart.

"Her family goes south for the winter, Nettie. You knew she was only here until…" He glanced at Marigold, seeming perplexed as he realized she could also be temporary.

Don't dismiss her feelings, Marigold wanted to scold him, but Leyohna was already crouched and hugging Nettie, speaking to the girl in a tone of comfort.

"I have to check on the diggings," Virgil said in a grumble. "Men will be looking for their mail."

"Can I come?" Levi asked him.

Virgil nodded, saying curtly, "Nettie, you help

Mrs. Davis settle in while Leyohna goes across to tell her family—" He left it hanging, nodded once, and stalked off.

Coward, Marigold wanted to shout at his back.

An awkward silence ensued between her and Leyohna. Harley was oblivious. He crouched to dig at something in the grass with his finger, but Nettie was fighting tears. Her little fists were in hard knots at her sides. She sent Marigold a death glare straight from her father's arsenal, one that reviled her for being the instrument of her loss.

"Nettie, are you able to speak to Leyohna for me? I'm hoping she's staying a little longer. Will you please ask her to help us both get used to our new situation?"

Nettie did, tearfully, and Leyohna assured them she wouldn't leave without saying a proper goodbye. That seemed to mollify Nettie a little, and Marigold picked up her things from where Virgil had dropped them on the ground. She followed the baby's pace as they made their way toward the door of the cabin.

Marigold had been truthful when she had said she was good with children, but she was realizing how cavalier she'd been about what it meant to *care* for children. This was not a Sunday picnic where she would hand out cups of lemonade and marshal a sack race. These children had lost their mother and were about to lose their surrogate. Marigold knew as well as anyone that it was hard to extend trust and affection after suffering such harsh blows. The way they'd looked with starved little eyes to their father made her want to open her heart to all of them, but could she commit to them?

Virgil hadn't been as forthcoming as he could have been. His letter to Pearl had left her sister convinced he was a "gold baron" who would provide her a very comfortable life.

Instead, Marigold suspected her cookstove was that smoldering fire with three saplings tented over it and a covered pot tucked into the coals beneath it. The water pump was a worn path from the empty bucket by the door down to the edge of the stream. And goodness, wasn't the cabin cheerfully bright with all these *gaping cracks* between the logs? How wonderful to be able to see so clearly how small and primitive the single room really was.

There were two beds built at angles to each other in the back corner. Judging by the number of scattered blankets and the rail on the wider, bottom one, it belonged to the children. There was a bench secured to the wall closer to the door. It had a narrow table set before it. No fireplace. The only heat was the warmth of the sun coming through the single window and the south-facing door.

Leyohna showed her the crate beneath the lower bed where folded clothing was kept. Three rows of shelves hammered into the wall cracks were the pantry. It was stocked with dried beans, oats, cans of corn and peaches, and one tin of evaporated milk. Alongside those were a few small baskets that appeared to be woven from some type of inner tree bark. They had lids perfectly sized to seal them and were filled with fragrant needles, herbs, dried mushrooms, and ground roots.

Nettie translated for Leyohna as she explained which were used for cooking and which had medicinal properties. She tapped her head and her swollen belly to indicate headache and monthly cramps. Marigold could have hugged her. She always felt as though her stomach was made of knives when her menses came on.

Nettie nodded that she could show her where to collect more if it ran out.

Leyohna then went to tell her family that they could begin preparing to leave the valley.

Marigold smiled bravely, but self-doubt washed over her like storm waves on the ocean. She was starting to feel as distressed by Leyohna's departure as Nettie looked.

Marigold picked up the whittled cow and horse and dog and pig from the floor and made a little vignette of them on the bench.

Harley promptly toddled across to knock them all down again.

"He always does that," Nettie said heavily. "No, I don't want to play right now," she added when Harley tried to give her the horse. She flopped onto the lower bed.

Marigold sank onto the bench and set all the animals beside her so Harley could bat them down with the horse.

"I'm sorry you lost your mother, Nettie. I was about Levi's age when my parents died. My younger sister was your age. I remember how angry I felt when our uncle sent us to school in Philadelphia, not giving us any say in what happened to us."

"*My* uncle sent us *here*."

"Oh? I presumed your mother brought you."

"No. She died of fever, and Auntie said she would

write to Albert to see if he would come back for us, but Uncle said he wouldn't and that we had to go live with Papa. He doesn't even *like* us."

"Your papa? Of course he does." Marigold didn't ask who Albert was. She had a suspicion. She left Harley bashing animals at the bench and went across to perch on the bed beside Nettie. She patted the girl's leg. "I think your father is trying very hard to make a good home for you." She thought of his saying how he had nearly starved in California the first winter after sending his pittance of gold to Clara. "He wouldn't have kept you here with him if he didn't care about you."

"You really think so?" Her voice was forlorn, her mouth trembling at the corners.

"I do." She hoped so. Fervently. "And I know I'm not your mother or Leyohna, but I want you and I to become friends because…" Her emotions were catching up to her. Her chest and throat grew tight. She had to blink a sting from her eyes. "Because I already miss my sister. When I decided to come here, I was feeling very disheartened and unlucky. I thought doing something that was *my* decision would make me feel as though I had control over my life. I thought doing something courageous would mean I *am* courageous, but…"

I'm scared.

She had landed herself in a remote, untamed wilderness with a remote, untamed man. She was facing more responsibility and fewer resources or protections than ever. The trapped sob in her throat stung so sharply, Marigold sniffed and wiped at the tear that started to trickle down her cheek.

A similar misery was welling in Nettie's eyes. Her chin crinkled and her lips quivered.

Marigold gathered her up. It was instinctual and incredibly comforting to hold Nettie's wiry little body and feel her small arms cling around her as they both snuffled with self-pity.

She knew she should be saying, "It will be all right," but in this moment, she really wasn't sure. She refused to start her relationship with this darling girl by lying to her. She hugged her instead, fighting to stifle her own sobs, sniffing back her tears, silently begging for a sign that she had done the right thing in coming here.

A loud fart echoed inside a metal tub.

Startled, she and Nettie pulled apart.

Harley sat on a board set across a squat chamber pot. Presumably it had a hole in it because he said, "Poop." His grin faded as he strained.

"Oh, Harley!" Nettie fell back on the covers, arms splayed helplessly.

"He *does* use the pot." Marigold's dejection flipped to hysterical amusement at the farcicality of it all. She grasped tickling handfuls of Nettie's tummy, saying, "That noise was the best thing I've heard all week."

Nettie released squeals of laughter.

CHAPTER SEVEN

Four hours later, Virgil approached the cabin with caution, not sure what to expect.

It was still standing, but something told him it was empty.

Damn. Nettie was likely still upset with him for Leyohna's impending departure. The baby had his stubborn moments, and Levi had been roundly peeved when Virgil had told him the bed he was making would have to go to Marigold.

Levi had marched home with his shit in a knot. He may or may not have paid Virgil any mind when Virgil had called out that the boy should fetch water for Marigold when he got here.

God knew Marigold had to be ready to string Virgil up, now she'd had time to fully appreciate how rough they lived. Maybe he should have tried harder to talk one of the other Ute women into staying through the winter. They were all determined to head south with their families, though. Sharing this valley with his crew for a summer was about as far as their trust in white folk went.

No, Marigold was his only feasible choice, but Virgil wouldn't have been the least surprised to hear she had started walking back to Denver on her newly shod feet.

Huh. Promisingly, the fire was snapping and flickering beneath the stew pot hanging over it. A full bucket of water was tucked near the embers to warm. Voices were coming from the shadows near the stack of logs.

Virgil found Marigold with Harley on her hip. Levi had assembled the pieces for the bed on the grass to show Marigold how it would come together.

"And the ropes pull it up flat against the wall every morning?" Marigold asked.

"So it's out of the way, yeah."

"That *is* a practical piece of engineering."

"Pa!" Levi leaped to his feet. "Marigold said she'll sleep with Nettie and Harley so I can have my own bed."

"Oh?" He glanced at Marigold.

"Nettie said she doesn't mind. Harley promised not to wet the blankets." That made the older kids snicker.

"Marigold says she can show me how to make a doll from the oat sack when it's empty." Nettie took two quick steps toward him in her excitement. "If you say I can have it."

Why did he get the feeling there would be a lot of "Marigold says" in his future?

"The oat sack? Sure."

Nettie grinned and brought fists of anticipation together under her chin.

"The children have eaten, but there's plenty of stew left. I was about to wash hands and faces, then put this one into bed." Marigold looked down to where Harley's head rested on her shoulder. His eyelids were drooping.

"I'll serve myself." He caught Levi's expectant stare and said, "After we nail the bed together." Virgil was bone tired and his stomach was about to eat the rest of him, but there was just enough light to hammer in the needed pins. He had picked up the nails and rope on his way home, figuring Marigold would need the bed tonight.

Of course, calling it a "bed" was generous. Levi had helped Virgil build the outhouse, and these six boards nailed onto a Z were exactly the same as the john door.

Still, the boy had measured and cut the boards himself and took care which board went where, obviously having spent a lot of time working out the best configuration. Damned if he wasn't looking proud as a new father once they had it ready to install.

"I'm starting to think you have a talent for woodworking, son."

Levi's mouth hitched with his crooked grin, but it faltered as he thumbed an uneven end on one of the boards. "I didn't cut this one very good."

"It's fine to notice things you wish you'd done different. That's how you learn to do better next time, but it's sturdy, and all your cuts were measured right so there's no waste. I know plenty of full-grown men who don't take the time to be sure. You did well."

"Thanks." Levi's head turtled into his shoulders. "I guess we could put that end against the wall where no one will see it."

"Now you're thinking." Virgil had an urge to ruffle his hair or pat his back, but Levi turned away for the rope.

Twenty minutes later, Virgil had the bed suspended off the wall in the only space available. They would have to shove the table under the window every night to lower the bed, but so be it. Levi didn't have a mattress, either, only a spare blanket Virgil used with his bedroll in winter. Marigold promised to see Gristle about setting aside some potato sacks that she could sew together and fill with dry grass to make Levi his own mattress.

Harley was scrubbed and fast asleep when Marigold returned from escorting Nettie to the john. Both had washed their faces and combed out their hair, leaving it in a braided tail.

Virgil had to consciously drag his thoughts from imagining unraveling Marigold's and feeling it across his naked chest and thighs— No. Just no.

Levi couldn't wait to put himself to bed, so Virgil left Marigold to settle them and went outside to finally plant his ass onto a log round and eat.

He stirred up the fire enough to throw some light so he could see what it was.

"Leyohna made it. I only had to warm it," Marigold said as she joined him a few minutes later. She scooped a tin cup into the bucket of hot water and dropped some pine needles into it.

"Have you eaten?" He paused his shoveling of stew into his mouth. She looked as weary as he was.

"I have. It's good. Leyohna was kind enough to give me a tutorial. Nettie said she would show me where to collect more herbs after Leyohna leaves. With her two burrows."

Virgil tugged his earlobe. What could he say? Tom drove a hard bargain when it came to letting his family do favors for white men.

"I don't think the children realize that Leyohna is

expecting," Marigold said quietly. "I imagine that's why she feels such urgency to head south with the rest of her family. Is that something you would like me to explain to them?"

He sure as hell didn't want to tackle it. "You think Nettie is old enough?"

"I think it would help her understand and feel less abandoned."

Shit. He had known that's how the girl felt, but it was hard to hear it blunt like that.

"I presumed you had written to your wife to join you here and something happened after she arrived," Marigold continued. "Nettie told me their uncle sent them here with a couple who carried on to Oregon. I don't expect you to talk about it if you don't want to, but it makes me concerned that they lost their mother, then the aunt who was caring for them. Now they're losing Leyohna."

The same thing had been chewing at him. "That's why I wanted them to have a mother."

Maybe he said it with more blame than was fair, because her mouth became a flat line before she touched her cup to it. Her gaze was in the fire, the flicker of the flames reflecting in her eyes.

He kept eating, piling food into his mouth in an effort to swallow down a frustrated defensiveness. He didn't know how she put him on his back foot by saying nothing at all, but she did.

"You don't want to marry, either. You said that," he reminded.

"I did."

"Well, then."

"'Then' what?" She sat taller.

"Then you should be happy I put a stop to things this morning. You want to risk a *reason* to marry?"

"No." Her answer was prompt and sullen. "And *I* would have put a stop to it before that happened."

He choked on a chewy bite of venison. "Is that right? I'll leave it to you to call a halt next time, then."

"There won't be a next time," she snapped back, quick as a wet cat.

"Damned straight there won't." Though it stung to say it.

Her brow might have flexed with what might have been hurt, but it was hard to read her expression in the firelight. Why was he even trying? He scraped the last of the stew and set the pot aside.

The fire crackled and threw sparks into the air.

Just when he was thinking about taking that water for a rag bath, she gave a small sigh that was impatient, but also sounded injured and frustrated.

"You don't have to be so mean about everything. If you want me to stick around and do my best for your children, we have to get along. Without…complications."

This was the thing he found most annoying about her. She said frank things that made him feel in the wrong simply because she was right.

"Look…" He wanted a wife so his children would have a mother, someone they could trust to be there as long as God was willing, but it had to be someone *he* could trust.

His throat closed over bringing up her history, though. He didn't usually mind speaking plain, but he balked at flat-out calling her things he didn't know were true.

After a second, he spilled the bald facts.

"When we staked our claim on this valley and started to work it, I went to Fort Kearney for supplies. While I was there, I sent a letter and some gold to Clara, telling her where I was. By the time a return letter from her brother caught up to me, the lawyer he'd hired was in Denver City with the children. I hadn't seen Clara since she was carrying Nettie." He left a nice long pause for that to sink in.

"I wondered," she murmured, chin dipped so her gaze was in her cup.

"Everyone does," he said flatly. "I had words with the lawyer, told him what I thought of the situation." He was still feeling that punch in the gut when that man had accosted him at the Express station, dragging him across to a wagon where everyone in the camp had heard his business. "But Archie had paid him to leave all three children with me, and that man was determined to do it."

"Lawyers are vile."

"And slick enough to keep Archie from putting anything incriminating into his letter. The lawyer said Archie told him Clara had taken in a boarder—Albert—and that she 'showed no regret for any lapse in judgment.'" Virgil had understood that to mean she'd taken Albert to their marriage bed of her own volition. "Archie's letter said that as Clara's husband, her children were my children and therefore my responsibility."

"When did they arrive?"

"May. She died last Christmas. Archie sent them with the first wagon train west. The lawyer and his wife were carrying on to Oregon and anxious to get back to the trail. I could see plain as day that Nettie and Levi couldn't do without their baby brother. Levi is protective of the both of them. Nettie clucks over Harley like he's her own little chick. He's all they have of their mother. What the hell was I supposed to do?"

"You did the right thing. The only thing you could do." She lowered the cup to her knee and regarded him with the eyes of a doe, gaze wide and dark and open.

It made something seesaw in his chest. He shrugged a prickle off his shoulders and ran his hands up and down his thighs. God knew he'd tried to find other options but hadn't come up with anything except bringing them home and placing ads to find them a mother.

"There was no word about whether this Albert might want them?" she asked.

"I wrote to Archie. Got what information I could out of the children. It sounds as though Albert went up to Canada for work, but he could have been running." Whether Albert was free or enslaved, Missouri was a slave state, and Albert hadn't been safe there. "What sticks in my craw is that Clara likely took in a boarder because I wasn't sending her enough to live on." Virgil rose and paced into the dark. "That's why I had to accept Harley." It was twisted logic, but it felt straightforward to him. "Clara must have felt abandoned, me being away for years and only sending dribs and drabs. If I'd been there, she wouldn't have taken that man into our home, let alone our bed."

"Did her brother not help her?"

"Do you know what that fucker did?" Virgil spun, still outraged by the man's gall. "He kept the gold I sent to her. Said it was for the care he'd given my children since her death and the cost of sending them to me. They arrived with a change of clothes and empty bellies, not a toy between them. Son of a bitch." If he ever got his hands around Archie's throat…

"Well, it sounds as if they're better off with you for many reasons."

"Here?" he scoffed. "Jesus, that tells you where they've been, doesn't it?" He squeezed the back of his neck, trying not to contemplate too deeply why they were so fearful of him. They spoke fondly enough of their aunt and cousins. As far as he could tell, Archie hadn't struck them or been outright cruel, but he hadn't wanted the responsibility of his sister's children. They'd sensed Archie's resentment.

"Don't tell them about Leyohna's baby," Virgil decided. "It's liable to raise questions I don't want to answer just yet."

She nodded. "I understand. And I realize now why you don't trust me. Especially after…" Her voice thinned. "…this morning."

He had dredged his sordid history from the depths of his gut to avoid making accusations that would hurt her, but he'd hurt her anyway. He could hear the ache of it in her voice.

"Marigold—"

Her head came up, but he didn't know what to say. His brain was trying to hang onto his doubts, but his gut told him to believe her. She'd been the victim of infidelity, same as he was. Hell, she adjusted her shoulders every time the subject came up, as though she was trying to carry all the lingering humiliation still sitting on her like a yoke.

Same as he did.

"I'm tired," she said when he failed to speak. "I'll turn in. Good night."

She was almost at the door before he managed to say, "Sleep well."

CHAPTER EIGHT

Marigold slept surprisingly well, considering her mind was in turmoil when she lay down. No wonder Virgil was so suspicious of her. She had been found guilty of infidelity, while his wife had committed the same crime and left him with the consequence of it.

You'll find me to be a fair, respectful man to all but liars, cheats, and thieves.

She wasn't guilty of adultery, though. It got under her skin that he refused to take her word for it.

It was hard to feel scorned and resentful of injustices, however, with two little bodies snuggled up close in the night. She settled her arm across them and didn't hear Virgil come to bed. Or rise.

In fact, she slept so hard she was completely disoriented when Harley sat up and said a sleepy, "Peas?"

"Shh." Virgil loomed over the bed before Marigold had properly remembered where she was. He plucked Harley from the blankets and carried him away.

Marigold rolled and resettled, peering through the pre-dawn light creeping through the cracks in the walls. Virgil set Harley on the pot and fetched a can from the shelf. He gave two jabs into the lid with his pocketknife, then poured milk into a cup, adding water from the pitcher.

When Harley sleepily toddled over to him in his nightshirt, Virgil lowered to the bench and gathered the baby onto his lap. They took turns drinking from the cup, Harley sitting limp and trusting in the curve of Virgil's arm, head resting on Virgil's chest.

Yes, Nettie, if your father can be that tender with a child who was thrust upon him by an estranged and wandering wife, he loves all of you very deeply.

She saw Virgil's head turn as though he sensed she was awake and watching. She closed her eyes, pretending to be asleep.

When the cup was empty, Virgil rose and started to bring the boy back to Marigold, but Harley pointed at Levi and gave a questioning grunt.

"Levi." Virgil gave the older boy's shoulder a squeeze, speaking softly. "He wants to sleep with you."

Levi lifted his blanket, and Virgil tucked the baby in beside him.

"Tell Marigold to get more milk today."

"I will."

Virgil left, and Marigold strained to hear his footsteps.

After a few minutes, Harley sat up and began to crawl around, eager to explore Levi's new bed.

"No, it's too early. Lay down and I'll rub your back." Levi wrangled his little brother back under the blankets.

A few minutes later, everyone was fast asleep again, but Marigold was wide awake. She was still pondering Virgil's feelings about his wife and her own reasons for coming here. She needed a home as badly as the children did, but could she make this shack into one?

She must have a little of Pearl's ability to conjure

rose-colored fantasies, because a fresh start had struck her as easier than trying to make something of the broken life she'd been mired in. She hadn't expected to have *quite* such a blank slate to write on, but she rose to get a jump on the day.

When she went outside to stoke the fire and fetch water for porridge, she found the bucket by the door was full. Flames were licking at fresh wood in the firepit, and the pot that hung over it held water and oats that were already thickening.

A small sigh escaped her. How was a man so gruff and objectionable also this thoughtful?

She hugged her shawl around her, moving to where she could see men striding between cookhouse and outhouse. The sun was only touching the highest peaks on one side of the valley, but it landed on some leaves, illuminating them with a bright yellow glow. The air was morning crisp and rich with the scent of pine and earth. The river trickled musically, and right in this moment, Marigold found this to be a very peaceful and pretty place.

"Marigold?" Levi came out of the cabin. "I thought you were going to the john, but you didn't come back."

"I'm here." She turned to see him hugging himself against the morning chill. "I was going to make breakfast, but your father did it already, so I was looking at the valley." She opened her shawl. "I'll have to make you a shirt for these cool mornings."

"Leyohna made me a vest. She said she'll make us boots for winter before she leaves." He stood in front of her, facing out, backing into her as she closed her shawl across his front.

"Too bad we're not up there where the sun is already shining." She pointed with the corner of her shawl.

"That's where Pa and the men lived when they got here."

"Oh?"

"Uh-huh." He nodded. "Pa said he wants to build a house up there one day. For now, we have to live here, but we're going to make it a proper house. Pa bought a stove, and me and Nettie help him make bricks at the clay pit for the chimney, then Ira cooks them in his fire. We're going to make it bigger, too. That's what these logs are for." He used his elbow to point. "After we build the extra room, he'll show Nettie and me how to plug the cracks with mud and straw. It's okay to be drafty in summer, but not winter."

"True."

"He said at Christmas we can go up there and have a hot bath."

"How?"

"There's a cold creek and a hot one. Pa and Uncle Owen and the rest of the men dammed it into a pool. Tom helped them make a wickiup to live in. Pa says they would have all died if they didn't have the hot water to sit in. He said icicles were hanging from all the trees and off their beards even."

"Goodness." Marigold wondered if Leyohna's family wanted company on their trip south.

"I should eat and let the critters out. Pa said you should get milk today."

"I will. Do you want this?" She offered her shawl as he stepped away.

"No, thanks. I'm not cold." He walked to the john, and she had to wonder if he'd stood with her for warmth or human closeness.

Either way, he'd caused her to look at this valley with new eyes. It was hardship and challenge and isolation, but it also held glimmers of potential.

A sense of buoyancy arrived, something she hadn't felt in so long, she didn't immediately know what it was. It might have been hope.

• • •

Marigold was used to being notorious. For several years now, her reputation had been preceding her. Therefore, it was no surprise to her that people knew her name as she walked with Nettie and Harley to the cookhouse.

The surprise was the way men tipped their caps and said, "Howdy, Mrs. Davis," in a way that sounded pleasant and friendly.

When the thin, gnarled man scraping dishes at the cookhouse saw her coming down the aisle between the two nearly empty tables, he set his work aside and swiped his hands on his long apron.

"Mrs. Davis." He spoke her name with far too much awe and deference, as though he was meeting a playwright or the First Lady. She almost thought he was mocking her, but he flushed so hard his scalp reddened beneath his thin white hair.

She smiled and held out her hand. "Hello. You must be Mr. Gristle?"

"Just Gristle, ma'am." He stepped forward so fast he kicked a stray tin can into rattling across the gravel floor. He barely glanced at it before giving her hand an enthused shake. "You can call me John, if you want to," he said bashfully, smiling with closed lips in what she took to be an attempt to hide his missing teeth.

"Thank you, John. I'm told you're the man to ask if one needs empty potato sacks."

His face went an even deeper shade of red at her use of his name. "I got four right here." He practically stumbled over his feet getting to a crate. "How many you need?"

"Two will do," she decided as she eyed them. "I'm making a mattress tick for Levi. He only comes up to here on me." She set her hand under her chin.

"We don't get husks to use as stuffing, only corn in cans."

"I thought I would use long grass. I'm off to view Yeller's fabrics, to make a suitable cover. If it's thick enough, it shouldn't be too prickly."

Gristle nodded with admiration. "Is that something you could make for me? I sleep on the ground and don't have time or patience for needlework. I'll pay you."

For a moment, Marigold was too startled to find words.

"I think we could work something out. May I come back for these after I've seen Yeller?"

"'Course." Gristle gave her a salute with his ladle, then turned and snarled at a miner. "Are you trying to pickle it for winter? You're making a meal of my salt."

She and Nettie exchanged looks as they left, and Nettie whispered, "I've never heard him be nice to anyone before. I think he likes you."

"I feel quite special, then." There were perks to being the only woman for miles, she supposed.

Yeller greeted her and the children with booming enthusiasm, cheerfully handing off three tins of milk, a small sack of flour, a needle, thread, and four yards of heavy cotton.

Back at the cabin, Marigold washed the sacks and draped them on the logs to dry. Then she found a pickle jar suitable for a sourdough starter.

Once that was tucked on the shelf, she took the children into the hills above the cabin to pick berries. Harley amused himself by eating what he picked while Nettie only ate every second or third berry. When Harley started to look sleepy, Marigold removed her apron and set him to playing with a feather they'd found.

She and Nettie had been exchanging little stories about their travel across the plains, but they quieted while Harley dropped off. It was a pleasant, companionable silence with only the buzz of bees and the odd birdsong. Such a fine summer day made her miss Pearl, but she also felt at ease, thinking this life she had chosen was not so bad. Not bad at all.

When she heard the rustle of a step behind her, she turned, expecting Virgil.

It was the biggest, blackest dog she'd ever seen.

No. It was a *bear*.

Nettie let out a piercing scream, startling the beast into blowing a grunt. It stood up on its hind legs and opened his mouth to show his teeth.

Marigold reacted on instinct, placing herself between the creature and the children.

"Git!" She threw her pail right at the animal, hitting him in the chest and dumbfounding him into dropping onto his four feet. He glared sideways at her, trying to decide if he wanted to charge or snuffle for the dropped berries or run away.

"Nettie, get Harley. Run back to the cabin. Hurry." Marigold never took her eyes off the animal. She ruffled her skirt and shouted, "You get now! Go on! Git!"

Harley wailed at being snatched up by Nettie. As she tried to carry him while running pell-mell down the hill, she screamed at the top of her lungs, "Papa! Help! Help us, Pa! *Help!*"

The bear didn't seem to know which way to look, glancing at the children and lifting his nose for a sniff of the breeze. Dear God, his paws were massive.

Marigold shifted to keep herself between the beast and the children. Her heart was threatening to crash itself right out of her chest.

"Go on! Get!" she shouted, trying to kick up some dirt at him.

With a disgusted huff, the bear lumbered into the trees.

Marigold waited one more second to be sure it was gone before she raced after the children. She was catching up to them when another animal charged at them from her left. She let out her own bloodcurdling scream and snatched the children into her, but it was a man on horseback.

"What is it?" He brandished a rifle.

Nettie looked up with her tear-streaked face and pointed. "Bear!"

The man kicked his horse into a gallop up the hill.

Marigold folded onto the ground, a shaking mass of overwrought nerves. Nettie fell onto her, clinging for comfort while Harley stood beside them letting out confused wails, rubbing his sleepy eyes, not sure why he was frightened and angry, but certain he was both.

• • •

Virgil heard Nettie's scream from the bottom of a gulley. He leaped onto a sluice box, kicking it over in his scramble to get up to even ground.

Owen galloped by, but Nettie was still screaming and Harley was wailing. Virgil ran harder than he ever had in his life, legs pumping, feet pounding. When he would have veered into the cabin for his gun, he heard Marigold's bone-chilling scream and saw them falling into a huddle on the hillside above the cabin.

He ran up to them, thighs hot, lungs aching, barely able to gasp out, "What?" Harley lifted his arms so Virgil snatched him into his chest.

"Bear." Marigold was shaking and white.

"Jesus." He crouched and touched Nettie's shoulder where she was clinging to Marigold. "You hurt? Let me see."

"I'm okay." Nettie stood to demonstrate.

Virgil reacted on instinct. He scooped her into his arms so tight he was liable to crush both of these tiny bodies to death if he wasn't careful, but Jesus Christ. He'd seen a man mauled by a grizzly once, when he'd been in the army. It was horrifying.

"What the hell were you doing up there?" He

glowered at Marigold, so scared for the bunch of them his guts hurt.

"Picking berries." She was shakily trying to get to her feet.

"Why do you think they're called bear berries?" he shouted. "You should have taken the gun. Or Levi, with the slingshot." He stood, keeping both children in his arms. His muscles shook, but he couldn't unlock his arms to let them go. "Pick near the Ute camp where the smoke from the fire keeps the animals away. *Think*, Marigold!"

"Well, I didn't know, did I?" She brushed at the grass clinging to her dress and glared up at him through eyes that were teary with fear.

His old guilt of "should have been there" reared inside him, and his mouth filled with a sour taste of failure.

A rifle shot sounded above. They all looked up the hill.

There was a crash of dry branches, an angry whinny from the horse. Owen wasn't taking time to reload. Virgil gathered himself, half expecting the animal to break from the trees and charge them.

"Get to the cabin," he started to say, but there was another shot. The revolver.

A faint but triumphant, "Whoo-hoo!" echoed down to them.

"He *killed* it?" Marigold stacked her hands on her chest.

"I'll go help him skin it." Virgil stooped to set the children on their feet. His heart was still rolling like a paddlewheel. "You get back to the cabin."

• • •

Two hours later, Virgil walked back to the cabin with the recovered pails, one half full of berries, the other holding Marigold's apron.

Walker and Antelope had turned up to help skin the four-hundred-pound animal and get it down to Yeller for quartering and hanging. They had accepted the hide and a portion of meat in exchange.

All the miners would get a small cut for their pots tonight. Gristle would turn the rest into roasts, sausage, jerky, bear grease, and bone broth. Levi had claimed one of its biggest teeth.

Owen paced alongside Virgil. He was in high spirits, and Virgil had a feeling it came from more than making such a dangerous kill. Owen was anticipating a proper introduction to Marigold after catching a glimpse of her when he'd galloped by on his horse.

She was behind the cabin, dulling Virgil's best knife by cutting handfuls of tall grass, leaving it in bunches to dry for Levi's mattress, judging by the sacks on the logs.

"The infamous Mrs. Davis," Owen said.

Marigold stiffened. Virgil snapped him a glare, but Owen wasn't looking at him. He was watching Marigold straighten and turn and find a polite, but cool, smile.

Virgil switched his attention to watching her, maybe a little too closely. Women tended to appreciate the look of Owen's sandy-blond hair and boyish grin and sky-blue eyes. He wasn't as tall as Virgil, nor as broad across the shoulders. Today he had blood on his shirt and dirt on his knees, but he didn't show his age as obviously as Virgil did, or have a nasty scar on his face from a saloon fight.

"Please call me Marigold." Her features eased slightly as she recognized him. "Thank you for coming to our rescue, Mister...?"

"Stames. You can call me Owen." He gave her an appreciative look that made Virgil want to elbow him in the ribs. With his pocketknife. "I wouldn't have known you needed rescue if I hadn't heard this one scream."

Nettie was tossing a small sack of beans back and forth with Harley. Owen snagged it from the air and set it on Nettie's head.

"Yeller's feelings are hurt. You were so much louder than he could ever be. You prit-near scared the bear into the next valley."

Nettie giggled and caught the sack as it slid off her hair. "I didn't scare it. Marigold did. With her *skirt*."

"What now?" Owen bit back a laugh.

"Like this." Nettie demonstrated, darting forward at the invisible animal while ruffling the bottom of her dress. "You git! She told me to run with Harley, so I did."

"Jesus Christ." Virgil's heart was a chunk of jagged ice in his chest. He rubbed his hand over his eyes, trying to clear his vision of the near miss with tragedy.

Owen choked on a guffaw while Marigold's cheeks went bright pink. She leaned down to saw through another handful of grass. Aggressively.

"We've been wasting bullets," Owen said to Virgil, not getting the message that he was upsetting

Marigold. "Gotta get us some bloomers and a few yards of calico—"

"Don't you have places to be?" Virgil snapped.

"I'm waiting for my invitation to dinner." He offered Virgil's paper-wrapped portion of meat to Marigold. It was dripping red out one end. "There'll be roasts and stew meat later, but this backstrap makes nice steaks. Whole valley's grateful you got us such a treat."

Marigold's expression turned so horrified, it was almost comical, but rather than make one of her smart-ass remarks while wearing her cool air of capability, she blinked fast and swallowed. She was still shaken, and that made Virgil sorry for her.

"I'll set up a wood grill." His partners had been interrogating him all day. He might as well use this as an excuse to get them all introduced and have done with it. "Nettie, can you fetch a few more potatoes from Yeller and help peel them?"

"Yes, Papa." The way she had called for him— *him*—was still in his ears. She had hugged him back so hard she'd busted something inside him.

Now, she was all soft blue eyes, anxious and tender-hearted. She was turning the rough hide that surrounded his heart into melted butter, but there was no room for that kind of softness out here.

He couldn't bring himself to stomp on such a tiny wildflower, though. He gave her shoulder a clumsy pat. "You're a good girl."

She beamed, and he felt foolish, especially when he noticed Marigold watching them.

He nodded curtly at Marigold. "Stay out of trouble until I get back."

CHAPTER NINE

Marigold was not in the mood to be sociable. All she could think was that she'd nearly died on her first day here. She could have gotten those beautiful children killed through blind ignorance. Arrogance! Did she think this valley was some farmer's field with nothing but Ol' Bessy to disturb them?

She'd had the sense to keep her sister from making the mistake of her life in coming here. What had made her imagine *she* would fare better? The older she grew, the farther from Bedford she went, the worse things became. It was a pattern she should have recognized years ago. Once, just once, she would like her choices to work out for her betterment.

And how on earth was she supposed to cook for a crowd when she had nothing to cook *with*? She filled the stew pot with potatoes and set them to boil, then stole a little of the onion greens from down the hill.

Having come that far, she went to see Yeller to ask if he had a sieve.

"Let's see what's tucked away," he said. "Different things get abandoned on the trail. If the men have time when they're passing by, they pick through and bring anything that looks useful, usually trade it for whiskey."

She followed him into the depths of his cool storehouse where free-standing shelves made from rough-hewn planks stood floor-to-ceiling. The front ones were tidy and organized, but as they moved farther back, the shelves were cluttered with odds and ends she promised herself she would examine more closely another day.

"This?" He reached into a shelf and showed her a conical wire strainer. Its stand was dented so it sat crooked, but inside, tucked next to the wooden pestle, was what looked to be an untouched tin of saleratus.

"Does that come with it?" She opened it and saw the white powder looked clean and dry. There was no unpleasant odor. She could use this for baking. "How much?" She was mindful of her debt to Virgil.

"Take it." He winked. "Sounds as though you've had quite a day."

"Thank you." She could have cried at his small kindness and silently promised him some biscuits in repayment. "I'm sorry to rush away, but Levi is minding the younger ones."

It wasn't dusk, but the sun had gone behind one of the peaks, and the valley was shadowed by the time she got back to the cabin.

Marigold gave Nettie measures of flour and water to mix with a little salt, butter, and saleratus. Levi had instructions from Virgil to cut sticks for the griddle. She asked him to also cut a few roasting sticks, since he knew which trees to avoid.

Marigold left a handful of loose berries on the bench for Harley to keep him happy, then stirred a little sugar and warm water into the rest and set it aside as a light syrup for the biscuits. She had just retrieved the boiled potatoes and was working them through the strainer to make a thick soup when Virgil walked in, face and hands clean, hair wet.

"I'll take that haircut." He held up a pair of scissors.

Did he think she had ten hands? The two she had were covered in potato starch, Harley was clinging to her skirt, and Nettie couldn't keep her fingers out of the syrup.

Whatever persecuted look was on her face had him quickly ducking his head.

"I'll get the meat started. Nettie, you carry this." He took the bloody package off the shelf and gave it to the girl. "And you…" He picked up Harley with a scoop of one long arm, holding him upside down against his chest. "Can start chorin' with the rest of us."

Harley squealed and grabbed his shirt. Nettie giggled. They left the door open as they departed, but at least Marigold had a moment to catch her breath. She got the last of the potato through the mesh and put it back into the pot with the chopped onion greens and a dollop of evaporated milk.

She tidied up as best she could, putting off going outside. She could hear the men had arrived. The potato soup needed to go back over the fire, since it had grown tepid while she finished it, but she wasn't looking forward to all the jokes at her expense.

Virgil strode in. "Everyone is asking to meet you."

She looked around, ankle deep in an imaginary pool of muddy humiliation. "I hope they've brought their own dishes. We don't have enough."

"And their coffee cups."

"Coffee?!" She snapped her head to search the shelf. "We don't have any."

"Owen brought the pot from the office. He'll make it. I always drink mine at the office, but get some for yourself if you want it."

"Thank you," she murmured, hating that she couldn't seem to catch a grip on herself. She started to pick up the cup of syrup and the bowl of biscuit dough, but her hands were shaking so badly, she had to set them down again. Her eyes started to sting. "Can you take the soup?"

He was frowning at her, which only made her defensive. She crossed her arms.

He tested the heat of the cast iron before he picked it up and tipped the lid, giving the contents a sniff. "Smells good."

Did he have to sound so surprised? She bit her lip, afraid it was quivering.

He wasn't looking at her. He put the lid back on and took a half step, paused when he realized she wasn't moving.

She was going to cry, and she didn't want to. She looked to the side and hugged herself tighter.

"Marigold." He said it in the way that questioned how she could possess such a silly name, like his patience was being tested. He set the pot back on the table. "I'm not angry anymore if that's what's got you looking so vexed."

"*I* am! I'm furious with myself. You *told* me there were wild animals, named them all, and I *didn't* think. What if something h-hap…" She started to bring her apron up to her dampening eyes, but it was stained and crusted with soggy potato, and that really felt like the final straw.

She stood there with her head hanging, the back of her wrist pushed against her mouth, stifling sobs that were filling her chest and trying to split her throat. Everything ached—behind her nose, inside her shoulders and chest, all the way to the bottom of her stomach.

"Hey, there. It didn't." His voice was grave. His boots came into her blurred vision, and firm hands took hold of her upper arms, giving a bolstering squeeze.

He dipped his head, catching her gaze with his own, silently demanding she lift her sorry expression to look him in the eye.

Her insides wobbled even harder because he wasn't angry, just very, very serious.

"Now you know," he said. "And it won't happen again. We'll have a good meal, and it will all be forgotten."

"No, it *won't*. They'll tease me forever." She flung her hand toward the door to indicate the men outside. "I'm so tired of being the person everyone points at and mocks. The worst part is this time I deserve it."

His hands dropped away, making her feel even more bereft. Why couldn't he hug her the way he'd done with Nettie? As if she was precious and he'd lay down his life for her.

She looked to the cracks in the walls and sniffed back the tears that were right there, trying to fall.

"Come on, now. You think there's anyone in this valley who hasn't made mistakes? The good people stay where they are and live their good lives. This is where the desperate misfits come, following rumors of riches and whatever else they think will lead them out of the shit they're standing in. Then they discover it's just a different pile."

She choked out a startled laugh. "Thanks very much. I feel much improved now." She did, though, even if the shoe fit a little too well.

His mouth curled at one corner. It wasn't a proper smile. It was wry amusement and a hint of self-deprecation, telling her his disparagement applied to himself as much as to her. It made her feel… *like* him. As though they were…not equals, exactly, but not so very different.

She had a profound urge to set her hand on his chest and maybe her head as well.

One of the children shouted, and she glanced guiltily to the door.

Virgil cleared his throat and picked up the soup. Marigold scooped up her dough, told her heart to settle down, and followed him out into the fading light.

Only three men waited. They'd added log rounds as seats near the fire, but the fire had been allowed to burn down to bright embers so the flames wouldn't scorch the meat.

"There she is." Owen rose and flashed his too-handsome smile. He was the only one clean-shaven and reminded her of Ben with those boyish good looks he seemed to know how to use to his advantage.

"It's nice to see you again, Owen," Marigold said politely.

The biggest man she had ever seen, bigger even

than Virgil, stopped wrestling the older children by the log pile and set them on their feet. When he stood over her, he loomed like a mountain.

Virgil said, "This is Stoney."

He tipped his cap. "El gusto es mio, Senora."

She felt like a child as she offered her hand and watched it get swallowed up in his big one. "It's nice to meet you, Mister…"

"My mamá called me Salbatore." He rolled the "r" while gently squeezing his callused grip over hers. "But Stoney, por favor."

"We don't fuss with last names here," Virgil said.

"Of course. Thank you, Stoney," she murmured.

"And Emmett."

"Ma'am." Emmett stood. He was tall with a wiry frame and flashed a wide grin. He removed a battered, brimmed hat, and his black, tightly curled hair immediately sprang outward in frayed wings.

"Peas?" Harley said, reaching up.

Emmett plopped his hat on Harley's head, and they fell into what appeared to be a familiar game of, *You wear it, no, you wear it.*

It was sweet and reassuring. These men must be decent enough if Virgil entrusted them with his children.

"Bing Sun is eating with his camp. Same with Tom," Owen informed her, jerking his chin toward the Ute camp. "Ira doesn't eat meat unless it's life or death, and someone had to stay back to mind the vault."

"You have a vault? I wondered where you kept the gold. I presumed a safe."

"Too easy to steal." Virgil nestled the soup pot

into the coals at the edge of the fire. "We dug a hole beneath the floorboards of the office. Stoney lined it with bricks, gave it a metal lid and a couple of padlocks. This bunch sleeps on top of it, and we never leave it unguarded."

"I see. Well, I'm sorry I'm not meeting everyone tonight." She was relieved beyond measure, truth be told, that it was only the three of them. "At least now I won't worry that I haven't made enough food." She smiled with welcome. "Thank you all for coming."

The men nodded, and there was an awkward silence.

It struck her that they were waiting for her to sit down. Silly her, she hadn't realized this was the governor's mansion.

"Virgil, will you hand me that cup, please? I'll take a little of the soup for Harley before it gets too hot for him." She lowered onto a log with her bowl of dough in her lap.

"I'll do it." Virgil scooped the soup himself, then picked up Harley and sat with him on his knee while he helped the boy drink it.

"Children," Marigold called to where Levi and Nettie were chasing each other in the growing darkness. "Do you want to roast your biscuits?"

They ran over and took up a pair of sticks. She showed them how to twist dough around the end and hold it over the fire to bake. Owen and Stoney used the other two sticks, moving aside a little of the meat to find a spot with some heat.

The "steaks" had been laid out on a grill of greenwood saplings set across a triangle frame of bigger branches.

"I don't know what I expected, but this meat doesn't smell very different from beef or venison, does it?" Marigold noted.

"Depends what the bear's been eating," Owen said.

"This one ate nuts and berries. I watched Yeller gut it."

"Levi." Virgil's voice was a low warning. "Ladies don't care for talk like that."

"Yeah." Nettie let her tongue hang out with disgust.

"I'm not bothered by talk of butchering," Marigold assured him. "Two years ago, we had wild pigeons come through our farm. My uncle killed a hundred in thirty minutes, swinging a fence picket. We lost all our corn, and they broke four fruit trees, snapped them right onto the ground, there were so many sitting on the branches. I plucked and gutted while my sister pickled and jugged. I can't say I enjoyed it, or that I'm in a hurry to eat it again, but we didn't go hungry."

"I used to see them when I was a boy," Virgil said. "Flocks a mile wide passing over for an hour, blocking out the sun and sounding like a tornado. My mother would hold me under the steps of the big house, praying the whole time. We'd come out and find shit on the ground an inch deep, like it had snowed."

"Is that real, Pa?" Levi asked, eyes wide.

"'Tis." Virgil nodded.

Marigold's attention was caught by more than the spectacle of what he'd described. She'd only ever heard people who were or had been enslaved use the term "big house." Emmett distracted her by claiming to have eaten alligator. Stoney explained how to roast rattlesnake and turtle.

"Hell, when we were in the army, Virgil and I would have eaten the ass out of a live skunk if—"

"Owen," Virgil growled.

"Let's all of us enjoy what's here tonight," Marigold said, biting back her smile. "The soup should be warm if your biscuits are baked."

• • •

Two hours later, Marigold coaxed the children to say good night.

"I'll turn in with them. Thank you all for coming. It was nice meeting you, Emmett and Stoney. Thank you again for your assistance today, Owen."

The door of the cabin closed, but the men didn't take the hint. They stayed around the dying fire with Virgil, all of them mellow from whiskey-spiked coffee and a full belly.

Emmett broke the silence with a suppressed burp. "That's the best meal I've had in years. If you don't marry her, I will."

"Hell, you will." Virgil meant it to come out as a good-natured drawl, but he spoke a little too fast and hard, turning it into more of a warning rumble.

The men exchanged looks, and Virgil saw their mouths twitch.

Shit. A prickling sensation went up his arms and into his scalp. He cleared his throat, annoyed with himself for sounding so possessive. For feeling it.

"She's here to mind my children, same as

Leyohna. You want a woman to cook for you, place an ad in the papers and take what arrives, same as I had to." He drained the last of his coffee.

"She could still watch your children and be married to someone else. Leyohna is," Owen pointed out.

"I told you more than once tonight to shut up. I'm starting to mean it," Virgil warned, still missing the mark on keeping a friendly tone.

Stoney snorted and said, "Buena suerte," under his breath because Owen had lost more than one bet trying to keep his trap shut longer than a full minute.

"She's not hard to look at," Emmett commented to Owen, as if this was a conversation they had every right to continue. "Anyone would want her."

"No shit," Owen said into the dregs of his cup. "A woman who can smother a bear with her skirt, skin it herself, then throw it on the fire and feed half an army?"

"Is that the story we're going with?" Virgil rolled his eyes to the stars. It wasn't enough for Owen to talk more than anyone else; he had to talk the tallest, too.

"Ought to call her Bear-igold," Stoney said.

Emmett spit out his coffee, and the men guffawed so hard, they wobbled on their seats.

"Jesus Christ." Virgil rose, thinking of how upset Marigold had been earlier, worried they would tease her to death. *Sad news, Bear-igold. They would. Mercilessly.* Bunch of dumbasses.

He kicked the last of the fire down. "You can all go home now."

• • •

In the morning, Virgil kept thinking about what his partners had said about how anyone would want Marigold. It was true. In their short acquaintance, he'd seen that Marigold wasn't afraid to work, was good with his children, and was easy enough to look at.

He caught himself staring at her when he checked on Harley. The kid had spent the evening stealing bites off of every plate he could reach, flashing his cheeky grin as he did. For the first time since he'd gotten here, he wasn't waking up hungry, begging for something in his belly so he could finish sleeping.

Virgil was pleased about that but missed his morning cup of milk with the little squirt. It had become his habit to take a few minutes with his children in this dawn hour, checking in with whichever older one was stirring enough to be left in charge of the baby until Leyohna came across.

That was on Marigold now. Should he wake her to tell her he was leaving? Her mosquito bites were fading, leaving her cheek pale and smooth in the dim light. Her lashes were sooty and thick, her hair a ribbon that trailed outside the blanket, tempting him to give it a tug.

As if he had, she took a long inhale and snapped her eyes open, turning her head and widening her eyes as she found him hanging over her like a vulture looking to pick bones.

He gestured toward Harley to explain himself,

then got the hell out of the cabin before his cheeks turned a guilty pink.

When he came out of the john a minute later, Marigold was coaxing the fire to life with one hand, clasping her shawl over her shoulders with the other.

"You didn't have to get up." The sky was still purple-gray, the stars not yet faded.

"I'd like to cut some fabric for the children's clothes today." She copied his quiet undertone. "So I can sew in the evenings. I wanted to ask you where you left the scissors?"

He looked around, trying to recollect. Somewhere Harley couldn't reach them. The shelf outside the door?

"Since you're up…" He fetched them. "I'll take that trim."

"Oh. Um. Of course." She nodded at one of the log rounds and removed her shawl so it wouldn't hinder her.

"Not too short. Nights will be cold soon," he warned and took off the straw hat he wore to keep the sun off his head. "Take my beard up, too."

"All right. Um." She moved behind him and began tucking his collar down.

Her fingers caressed the back of his neck in a tickling touch that feathered its way straight down his spine, slithered under his tailbone to tickle his balls, and filled his cock with heat.

Oh *shit*, this was a terrible idea.

He gathered himself to stand, but the weight of her hands came onto his shoulders.

"Sit straight. Dip your head forward."

He swallowed and tucked his chin.

The cold metal began to clip along his nape. He watched his broken, dirty nails curl into his palms.

The blades made a few passes against his neck, barely warming from the heat of his body, then began to clip around his ears.

"Don't move," she warned softly.

It was downright erotic, holding still like this while she petted his hair and gathered it in bunches. He held his breath but heard hers along with the soft rustle of her clothes. Her short skirt brushed his knees and the back of his hands.

The *clip-clip* of the scissor blades worked around his head and down the side of his face, making his beard itch. Just as he was about to scratch into it, she began pinching sections of whiskers. Her knuckles brushed his cheekbone and grazed his lips.

He was caught in ecstatic torture. His mouth watered. His pulse was throbbing in the tip of his stiff cock, dampening the eye. Her clothes smelled of flour and the familiar must of the cabin and the warm musk of a woman.

As he spread his knees, she stepped between. He opened his eyes enough to see the swells of her breasts beneath her coat. Were her nipples hard? Did she like them to be sucked?

He felt as though his skin had shrunk and he would split right out of it if he didn't put his hands and mouth on her. Everything in him wanted to grab her and kiss her and fuck the daylights out of both of them.

"You have a widow's peak. I didn't realize…"

"Why does that matter?" Through his haze of arousal, he lifted his attention enough to catch her pulling her face into a grimace of apprehension.

"It doesn't." Her voice was high and sharp enough to cut through his sexual trance. "I'll just…" She pinched and clipped and wrinkled her nose, face confounded.

"Marigold." His blood cooled. Fast. "You said you knew how to do this."

"You're my first man. I understand most find that to be a thrill. I've never understood why. The first flapjack is always the worst of the batch. Everyone knows that."

"Very funny." He brushed her hands away and ran his hands over his hair. It didn't feel anything like after the barber had finished with him. "How bad is it?"

"It's *fine*," she insisted but looked as if she needed to pee. "Maybe if these were sharper?" She snipped the air twice. "You're not paying for it," she reminded him.

"Jesus Christ." He rose and went to the window, shifted to glimpse his reflection in the glass. "I look like a half-peeled potato!"

She bit her lips, showing no contrition at all. "I'll get better now that I know what *not* to do."

Muttering every curse word he knew, he slapped his hat over his chewed-up head and stalked off to work.

CHAPTER TEN

After such a blundering start to her new life here, Marigold was determined to be more cautious and try harder to think ahead. To that end, she squeezed as much knowledge as she could from Leyohna, making copious notes on foraging across the valley for seasonal roots, berries, spring greens, and fall mushrooms.

Leyohna was a wealth of practical ideas, too. She pointed out that dry needles were in abundance on the forest floor. She helped Marigold find a tree that shed ones with blunt tips and showed her a tree that had soft inner bark suitable for stripping and using as well. Marigold had to add an extra layer of thick cotton to the tick, but it saved her the work of cutting grass. The needles brought a pleasant fragrance into the cabin, too.

Gristle was so pleased with the mattress she made for him, he gave her a cotton sugar sack that Marigold was able to quickly sew up as an undershirt for Leyohna's newborn. She ran it across to give it to her before she left.

They hugged a final time, and Marigold felt as orphaned as the children when Leyohna filed out of the valley with the rest of her family two days later.

The children were out of sorts from losing yet another mother-figure. Marigold knew it wasn't personal to her, but she felt as though she wasn't meeting their expectations and there wasn't any way she could correct it. Levi was grouchy that he had to release the animals and mind them without Chevano. Nettie lost her temper with Harley and refused to play with him, which turned him whiny. Harley was usually a cheerful and curious little scamp. He squawked if he bopped himself while bashing his wooden animals, but he loved to snuggle and could amuse himself endlessly with a spoon or a blanket or a dribble of water on a tin plate.

She wished Virgil would spend more time with them. She thought that might reassure them, but she'd been here more than a full week, and aside from a few words in the evening, she hardly saw him.

If he'd been coming home drunk each night, Marigold would have had a reason to complain, but he was always filthy and dog-tired and hungry, rarely having eaten since morning. He obviously worked very hard, and even though he wasn't the most demonstrative father, he was always patient with his children. He admired Nettie's sack doll without saying a word about the clumsy stitches or the cock-eyed buttons placed for eyes. He helped Levi fix his slingshot and whittled a pair of interlocked rings for Harley that kept the boy busy trying to pull them apart.

"Did you tell Yeller you would write letters for the men if they needed one?" Virgil asked her one evening, as he was scraping up the last of the pea soup.

"Do you mind?" Marigold caught Harley's arm, trying to keep him in place as she washed him for bed.

"Not at all. We try to do it at the office, but we don't always have time. I said if you're up to it, we'll eat at the cookhouse tomorrow. Anyone in need of a letter can see you then. It's payday. Gristle will have ham and cornbread."

"That's a nice treat. Thank you."

"Gristle's talent is quantity, not quality," he warned. "But it fills the hole, and having you and the children there might keep the men from drinking and gambling away a week's wages before midnight."

Marigold had learned the men could choose one of two methods for receiving their pay. Some preferred carefully measured gold dust stored in the quill of feathers. Others took promissory notes that were accepted by the mercantile and saloons in town. When Virgil or one of the other partners went for supplies, they settled up at all the establishments, buying back their notes with gold dust.

Marigold understood shipments of gold had also been sent to the mint in Philadelphia under armed guard. Whether those coins had come back and were stored here, she had no idea. They wanted to invest some of the company's earnings into a railroad, but each of the partners also had personal interests, too. Emmett had shares in one of the lumber mills in Denver and had ordered equipment to build his own mill here. Bing Sun supported family in San Francisco. Owen was determined to open a saloon—"Mine gold from men's pockets"—while Virgil was building a house for his children. She didn't know what the rest planned.

The cookhouse was full when they arrived. The

miners ranged in age from a boy who looked like he had only a few years more than Levi to ones with leathery faces and thin, gray hair. They were all rough mannered and had to be reminded by Virgil not to swear, but they seemed to appreciate the family atmosphere with the children there. After they'd eaten, the men delayed their poker game and turned their cards face down in a memory game that amused the older children.

Marigold took out her supplies and wrote a letter for a young man who wanted his mother to know he was well and staying out of trouble. Another asked her to warn his brother that prospecting was not the path to quick riches they had been led to expect. *Don't come. You'll regret it.*

While she wrote, she kept an eye on Virgil. He wore his straw hat, so his hair was covered, but with his beard still chopped up like a rag mat, he looked more disreputable and dangerous than ever. He was watching his children, however, and his expression had softened into an almost-smile. It was pure tenderness by his standards.

The children were eating up the attention, and the men seemed cheered by their high spirits. One pulled off his sock to use as a puppet, and the two older children had to do the same. Their silly antics sent Harley into fits of giggles that were so infectious, everyone was laughing.

With a bubble of laughter in her own throat, Marigold smiled at the next man who approached her.

"Hello. I'm Marigold. Are you needing a letter?" She started to reach for her pen.

"Buster, Ma'am. And no. I can write my own letters, but I wondered if you'd give me a trim?"

Marigold sat taller, smile falling away. She'd already been teased about the bear and Virgil's haircut tonight. She was ready to make a sharp remark about not wishing to be the butt of everyone's jokes, but Buster was serious. He removed his hat to show her the matted knots that had formed in his fringe of fine gray hair.

"I can't get a comb through it." He frowned with distress.

"I'm so sorry, Buster. I didn't bring any scissors." She showed her empty hands.

"I asked Yeller if I could borrow these. I sharpened them myself." He set a pair of thin-bladed scissors on the table next to her bottle of ink. "I'll go wet my head."

Marigold wasn't given an opportunity to decline. Buster went out to the pump and came back with his hair and beard dripping.

When he returned, he seated himself on a bench beside her, expression patient.

"What's going on here?" someone asked as Marigold rose and picked up the scissors.

She hesitated, not realizing she was looking for Virgil until she met his gaze across the cookhouse. If he had seemed to relish her becoming a spectacle, she would have refused and gone home, but he quirked his mouth with wry amusement. *You're standing in it now.*

She bit her lip, trying to think how to rescue herself.

"I'm not sure I should charge you," she confided

to Buster. "I'm not very good."

"You can't make it worse," someone drawled nearby.

"Have you seen Virgil?" someone else asked. "She definitely can."

Snickers followed. An audience was gathering. *Oh no.*

"I *will* charge for providing entertainment, though," Marigold decided, sending a warning look around at the men. "Shall we send your hat around, Buster? Split the takings?"

It was a bluff, but Buster craned his head back to see her.

"Yes, ma'am. If someone wants to say I'm so bald there's nothing for you to cut, he can ante a half-dime for the privilege."

"Hear that, gentlemen? We will not be made a mockery," Marigold informed them.

"These men just got paid, Marigold." Owen flipped Buster's hat and threw a coin into it. "I'm going to put my dime in, purely out of appreciation for what a greenhorn move that was on your part."

"Oh, for—" She was definitely standing in it. Virgil had his tongue tucked firmly in his cheek. She resolved to do her very best and tried to block out the comments as she got to snipping.

"He's gonna be too embarrassed to go to town after this."

"Virgil oughta be."

"That's his plan. Get us too ugly to leave. Keep us here 'til it grows out."

"Was that his ear? They grow back, don't they?"

"Is it supposed to bleed that much?"

No blood was shed and Buster's ears were intact when she finished, but Marigold vowed, *Never again.*

Two more men sat down, both with wet heads. *Damn it.*

If she hadn't heard more dimes going into the pot, she might have refused. As it was, between barbering and letter writing, she came away with nearly a dollar.

More importantly, even though they had been merciless, she came away feeling less intimidated by these hard-living men. Outside of that ribbing, they were always polite to her, calling her Missus Davis even though they didn't fuss with last names here.

Over the next days, they also began giving her things when she least expected it. The day after she had cut his hair, one young man gave her a wooden hand mirror. She was thrilled to have it, but he refused to take any payment for it.

Another ran to catch up to her as she was walking to see Yeller. "I found these feathers. They're pretty. I thought you might like them."

"They are pretty," she assured him, but she had no use for feathers. "Thank you," she said, bemused, and carried on.

With the day sunny and warm, and Harley and Nettie skipping alongside her so cheerfully, and friendly faces waving at her, Marigold felt quite nice. Accepted.

Dear Pearl. Forget everything I wrote last. I think I could feel at home here.

As she arrived at the storehouse, Virgil came out

of the office.

"Papa!" Nettie called, smiling and waving.

He halted, then veered toward them, frowning. "What's wrong?"

"Nothing. We need milk, and the children liked the cornbread so much the other night, I said I would pick up meal and make it again tonight."

"You can tell Levi in the morning what to pick up." He caught Harley and lifted him before he could throw himself against Virgil's dirty pant leg.

"I know, but it's a nice day for a walk." Also, she needed to borrow a baking pan from Gristle and ask him to bake the bread in his oven.

Virgil grunted, perhaps not as enamored with midday strolls as she was, but she imagined he walked several miles a day, checking in with all the crews and working alongside them.

"Peas?" Harley asked, digging into Virgil's shirt pocket.

"That cupboard is bare, son." He worked his own finger into the crook of Harley's neck, making the tot shrug and giggle as he squirmed into Virgil's shoulder.

"Papa, who's that?" Nettie asked.

"Hmm?" Virgil's relaxed expression shifted to his daughter.

At that moment, there was a short, piercing whistle. Emmett appeared from seeming thin air, saying, "I'll get Levi."

Before Marigold could turn to look, Virgil had thrust Harley at her, his features grim.

"Get the children into the office. *Now*." He herded them in there while Gristle gave a clatter on the dinner bell.

Marigold only had time for a quick glance but spotted two men on horseback coming in from the direction of where the Ute camp had been, galloping with purpose.

Inside the two-room office, Ira was at the table, hurrying to put away scales and fold the pile of gold dust into the oilcloth he'd laid out as a work area. Ira was tall, quiet-spoken, and looked younger than the rest. He used his knuckle to push his wire-rimmed spectacles up his nose as he asked, "Who is it?"

"Dunno." Virgil took a rifle off the rack behind the door.

"Fuck," Ira said as Virgil commenced loading. Then, "Sorry, Missus Davis."

As Virgil left, Emmett entered, pushing Levi in ahead of him. He shut the door and pressed Levi toward the bunkroom at the back. "Get up on that bunk and open the vent. Let me know if you see anyone sneaking up that way."

"Yes, sir."

"What can I do?" Marigold asked, feeling helpless and useless and frightened. Her pulse was pounding so hard, it drowned out the sound of the approaching hooves.

"Keep the little one quiet." Ira tucked the wrapped gold into a crate on the floor, then threw a dirty shirt over top.

"Of course." She picked up Harley and gave Nettie a reassuring smile, hugging the girl into her hip.

• • •

As the two strangers galloped closer, Virgil kept his rifle aimed at the sky but had his finger on the trigger as he positioned himself between the riders and the office.

They slowed as they saw him and sat taller, looking around the valley as they kept trotting forward. They didn't look as though they were signaling anyone, so that was something.

"State your business," Virgil called out. "Before we get nervous about your intentions."

"You got a thief here. Stole my gold watch. I came to get it back," one said. Virgil could tell he was the belligerent, trouble-making type.

"Who?"

"Don't know his name, but I heard he came here from Horsefly a month ago."

"Owen? Any of our men from Horsefly?" Virgil called out while keeping his gaze fixed on the men.

"Got a few. Is he French?" Owen called from off to Virgil's left.

"Nah. Freckles and a chipped tooth."

"That'd be Rufus," Owen said in a lower voice to Virgil. "He wouldn't be here if I thought he was a thief."

"Get him," Virgil said. "Tell him to bring the watch if he has it."

As Owen galloped away and the strangers drew closer, Virgil said, "You two get down and introduce yourselves."

"Most call me Sureshot," the talker said, staying mounted. "This here is Wildfire Will."

The sidekick looked nervous. There was definitely something shifty about them.

"You can call me Virgil Gardner, and everything you've heard about me is true." Virgil kept the rifle barrel resting in the crook of his elbow as he scratched into his beard, deliberately drawing attention to his scar. "Get off your horse and tell me about the watch."

The men exchanged sour looks and dismounted. They didn't seem to have long guns, but each wore a holster with a pistol.

"It's gold," Sureshot said. "It has B.E. scratched onto the inside. That's how you'll know it's mine."

"Those your initials? Sureshot?"

"I won it at cards."

'Course he did. Virgil would bet all the gold he'd ever touched that that was how he'd lost it, too. In his periphery, Virgil was aware men had stopped working and were peering out of the gulch to watch what was happening.

"I'll tell you how we settle things here," Virgil said. "A jury of miners will listen to both sides and decide. If you don't like those terms, you can wait in town for Rufus and settle it there however you see fit."

Sureshot curled his lip. Wildfire Will shrugged.

Gristle called out from the cookhouse, "We havin' a trial, boss?"

"Call the men in, yeah."

Gristle sent his ladle around the iron triangle with a clangetty-clang, this one less forceful than the alarm he'd sent up when the men had been spotted, more like the call of the dinner bell. Men left their work areas to amble in from all directions.

Which suited Virgil fine. Their men regarded the

office as the bank since that's where their earnings were kept. They would fight to protect it if it came to it.

This would be a really good time for Tom to turn up, but he was still escorting his family south and collecting news from that direction.

After a twenty-minute wait of kicking dust and fat chewing, Owen rode up with a scared-looking knot-head of a kid on the back of his horse, maybe twenty. The boy looked like a dog who'd lost a cat fight.

"Mrs. Davis give you a trim, son?" Virgil asked as the boy slid to the ground.

"Yes, sir."

"Looks like a blowdown in the back woods," someone said.

"That's what I said. Looks like the cow got into the cornfield."

"Quiet," Virgil said in a terse order for silence. "You got a gold watch, son?"

"I won it at cards." He drew it from his pocket while eyeballing Sureshot. "From him."

"Hell you did," Sureshot said through chew-stained teeth.

"Let's see it." Virgil took the worn timepiece and opened it to see a B.E. engraved on the inside of the face cover. "This is valuable. You could have sold it and gone home to... Where you from, Rufus?"

"North of Chicago, sir. I thought about it, but then I thought, um..." He gulped down his entire Adam's apple. "I thought Mrs. Davis might like it?"

"Why the *hell*—" *Oh, fuck.* Okay, that was a problem for another day.

"Who's Mrs. Davis?" Wildfire Will asked, looking around. "You got women here?"

"None of your business. Stoney here will hold onto this watch until the rightful owner is determined." Virgil thumbed at his friend, who was more inclined to scoop up a spider and take it outside than squash it, but Stoney knew how to stand tall and look mean. "Do you both agree to let our jury decide? Or do we take this watch to town, sell it, and split it even?"

"I want to do it here," Rufus said, scowling at Sureshot.

"I don't want to go to town," Sureshot grumbled but sent a suspicious eye across the workmen, all colors and sizes, all filthy, most wearing beards. Several had taken off their hats to fan themselves in the afternoon sun. "They're all your men, though."

"They all have their own opinion. You'll each count off six and Yeller will break a tie if there is one."

Sureshot and Wildfire stuck their heads together as they looked over the motley offering.

"You got some kind o' mange here?" Wildfire asked with a worried look on his face.

"Just get counting."

Virgil waited while the jury was chosen. Once the twelve men were standing to one side, he asked, "You got any witnesses besides Bonfire Bill?"

"Wildfire Will," he corrected. "And, yeah, there were other men—"

"No, there weren't," Sureshot corrected him.

"I mean, no." Wildfire squeezed his hands into

fists. "But I saw him steal it." He nodded at Rufus.

"You saw Rufus take the watch, but you didn't stop him?" Virgil clarified.

"Well, no. I…" He looked at Sureshot.

"You saw him—" Sureshot started to prompt again.

"No." Virgil held up a warning hand. "You two had all kinds of time to get your story straight before you got here. Tell me, Whippoorwill, how'd he steal it? Pickpocket? Got into Sureshot's tent? Broke into his room at the saloon? What?"

Wildfire frowned at Virgil's adultery of his name. "He took it off a table at a saloon."

"Because he'd won it?"

"Sureshot was three sheets to the wind." Wildfire took off his hat to scratch into his sweaty hair. "He was supposed to save the watch and give the owner a chance to win it back, not—"

"Shut the fuck up." Sureshot stepped forward to point at Virgil, then at Rufus. "Your boy took advantage. I was drunk and he tricked me into gambling it."

"That true, Rufus?" Virgil asked, keeping his eye on Sureshot but motioning Rufus to come up where he could see him.

"Everyone was drunk in Horsefly," Rufus said, shrugging his shoulders up to his ears. "My claim wasn't paying, so I went looking for work. I sold some tools and played a hand of cards. I won the watch straight away along with a big pot. I stayed an hour and lost most of my other winnings, but I didn't have a hand worth gambling the watch, so I left. I thought I'd sell it to get home, but I met Frenchie.

He was coming here, so I came, too."

"That's true." A barrel-chested man with a thick French accent pushed out of the gathered miners. "Rufus showed me the watch and told me that story. He wanted to go sell it in Denver. I said we should come here, that I heard we'd have wages and meals. We do, so we stayed."

"I'm telling you, he stole it," Sureshot insisted.

"Who thinks Rufus stole it?" Virgil asked.

Wildfire's hand shot into the air, then sank as he realized he was the only one.

"It sounds to me like the man you won the watch from is after you to get it back," Virgil said. "So here's what I'm going to do. Rufus, I'm going to pay you twenty dollars for that watch. Is that a fair price?"

"Yes, sir." Rufus nodded so hard, the uneven line of his hair flapped against his forehead.

"Done. Now the watch is mine. I'll sell it to you— Let me finish." He put up a hand to forestall Sureshot's sputtering argument. "If you don't have twenty dollars today, that's fine. I'll let you take this watch back to Horsefly and settle up however you need to. But the next time I see you, whether it's here or a saloon or hell itself, I'm going to expect my twenty dollars. All these men are witnesses." Virgil pointed around the gathered group. "I'll warn you now that the owner of that watch is nothing compared to the hound on your heels I am when someone owes me money. If those terms are acceptable, Stoney can give you the watch and you can get the hell out of Quail's Creek. Don't come back without my money."

Sureshot curled his lip and gave a crafty look around. "I'll have it next week."

Sure he would. Virgil would never see him again, and that was easily worth twenty dollars, but it wouldn't even cost him that much. His partners would chip in. Virgil was only out two dollars and change.

• • •

As the horses galloped away, the tension in the office hissed out like a held breath. Ira opened the door and stepped outside. Emmett quit guarding the window and set his gun back on the rack behind the door. Levi said, "I wish my bunk was this high," before jumping down and landing with a *thud*.

Marigold had been rocking Harley to keep him quiet. He'd fallen asleep and was straining her arms, so she set him on a lower bunk and straightened with a sigh of relief.

As Emmett and Levi went outside, leaving the door open, Nettie poked her head out to ask, "Papa, is it okay now?"

"Sure is, little bug." Virgil gave Nettie's hair a pat as he came into the office. He briefly met Marigold's gaze, gave her the smallest nod of reassurance, then helped himself to a piece of paper and a pencil from the cup on the sill.

"Howdy, Miss Nettie." Rufus stepped aside to let Nettie leave, then he hovered in the open doorway. "Missus Davis. It's nice to see you again." He smiled wide enough to show his chipped tooth.

"Hello, Rufus. It's nice to see you, too." Marigold

nodded politely, still trying to shake off the fear that had gripped her.

Virgil scrawled a note and offered it to Rufus.

"Bring that back on payday. We'll settle up then, but I won't pay it out to anyone else, so don't bother gambling it. Now get on back to work."

"Yes, sir. Thank you, sir." Rufus smiled at Marigold once more before he left.

Virgil moved to give the coffeepot on the cold stove a swirl and released a disappointed sigh at the lack of slosh.

"I'll run across to the cookhouse," Marigold offered. "Make some fresh."

"Where's Harley?" He glanced around.

She pointed at the bunk.

He nodded. "I'll keep an eye on him. Thank you for keeping them quiet. I worry about my children being used as leverage against me." He squeezed the back of his neck, his first show of anything less than complete control over the situation.

"This is what you meant, isn't it?" She clasped her elbows. "When you told me there's no law here and you have to do it yourself? I didn't appreciate what that meant until today." She didn't know which was worse, a system so tightly woven that there was no picking out the threads of injustice, or this void where any sort of crime could go unpunished.

"Yeah, men aren't real worried about standing trial in Fort Riley if there's no one here to arrest 'em and take 'em there," he said drily.

"Weren't you frightened they might shoot you?" The empty pot shook in her hand as she accepted.

"Hey now." He stepped close enough to set his hand under the pot to steady it and covered where she gripped the handle. "We're safe." His hand felt warm over her chilled one. Callused, but gentle where he wrapped his palm over her sharp knuckles. "If they were the type to kill in cold blood, they'd have already shot the owner of the watch. It was plain enough they were scared of him. They'll be scared of me now, so I doubt I'll ever see them again."

"You managed to calculate all those risks in the heat of the moment?" An incredulous laugh scraped her throat.

"Done it often enough I'm good at it, I s'pose."

Another chuckle of mild hysteria escaped her.

His mouth quirked in a rueful half smile. Their gazes locked, and his thumb rubbed her skin where he still covered her hand.

Her lips felt as though they trembled, and she wasn't sure if it was from leftover fear or anticipation of—

"Oh. S'cuse me." Ira was three steps in and already turning to leave.

The bubble between her and Virgil burst. They stepped apart, leaving only a faint sting in her face and a scowl of annoyance on his.

"Stay," Virgil barked at Ira.

"I only thought I'd put the gold away." Ira wouldn't look at them. His bottom lip was pulled wide in a grimace at having overstepped.

"You're not interrupting anything," Marigold insisted, feeling foolish because her voice went high enough to make it sound like a lie. "I'm off to steal hot water from Gristle for coffee. I won't be long."

She hurried out and came up against a wall of curious gazes on the half-dozen men lingering outside. They'd probably heard all of that.

She showed them the empty coffeepot and hurried across to the cookhouse.

CHAPTER ELEVEN

Marigold was still trying to find her nerves a few days later. She had just got the children fed and was washing Harley tip to toe with a damp rag when she noticed Virgil coming up the path, earlier than usual.

Everyone's mood brightened, including hers.

"Evenin', Pa." Levi came up on his knees behind the checkerboard she'd had him measure out and scratch into a log round.

"Papa, look what Levi made us. It's a game! Marigold showed us. I found the pebbles."

"Look at that." He gave an admiring nod. "I haven't played checkers since my army days. Nice work with the straight edge, son. You have a double-jump there, Nettie."

"Pa," Levi complained.

"She's younger. And you're ahead." His hand hovered, almost as if he might ruffle the boy's hair, before he tucked it in his pocket.

Levi didn't notice, but Marigold did, and she wanted to say, *It's okay. Touch him. He's starving for your approval.*

Virgil let out a weary sigh as he sank down on a log round. "You're naked," he noted as Harley escaped Marigold's bathing efforts and scampered over to Virgil.

There was no holding Harley at arm's length. The boy presumed he was loved by all, and that seemed to be his trick to ensuring it.

Virgil picked Harley up and stood him on his thighs, warning, "Don't you dare tinkle on me."

Harley leaned to poke his hand into Virgil's shirt pocket. "Peas?"

"Still empty, son. Have to wait 'til I get back."

"Emmett said you said he should go from now on." Levi picked up his head and frowned with dismay. "He said he would take me to see the sawmill if you said I could go."

"That's all true. I will let you go, but there's a meeting on Monday that I need to attend, so I'm taking this trip."

"But Leyohna's gone," Nettie said anxiously.

"Marigold is here."

Levi's brows recreated his father's most displeased glower. Nettie looked to Marigold with a fretfully crinkled chin.

Marigold's stomach shrank and her blood stung her veins. What if Sureshot came back? Or someone like him?

This was her chance to say, *This was all a horrible mistake*, and go back to civilization. She could pick one of her contingency plans, which were all horrible, and try to make her way back to her sister. Beyond Pearl's eternal optimism, however, Marigold had nothing to go back *to*.

At least here she had the freedom to walk wherever she needed to go without being accosted. She might not have much by way of possessions, but Gristle had been so thrilled with a pillow she'd made him from a flour sack, he had given her this handy basin she'd just used for Harley's bath. The biscuits she'd made for Yeller had earned her a small wooden crate full of empty jars that she planned to fill with something—dried berries, rendered fat, nuts they would hopefully gather and roast in the fall.

She had an employer. More than one. Just this morning, a young man had offered her fifty cents to write a letter to his sister. Marigold had earned enough since arriving here to pay down five dollars and twenty-five cents of her debt to Virgil.

She still owed him well over a hundred dollars and had no way to pay him back if she went back to Topeka.

The owner of that watch is nothing compared to the hound on your heels that I am when someone owes me money.

Jaded shadows shifted in Virgil's eyes. Tension invaded his wide shoulders and around his mouth. He expected her to leave him holding a debt and children he didn't have time to mind. She heard his hackles rising as he pondered his own short list of contingency plans.

She couldn't stand for him to think she was so faithless. That's what it came down to.

So, with the same impetuous gamble she'd taken when she'd decided to use the ticket he'd sent, she said, "I wonder if I could give you a letter to post? To my sister." She had been writing one, when she found a moment here or there. In it, she put on a brave face and glossed over all the dangerous moments so Pearl wouldn't worry too much. "She'll want to know I'm settling in."

It felt like the burning of a bridge to say it aloud. Soon the weather would change, and getting back to Topeka would become impossible until spring.

However, despite the deprivations here, she felt as though she had more freedom to speak her mind and be herself than she'd had at any other time in her life.

"'Course," Virgil said gruffly as he set Harley on his feet. He gave the boy a nudge to come to Marigold as she held up the boy's clean shirt, freshly washed in the creek yesterday. "Make a list of anything you need. I'll get what I can."

"Do you think you could find slates for the children's lessons?" she asked.

"I'll look."

"Thank you."

Rather than an atmosphere of relief, their conversation felt even more stilted. Marigold wanted him to be pleased, she realized, but Virgil wasn't letting on whether he was happy or not that she was willing to stay.

"Lessons," Levi groaned.

He'd had two years at a Catholic school in St. Louis. From what he'd said of it, they had been very strict, but they'd taught him enough that he could read the most common words in the scraps of newspaper they used for starting fires and left in the john. Nettie recognized her numbers and letters, thanks to her mother's teachings before she passed.

There was plenty of room to continue with both of them, but Marigold reasoned she would have them captive once the snow kept them indoors. She was easing them into that eventuality by showing Levi how mathematics allowed him to measure out the checkerboard. Nettie had practiced her counting when she had found the black-and-white pebbles.

They were both learning subtraction as they captured each other's markers.

"Finish the stew. We've eaten." Marigold got Harley's arms into his sleeves. "One more game, children. Once you're in bed, I'll read the rest of Rip Van Winkle."

Ira had invited her to borrow from his small library so she could read stories to the children. They were currently working their way through *The Sketch Book of Geoffrey Crayon*.

"You don't want to read out here?" Virgil asked as he used a stick to move the pot from the dying fire onto a log round. "Light's better."

Only marginally, since the first stars were poking holes in the sky. She would need a candle either way.

"If you want to hear the story, you have to be in bed," Nettie informed him, repeating the rule Marigold had set.

"Huh. Knew from the beginning you were the sneaky sort," Virgil drawled.

Marigold paused in dressing Harley.

Virgil froze, too.

"That was a joke," he grumbled and began eating straight from the stew pot.

Was it? Most jokes had a basis in truth. That told Marigold exactly how far she'd come in earning his trust. Not so much as an inch, apparently.

She smiled tightly and went about getting the children into bed. A few minutes later, when she was about to begin reading, Virgil came in to say good night to the children.

"Levi, you'll help Emmett and Yeller build the winter paddock while I'm gone, but ask Marigold first if she needs anything, hear? Fetch the water and firewood for her."

"Yes, sir," Levi said solemnly.

"I know I can count on you." His hand landed with two pats on Levi's bent knee. "And Nettie, you'll help Marigold with our little turnip?"

She giggled. "I will, Papa."

"Good girl." Her braid was given a gentle tug. "As for you…"

He touched his bent knuckle under Harley's chin.

Harley held up the cloth dog Marigold had made him and flapped his lips in his version of a horse's neigh, because that's what he'd decided it was.

"As long as we have an understanding," Virgil said drily.

He didn't meet her eyes as he nodded at Marigold and went back outside.

• • •

As Virgil came back from cleaning the stew pot and fetching fresh water for the morning, he saw Marigold sitting by the fire. The flames had died down to a glow of red amongst the charred logs. They were headed to bed, so he wouldn't stoke it, but he almost went looking for wood just to put off talking to her.

He still felt like a shit for his remark implying she was dishonest.

She was, though. He was still taking grief over his haircut. *Is that what they're wearing in Paris this season? You have a head wound that needed stitching?*

*Singe your beard blowing out a candle, boss? Gotta
be more careful.*

Jackasses.

Even so, that moment earlier when he'd realized
she might jump ship, or more likely jump into his
wagon with the intent to get herself back to Topeka,
had driven a stake straight into his heart. In many
ways, Leyohna had been easier to have around because she knew how to live rough and being married
to another had killed any sexual tension.

Marigold was a pain in his hide and forced him to
spend way too much time double-thinking what he
said, but he also needed her. Leyohna was gone, and
starting over looking for a new bride or childminder
would take the rest of the summer, time that he
needed to be working alongside his partners.

It was a rock and a hard place, for sure.

"My letter to my sister," she said, holding it out
to him. "And this is my accounting of my wages
against my debt and expenses so far. I've added the
cost of purchasing a stamp."

He felt like the worst pinch-fist when he saw how
carefully she was keeping record of the things she
picked up from the storehouse and what she used
them for.

*1 lb. cornmeal (dinner biscuits, 3 leftovers to
Gristle for goodwill)*

Leyohna had been perfectly kind to his children
and had fed them well, but she had known she
would leave and had maintained a small distance
because of it.

Marigold, on the other hand, seemed determined
to turn this pile of matchsticks into a home. She kept

it neat as a pin, spent a good portion of each day preparing meals, and was putting up what she could for winter. Literally *up*. She'd asked him to suspend a rack from the ceiling that she had covered with paper. Berries were drying, and she'd added some onion tops the other day.

He pocketed her letter and offered her back her accounting. Maybe he'd buy her a proper ledger book. Would that only reinforce what a miser he was? He must be one, since he knew all the words for it. Parsimonious. Frugal. Tightwad. Churl.

"I meant to bring my sewing out, but it's nice to rest." Her eyes caught the moonlight as she looked up.

"Why do you think I make these trips to town? I finally get to sit down," he said facetiously.

"Is that another joke? Or—?"

"I don't know." He was dead tired, but he rose to pace out of the light, suddenly feeling like a boy who couldn't say anything right. "I didn't mean what I said earlier."

"I was beginning to hope you trusted me a little," she said faintly. "At least I know where I stand." She sounded hurt. That bothered him. A lot.

"I don't trust many, so don't take it personal," he said gruffly.

"Is *that* why you make all the trips to town yourself? You don't trust anyone else to do it?"

"No. Other way, maybe. I trust my partners with my life, but I don't want to risk theirs." That's why he'd taken the lead with Sureshot. That and, "Owen gets too friendly. People take advantage of that. A man big as Stoney shouldn't get harassed, but he does. Men want to test him because of his size." Virgil scratched under his hat. "The men go when they need something, but I've taken to doing the supply runs so I can stay informed on politics."

Marigold made a pained little noise at that dirty word.

"I don't have any passion for it, trust me. The damned paper printed my name as a representative from our mining district, after I went to a meeting in April. Ever since then, I guess that's what I am."

Maybe there was a part of him that liked that the men looked to him to handle their business. Not ego, but it felt good to know they trusted his sense. It was validating. He wasn't "nothing" if he was overseeing a mining operation and had the ear of future statesmen.

"Will you be very disgusted with me if I admit to being nervous that bandits will come while you're gone?" Marigold asked in a small voice.

"First of all, most know to keep their misbehaving over in Horsefly and not bring it here. If they do, Owen is a helluva longshot, and Emmett's fast with a pistol. Stoney doesn't like fighting, but he knows how. Bing Sun doesn't look dangerous, but *I* wouldn't creep up on him."

"What about Ira?"

"Ira was raised by pacifists. He'll do anything to avoid violence but isn't above it if it becomes necessary. I'll tell you what, though. He's not afraid to die, and that unnerves anyone who threatens him."

"Tom's still away?"

"Yes."

"Can I ask you something?"

"What?"

"Did Tom take gold with him?"

"I could tell you, Marigold, but then I'd have to kill you and explain myself to your sister. Who'd wash my kids' clothes after that?"

She snorted. "You couldn't just cut out my tongue?"

"Who would read to them? No, I'm afraid your curiosity will have to remain unsatisfied." As the words left him, he heard how suggestive that sounded and gruffly changed the subject. "I'll take the mules and the small wagon this time. That cuts time off my travel. I'll be gone three nights, tops."

"The children will miss you anyway."

He was still standing in the shadows, which was probably why he admitted, "It bothers me when they think I won't come back."

"You're the only father they have." She removed the kerchief she wore over her hair and left it in her lap while she began removing pins and combing her fingers through the tresses. She turned her head so she could better reach as she broke her hair into three sections and began to weave it together.

Let me.

He cleared his throat, realizing he'd left the silence to draw out, and strained to remember what they had been talking about.

"They had one in Albert. Far as I can tell." He was bothered by the fact they'd looked to another man to be their father. Bothered that they'd lost Albert, too. "Clara wouldn't have let him near them if she didn't think him a good and decent man. What I am is all they have."

"You're still miles better at fathering than my uncle was." In the dying light, he saw a sad smile touch her lips. "He had nearly two decades to learn but never really got there. Which isn't to say he was cruel or resentful, but he didn't welcome us. He did his duty, paid for our boarding school—with Father's money," she added as an aside. "He would send us a letter a few times a year, and he set aside funds for when we married. We had to use most of Pearl's for my legal fees, which is why I encouraged her fiancé to pursue her—"

Marigold broke off and pushed her mouth to the side.

Virgil folded his arms, sighing with impatience. "So this suitor of hers didn't just *happen* to come courtin' because he heard she had another offer. Damn it, Marigold, you had me wanting to cut out my own tongue for what I said earlier. Now you're admitting you arranged her a marriage so my ticket was free for you to snap up. You *are* sneaky."

"*No*. I wanted her to marry Hiram and refuse the ticket. Some of that was selfishness, since I didn't want to be left there alone, but I wound up needing a…situation." She used her kerchief to tie off the tail of her hair. "The point I was making is that my uncle is a decent man but lacks warmth. You're far superior to him as a father."

Virgil snorted at what sounded like blatant flattery being used to temper the fact he'd caught her in another lie. It wouldn't work. He was *not* decent, and he had about as much natural warmth as the mountaintops in January. As for making an effort at fathering?

He shoved his hands deep into his pockets. "I keep thinking that being soft doesn't do them any favors. The world is a terrible place, and they need to be prepared for it."

"They lost their mother, Virgil. They know how cruel life is."

He had to nod at that unpalatable truth, but his chest burned like he was breathing smoke. This was why he found her so frustrating. She wasn't always honest, but when she was, it struck sharp as lightning, illuminating everything inside him.

"Is it so hard to let them know you want them?" She folded her hands in her lap. "That you care about them?"

"Yes," he said with self-deprecation. "That's why I haven't done it."

"Are you telling me you don't trust *them*? They're children. They don't know how to be manipulative unless someone teaches them to be that way."

"It's myself I don't trust," he admitted reluctantly. He was tempted to kick his feet, they felt so close to a fire. "I don't know how to be a father. Not a good one." He hovered in the shadows, trying to hide from the truth same as he'd tried to hide from the man.

"Because you were only shown how to be a bad one?" she asked very gently. "I'm sorry, Virgil. The way you spoke of your mother the night we had the men over sounded… I don't know. I don't mean to pry."

His mother. He pinched the bridge of his nose, surprised he'd spoken of her so easily when he usually kept a firm distance between himself and his childhood.

The stew he'd eaten an hour ago threatened to come back up, but he wanted Marigold to know what sort of childhood he'd had, so she'd understand why he worried. So she would look for signs of him turning into that ugly old son of a bitch and put a stop to it.

"I saw my father outside a shop once. I wasn't even old as Nettie. My mother was running errands, and I was holding parcels. I saw him walk by and said, 'Morning, Daddy.' He caught me by the ear and threw me into the shit in the street, then whipped me with his riding crop until my mother got between us."

"Oh my God. Virgil, that's horrible." He heard her rise and start toward him, but he put up a hand to hold her off.

"My mother was indentured. He had a wife, and I wasn't supposed to exist, let alone make claims in public that he had sired me." Virgil could still hear the sing of the whip through the air and the spittle-raged voice yelling, *You're nothing to me. Hear me? Nothing.* Virgil had feared he would be cut clean in half.

"Is your mother still alive?"

"No," he dismissed, still trying to convince himself she was in a better place. "She died when I was fifteen. I lied my way into the army the day she went into the ground. No way was I sticking around to continue paying her debt to that asshole."

"Is *he* still alive?" Her voice quavered with outrage.

"Doesn't occur to me to wonder." That was mostly true. "But I can't stand the smell of tobacco to this day, so steer clear of that habit. Otherwise, I'll have to fire you, and then where will I be?" It was his poorest attempt at humor yet. As he reached for it, he realized how revealing it was that he was trying to use something so flimsy to shield himself.

In a voice soft as duck down, she said, "Here I was going to take up chew. I find the way the miners spit all over the ground so attractive, I thought you might, too."

"Idiot," he choked, fighting a grin and a sweet, painful ache as he stared up at the stars. He wasn't supposed to find her attractive. Did she remember that?

Without warning, her arms encircled one of his. She hugged it, and she set her forehead below his shoulder. He tried to swallow the lump that formed in his throat.

"You will *never* be like that with them," she assured him fervently.

"I'm not a child, Marigold. I don't need comforting."

"I do. So shush. Then you can go off to Denver and growl at the rest of the world for a few days. Give me a much-needed break from it."

"You are such a pain in my ass." The shard of glass in his chest stung, pressed by a chuckle he refused to release. The fact she made him want to laugh right after a walk through his worst memories was something he both resented and relished. Same as her, he supposed, and looked down the top of her head. How did such a little bit of a thing hold so much honey and vinegar?

"You think you're not a thorn in mine?" She

lifted her head. "Buy me another cushion while you're away. God knows I need it."

He lost his battle with what sense he had and scooped his arm around her, pulling her to stand in front of him so he could kiss that smart mouth of hers.

She gave a squeak of shock against the press of his lips to hers and went all stiff, but in the next heartbeat she melted. It was his undoing.

He wrapped both his arms across her back and slanted his head to get a full, satisfying taste of her mouth. Her curves were everything as she pressed into him and her fingertips caressed his collarbone beneath the bend of his collar. Then here was her tongue brushing against his and bringing his cock to full attention.

Even as he groaned, however, she drew a sharp inhale and pushed herself away from him.

Fuck. But also, good. They shouldn't. But fuck. He wanted to keep her right here but fought the urge. She was being sensible for both of them, pressing her fingertips to her mouth and shaking her head.

"That—"

"I know. You're my housekeeper. I won't treat you the way my mother was treated." His voice hardened as he saw the similarity. "That won't happen again," he vowed.

She was only a faceless silhouette, but he saw her nod.

"Safe travels." She hurried into the cabin.

CHAPTER TWELVE

Virgil's head was about to split under the pressure of holding onto his temper. For two days, there'd been nothing but debate on parliamentary rules and points of order. A single worthwhile motion had carried—yammer-mouths were limited to five minutes of listening to themselves expound on a topic. *Five minutes.* A man ought to be able to make his point in the time it took for an average piss. Anyone leaking anything into a john for a solid five minutes needed to see a doctor.

And, so help him God, if he had to listen to one more amendment to an amendment, he would set fire to this whole damned process.

By Wednesday afternoon, it had been resolved that the question of Statehood versus Territory would be put to a general vote. The business of drawing up committees for all the different special interests commenced, and Virgil walked away in weary disgust, eager to finish up his business and get back to Quail's Creek.

He went straight to the mercantile to ask after slates for the children's studies. They had a few and they were expensive, but Marigold had asked him special. Teaching them was the reason she was here. He didn't want Harley to feel left out, so he had three put on his account along with a double order of his usual lemon drops. Then he glanced over a handful of books, skipping past *The Scarlet Letter*.

No use rubbing Marigold's nose in her unearned reputation. He bought *David Copperfield*, since it was about a young man. Levi might enjoy it.

He stared at the cushions, wondering which was softer—buying it for Marigold or buying it for himself so his travels back to Quail's Creek would be kinder on his ass.

The fact he was hurrying through his errands, anxious to get back on the trail, was the part that made him soft. That's why he'd been so irritated by the ponderous proceedings at the convention. He had places he'd rather be and wasn't sure what that said about him.

He dropped by the Express office to pick up the mail and send Marigold's letter. It was odd to send a letter to the woman who should have been his wife from the woman he should have sent back.

Damn, but he'd been relieved when she had said she would stay. He kept telling himself that's what had been behind the kiss he had planted on her. He shouldn't have done it, regardless. He'd promised to protect her, and that meant from himself as much as anyone else. Kissing her was pure weakness, but he hadn't seen a lot of compassion in his life. Not the kind that came with physical warmth and gentleness. For such a salty woman, she was capable of real sweetness, and that got to him even more than the throbbing want that kept pulling at his crotch.

That lust was relentless. He'd woken from a dream about her this morning, on a cot in a room over the corral where he'd stabled his mules. He'd had his hard cock in his hand before he'd thought better of it and had come loud enough to spook the

horses in their stalls below him. A man in a neigh-
boring room had called out, "You got a whore in
there? Send her to me when you're done."

It was fucking embarrassing, and he had to quit
thinking of Marigold like that.

On his way back to his wagon, he checked on the
glass for his windows. It had arrived in a larger shipment and would need to be repackaged for the trail.
The mill promised the lumber for the frames would
also be ready by morning.

Virgil settled up at several of the saloons, but he
didn't have much taste for lingering in any of them.
He usually had a drink or two, which allowed him to
get the word out that they were hiring in Quail's
Creek. In the spring, he'd brought hungry miners
back with him more than once, but with Denver trying to catch up to Auraria, men were finding work in
town. They weren't interested in grueling labor and
the isolation of camp life.

Virgil spared time for a brief trek out to the trading post, always on the hunt for a bargain and the
latest gossip. He wasn't planning on shopping like a
lovesick suitor, but he hit the mother lode when he
got there. A trail picker had taken ownership of a
wagon that had belonged to an English couple
who'd passed from fever on their way to Oregon.

The women from the cathouse had already taken
the wife's dresses, but there was a bonnet and an
apron plus a sturdy basket of sewing supplies and an
entire crate of "clouded blue" wool. There were even
knitting needles and a book entitled *The Lady's
Assistant in Knitting, Netting, and Crochet*.

As Virgil stood there, hands on hips, wondering

what sort of fool got so tickled over buying something for a woman he wasn't screwing, the trader knocked a dollar off his price, determined to make the sale.

The children needed socks, didn't they? Virgil bought it all.

• • •

Marigold made herself stay busy so she wouldn't worry about Virgil's absence. Or think about their kiss. It had been little more than a peck, after all.

But she had never felt such a deep or unremitting yearning for her ex-husband. It didn't make sense that she would suffer it for Virgil, a man she didn't know very well.

She knew he was honorable in his way, though. He was loyal to his friends and devoted to his children's well-being. He was hard-headed to the point of arrogance, but with moments of uncertainty and humbleness.

She wondered what he thought of her, then quickly tried not to wonder. It ought to be a relief that he was away, but over the days of his absence, her longing for him only worked itself deeper like a splinter, becoming a swollen, tender thing she struggled to ignore even though she had plenty to distract her.

It rained the day after Virgil left, and the temperature plummeted. It was still July, but she took it as the warning it was and spent the next two days sewing warmer clothes for the children. She started Nettie making squares for a scrap quilt and kept

Levi home one day to help plug the gaps in the walls with mud.

On the third day of Virgil's absence, Levi came home proud as punch, having picked off a hare with his slingshot. Yeller had already helped him skin and clean it. He'd left the pelt in a bucket of saltwater and would stretch and dry it in a few days.

"Will you make me a fur hat, Marigold?" Levi asked as she cut strips off the skinned animal for cooking on a sapling grill. The rest would go into the stew pot tomorrow.

"Of course." She didn't have the first idea how to fashion one, but someone here would be able to guide her, maybe even Virgil.

"I want a fur hat." Nettie was so overcome with envy, her lip quivered and tears stood in her eyes.

"Don't worry. I'll get you a white one when they change color for winter," Levi promised, leaving Nettie smiling for hours.

When they were closing in on their fifth night and Virgil still hadn't returned, Marigold began to grow concerned. She put a brave face on it, but she could tell the children were unsettled as well. Levi was grumpy the next morning, and Nettie wouldn't leave Marigold's side even when Marigold used the john. Harley picked up on the general mood and became truculent as well.

At least the weather improved enough they could walk some sourdough down to Gristle and ask him to bake the rolls in his oven while it was still hot from breakfast. Marigold baked bread once a week, but if she found a few minutes—or made the time, as she had today—she made a batch of rolls. Today, she would leave a few as a thank-you to John.

They stayed while the rolls baked, helping Gristle grind corn, which kept the little ones busy. Marigold was hoping someone would offer up a word on Virgil's expected return, but even though Owen said, "Good morning," as he arrived and left with the coffeepot, he didn't mention Virgil.

When it had been a full week and Virgil still wasn't back, Marigold couldn't stand it a minute longer. She bundled up the little ones and wrapped the last of the sourdough with her latest batch of berry syrup. One roll was for Levi's lunch. The rest were a bribe for whoever might have some reassurance that Virgil hadn't abandoned her in the wilderness with three hungry mouths and no reliable means of feeding them.

Levi and Emmett came away from digging post holes when they saw her arrive at the storehouse. Levi offered a sullen thanks, chomping down his roll in three bites. Emmett ate his more slowly.

"I'm going to propose to Virgil that we pay you a dollar to leave a batch of rolls in the office when you're baking. Yours are miles more tasty than Gristle's. Is that something you could manage?" Emmett asked.

"I think so. On the topic of Virgil… Nettie, love, will you take this biscuit over to Yeller, please? Oh, Levi, fetch Harley before he gets under the fence." As the older children ran out of earshot, she asked Emmett, "Should I be worried?"

"About?"

"The fact he's not back yet."

"Virgil? No." His face went blank as if it didn't

occur to him to worry about his friend. "Well…" Emmett pulled at his earlobe. "What's it been? Five days?"

"A week," she said, voice edging toward strident.

"No wonder it's felt so much brighter around here." The glimmer of amusement in his eyes faded when she failed to laugh with him. She saw a glint of speculation grow in its place.

She folded her arms defensively and looked down at the muddy hem of her bloomers. "Three children in the wilderness may not seem daunting to you, but it is for me."

Humor lingered in his voice, but he said very sincerely, "I hope you know we'll look after his children one way or another—including the woman who's looking after them?"

Marigold relaxed a smidge, since that was reassuring, but it wasn't as though she wanted to live here, raising a man's children without him.

"He said he would only be gone three nights. It's been more than twice that." She chewed the corner of her mouth.

"Understood. But it could be a washout on the trail. It could be any number of delays that don't mean a thing. Virgil can take care of himself. He also knows we're short-handed and need supplies. He won't dawdle without good reason. He'll be back— well, I'd say any minute now." Emmett smirked and nodded beyond her.

Marigold turned and saw the wagon appearing on the hillock at the top of the track that wound down to the floor of the valley.

"Oh!" Her heart leaped so high, she put her hand

over it to keep it in her chest. It wasn't just relief. It was delight. Excitement at seeing him again. Reunion. "Now I feel silly, worrying for nothing."

She caught Emmett watching her with an expression that was a little too insightful for her comfort. She realized he could read her growing feelings for Virgil plain as day. It made her feel obvious and vulnerable to teasing or exposure.

A sting of anxiety climbed through her. *Please don't tell him*, she silently begged.

Emmett blinked and looked toward Virgil, expression mild, almost making her think she'd imagined that strange moment.

Still, it made her careful to keep a sense of decorum and not leap about the way the children did, waving and shouting, even though she wanted to smile so hard her cheeks ached at resisting it.

She picked up Harley so he wouldn't run with the older ones, asking the baby, "Who's that?"

Harley looked to where Virgil stopped the wagon long enough for Levi and Nettie to climb aboard for the short ride the rest of the way to the storehouse.

"Papa," Harley said, kicking his legs in excitement.

"Oh!" A sharp sting hit the backs of her eyes at little Harley using that word for the first time. She hugged him closer, ever so proud of him.

Yeller went into the storehouse, muttering about a busy afternoon of unloading.

"We were starting to think you'd gone to Washington to plead our case, you were gone so long," Emmett said as Virgil halted the wagon.

"If that convention was a taste of politics, I'd

rather take a kick in the face from one of these mules." Virgil's gaze hit Marigold's hard enough to send a fresh jolt of thrill through her. He nodded once in a greeting that made her cheeks sting with a blush, then stepped down from the wagon, holding out his arms for Nettie.

She leaped into them, making him stagger and say, "Oof." Her small arms squeezed briefly around his neck before he set her on the ground. His face turned pink with self-consciousness, as though he was pleased by her affection, but he didn't know what to do about it.

Levi came down from the wagon in a leap to the ground before his father. Both children hovered near Virgil, waiting with expectant expressions until he pushed his hand into his pocket.

Harley nearly went wild in her arms, so she put him on the ground. He scrambled across for his taste of a lemon drop. Virgil gave him his sliver, and the older children took theirs before Virgil held out his hand to her and Emmett. "Got a few extras this time."

Marigold went forward with all the shyness of a virgin on her wedding night.

"Thank you." Her voice held no substance. Her heart was battering inside her chest like a trapped bird, making it impossible for her to meet his gaze.

"You know I've got a sweet tooth." Emmett took one, then jerked his head at Levi. "Come on, slingshot. We're burning daylight. Unless you have news?" he asked Virgil.

"Yeah, I'll put coffee on. Whistle up the rest of them."

"We'll finish our post, then you can have the rest of the day off," Emmett told Levi as they headed back into the field.

Seconds later, there was a sharp whistle. One answered from a distance, then Emmett sent a couple of short ones in reply.

Virgil set Harley down, but the boy immediately started to cry as if he'd been abandoned by the side of a road.

"You hurt?" Virgil picked him up again and turned him sideways to look at his feet. They were shod in the leather moccasins Leyohna had made for all the children before she'd left. They were still big on him so his toes wouldn't be pinched the moment he grew.

As Virgil lifted him, Harley immediately stopped crying. He grabbed at Virgil's shirt, chortling.

With an exasperated noise, Virgil started to put him down again only for Harley to squawk and hold onto him.

"I think he missed you," Marigold said. *We all did*.

"Kid, I have things to do." Virgil straightened with the boy still in his arms.

Harley only burrowed his hand into Virgil's shirt pocket and said, "Peas, Papa."

"Ah, sh— When did he start saying that?" He was trying very hard not to let his pleasure show, but his cheek rounded beneath his scar as he pushed a reluctant smile into that side of his face.

"Just now, when he saw you in the wagon. I'll make the coffee," Marigold offered.

"Thanks." Virgil glanced around to ask, "Where'd

Nettie get off to?"

"I promised her a stick of jerky if she stacked cans for me," Yeller said, pulling down the gate on the back of the wagon.

"Enlist Levi soon as he's done with Emmett," Virgil said, then carried Harley into the office.

Ira was at the table, writing in a ledger book.

"Virgil. Good to have you back. Mrs. Davis," Ira greeted. "Ah, here comes trouble." He shifted in his chair as Virgil set Harley down and the boy ran across. Ira picked him up and stood him on his thighs. "I hear a whistle for a meeting?"

"Yeah. Got time?" Virgil walked into the bunk-room and poured water from the pitcher into the basin on the stand.

"Sure. No, you can't have my spectacles. We've talked about that." Ira pulled his face back from the boy's reaching hand.

"I'll start the coffee." Marigold picked up the cold, mostly empty coffeepot. "Do you want me to take him with me?"

"I'll take him outside while I set up." Ira stood with Harley in his arms and left.

Marigold hovered, caught by the sight of Virgil. He had hung his hat and was now bent over the wash basin, scooping water to splash his face and neck.

If the situation had been reversed, she would have accused him of leering, but only realized how inappropriately she was behaving when he straightened with the towel in his hands and noticed she was still here.

"Need something else?" He smoothed his beard

as he dried it and ran the towel over his hair and behind his ears.

"You had a haircut while you were away," she noted, overheating at how handsome he looked with his beard trimmed short, yet still wickedly dangerous with more of the puckered line of his scar showing.

"Cost me fifty cents." He hung the towel and picked up his hat, settling it in place.

"I expect it would have been more if I hadn't taken it down already." She lifted the cap on the coffeepot to see how much was in it.

"You got an answer for everything, don't you?" He sounded disgusted, but the corners of his mouth were deeply indented.

"If only there was a market for them. I'd be rich."

"Ha!" He barked out a reluctant laugh. "I'll bet."

Their gazes locked and held. His expression was warm with humor, hers likely reflecting the pride sparkling in her at having knocked a laugh out of him.

I'm glad you're back, she wanted to say, but it felt too revealing.

"Oh. Lo siento," Stoney said as he came in.

She blushed and said a flustered, "Excuse me, Stoney. I was about to make coffee." She hurried out to the cookhouse.

Pablo, a hollow-cheeked, bushy-browed man of fifty, was there, sitting with his foot up on the bench while he peeled potatoes for Gristle.

"Pablo, how is your ankle?" Marigold asked as she stole some of the water Gristle had started to boil for the potatoes. "Is the poultice helping?" She'd made one from mustard, onion, and castor oil.

She was fairly certain his ankle wasn't broken, only turned, but it had been swollen for a few days now.

"Almost went into my boot today. Back to work tomorrow, I think, but I've been waiting for a chance to give you this." Pablo struggled to stand up and dug in his pocket.

"You paid me already," she insisted.

"No, this is…" He offered her a rock the size of a chicken egg, oval and smooth. It was granite-gray like Pablo's hair and beard but had a streak of white and was still warm from his pocket.

"Um, thank you," she said, bemused.

"It has a ring," he pointed out. "My mama called that a wishing stone."

"Will you look at that." She rolled it to admire the way the white stripe went all the way around. "I'll have to think long and hard so I don't waste it."

"I can always find you another one," Pablo said with a shy shrug and sat down again.

She thanked him and dropped it into the pocket of her apron. They chatted a moment longer while she waited for the coffee. When it was ready, she used a pair of towels to take the hot pot back to the office.

Owen and Bing Sun had arrived, and they took over pouring the mugs while Marigold went across to pick up some hard tack and a can of peaches that she dished out for all the men, listening to Virgil as she did.

"I'll be shocked if Steele isn't elected governor," Virgil was saying.

"Of what? We likely to be a state or a territory?" Emmett asked.

"The debate continues, but the point was made by me and several others that we can't keep kicking this down the road. There'll be another hundred thousand fortune-seekers arriving next spring, some honest, some not. We have to be able to elect our own marshal."

"Will you run when the time comes, Virgil?" Stoney asked.

"I'd vote for you," Ira said.

"Me, too," Emmett said.

"I'm pretty busy with this mining company, in case you haven't noticed," Virgil said with a scowl.

"Steele came here to prospect. Now he wants to be governor," Ira pointed out. "You think he'll give up mining?"

"No," Virgil said flatly.

"If he can work and lawyer and govern, you can, too," Owen said.

"Jesus Christ," Virgil muttered under his breath. "Let's worry about who does what when it happens. For now, there's a committee drafting a constitution for Jefferson State. It'll be put to a vote in September."

"Will everyone vote?" Emmett asked, pinning an intense stare on Virgil.

"*Everyone*. Or I'll have something to say about it," Virgil promised him.

"Women, too?" Marigold blurted, pausing in feeding Harley a bite of peach.

All the men looked at her as if they'd forgotten she was here.

Virgil took off his hat to scratch the back of his head. "Well. Every man with a claim he's working.

That's how it went at our first meeting."

"I see," she said frostily. "I'll just go down to the stream and start panning, then. Oh, wait. I'll have to grow a beard first, won't I? And something else."

"We need law and order however we can get it, Marigold," Virgil said testily.

"Don't take that tone as though I'm too idealistic to understand how this works. I've been dismissed at more of these meetings than you will ever attend." She knew better than to let her temper flare so hot and fast, but this was so damned *typical*.

She grew more incensed when she saw Owen's shoulders come up in suppressed laughter while he sent a look to Ira that said, *Get a load of her*.

"In fact," she continued with snapped temper, "I can tell you right now that you're asking for something you won't get. The South controls Congress. Write whatever constitution you like. If they admit a free state, their balance of power will shift. They would rather ignore your request—which is exactly what happened in January when your Mr. Graham attempted to have your territory recognized, isn't that right? Now you've discovered gold. Do you really think anyone wants to give uneducated prospectors control over it? *You* are the ones who are the joke. But, by all means, deny me the right to vote, since my head is completely empty of what is truly at stake."

"You think they'll take us seriously if we come in with a demand they give *women* the right to vote?" Virgil scoffed. *Scoffed*.

"Governments are formed by the consent of the governed. How can I consent to this government if I have no voice in forming it?" she shot back.

"For God's sake, Marigold." Virgil stood with a clap of his feet onto the hard ground. "You're talking in circles like the men in those meetings. It's exhausting. All I want is a goddamned sheriff to keep outlaws from taking over my valley."

"You think I don't want to keep men out of *my* valley?" That pun was very much intended. She left the bowl in Harley's lap and stood to confront Virgil. "I should not need a man to stake a claim to *me* in order to have a voice in my own future."

The profound silence that followed made her realize she was shouting. And that she and Virgil weren't arguing by the fire next to his cabin, but in the middle of the camp. They had an audience of his partners, Harley's tender ears, and whatever men had stopped working in nearby ditches to stare in astonishment.

"Are you finished?" Virgil asked in a growl of warning.

For one second, she had spoken exactly what was on her mind, and it had felt fantastic, but no. She wasn't even supposed to do that.

CHAPTER THIRTEEN

Marigold stormed away, and Virgil grappled to regain control of his temper. *Damn that woman.*

"Papa?" Nettie was suddenly at his side, mouth quivering. "Is Marigold leaving?"

"What? No."

"Sure about that?" Stoney asked under his breath.

"Have *you* staked—" Owen began.

"Shut up. *No*." Virgil sent Owen his hardest look ever, then a warning glare toward Stoney and the rest. "She just needs a minute to cool off," he assured Nettie.

"You should go talk to her," Emmett said.

All the men nodded.

"Make sure she knows we're all looking out for her," Ira said. "That we appreciate what she's doing for you."

"I'm *paying* her," Virgil reminded them. "She's not doing me a favor."

"We're all paid to be here, but the company would fall apart if one of us dropped out, including you. She minds the children, and that makes you available to us. That's important and necessary," Emmett said with the calm, annoying logic that had made Virgil want him as a partner in the first place.

"We can watch the children while you make up with her," Bing Sun said, doing something with his hands as he reached from the shade out to the sunshine and cast a shadow of a bird onto the dusty, packed ground.

Nettie gave a soft giggle and moved closer. "Can you show me?"

"Why am *I* making up with her? Do any of you seriously think we'll get anywhere in a population of men if we start asking for women's rights?"

"Well…" Emmett shrugged. "If there are only a few women here, they'd get outvoted anyway, so where's the harm?"

"What did she mean about sitting in on meetings? Does she know about constitutions?" Ira asked. "Because I don't want to vote on something I don't understand. If she could explain it to us—"

"Si." Stoney leaped on that. "I don't read English. Tell her we'll pay her to help us read it when it gets printed in the newspaper."

Bing Sun nodded. "She can tell us about lady rights, too. She wants to be heard. We should listen."

"You're our talker," Virgil snarled at Owen. "*You* go talk to her."

"About what? I wasn't paying attention."

Jesus Christ. Virgil looked to the sky.

"Fine. I'll order bloomers for the lot of us. Nettie can leave for Washington soon as we finish reading out the minutes from the temperance committee."

• • •

Marigold had been so distracted by Virgil's arrival and the subsequent meeting, she had forgotten the things she'd meant to pick up from Yeller. That meant she would have to go back to the storehouse, and she would rather remove her eyeteeth with a shard of broken glass.

She was saving the bear jerky for winter but decided she could use a tiny nip of it to flavor a bean stew. After last week's rain, she had picked wild mushrooms that Leyohna had told her were safe and set them to dry, but she would forage more as soon as it rained again.

What she wouldn't do was have another cry. What was the point? Despair might float around her like a wraith, but giving in to it had never once improved her situation.

It was just so frustrating that Virgil seemed to like her one minute—had kissed her, even—yet dismissed her the next. It was hurtful. Infuriating and lowering.

A firm step outside the door was her only warning before he walked in.

Her heart leaped into the cloud of dejection swirling around her. She felt clawed apart and left in tatters. She defensively folded her arms and lifted her chin, unnerved by the fact the children weren't with him. They were a buffer she could really use right now.

After a long silence where he studied her, the shelf behind her, and the table before her, he folded his own arms.

"What's that?" He flickered his gaze to the rock she had pulled from weighing down her pocket and left on the corner of the table.

"It's called a wishing stone. You wish someone would leave you alone, then you throw it at their head."

His mouth tightened. "I am not responsible for all men, Marigold. I won't be hung for their crimes."

"You *are*, though." Her temper flared again. "Maybe you're not responsible for their actions, but you lead all of these men." She waved toward the river where his workers shoveled gravel into sluice boxes all day. "You set an example, and you're their voice when you go to Denver. Don't pretend you don't have influence."

"I'm still only one man. I have to pick my battles, and they have to be battles I can win." His scarred cheek ticked. "Otherwise, I lose what influence I've managed to gain."

"Yes, I know how that works. I tell myself every day that I should have put up with Ben's cheating because I was never going to win that battle. At least I would still have a place in society there. It's been proven to me again and again that self-respect is far less important than what others think of me. I should have thrown myself into the Delaware when I had the chance!"

"Don't say things like that," he ordered in a grumble.

"See?" she cried, waving her hand at him. She blinked past the hot tears gathering in her eyes. "It's not even allowed for a woman to decide how she *feels*."

"That's not what I meant."

He came forward so quickly, she fell back a step.

His mouth tightened. He looked down. "I don't like to hear that he hurt you so bad he nearly broke you. Makes me want to crack his skull in."

He picked up the rock, turned it over, then set it

aside again. When his eyes came up, he met her gaze straight on. His voice was grave enough to still everything inside her.

"I wish I could tell you why life is worth living. I've struggled with that question myself. Life is pain and hardship and scrapping over the few bones that are out there. For what? Shiny chunks of rock? I wish to hell you were the kind of woman who only wanted a fancy hat or a lace parasol. I could give you those things and we might be able to live a happy life, but you want more, Marigold. I understand that because I do, too. I respect you for it, but it's not in my power to give you what you want, and now it's one more pebble in my boot."

"Why would you care what I want?" He had every right to fire her for insubordination after her outburst in front of everyone.

"Since when have I been able to ignore you?" he asked grouchily.

The tiniest smile tugged at the corners of her mouth. She tilted her wet lashes up at him. "You're very confusing when you're nice to me."

"I don't want to be nice to you. If I let down my guard around you, then I want to do more than be nice. I want to touch you." His brows came together in frustration while his heavy hand set itself against the side of her neck, palm warm and faintly rough with callus. "And this here is a battle neither of us can afford to lose. You're my housekeeper, not my wife."

"I know, but…" Her feet moved without her permission, inching toward his. Her hands went up to touch the silky whiskers of his beard. She'd been longing to touch it again since she'd cut it.

When her petting fingertips grazed his ear, he made a noise in the base of his throat and covered her mouth with his.

This was worth *living for*, she thought distantly, as he rocked his lips across hers, tender and possessive, beard softly scraping her chin and arms closing around her to draw her into the powerful strength of his body. She drank in the taste of coffee and peaches, the scent of trail dust and summer heat and salty, sweaty man.

This was worth throwing away her education and marriage and reputation. It was worth crossing half a continent and living at the mercy of nature. When he kissed her, he made her feel pure even as his tongue slid in to touch hers and his hand roamed to stroke the side of her breast. He made her feel free even as he pressed her backside to the edge of the table and caged her with his weight and caught her earlobe with his teeth.

He made her feel powerful even as her muscles trembled with weakness and her loins turned to liquid because she only needed to tug at his shirt and slide her touch beneath the edge and she made him shake. When she opened her legs and let him press the thick shape of his arousal against the heat beneath layers of skirt and bloomers, he swore and gripped the edge of the table and hung his head against her shoulder.

When she palmed him through his trousers, he said, "Fuck, Marigold," in a groan so helpless, she smiled against his throat.

Then he did the same to her, sliding his touch

beneath the shortened skirt of her gown. He found the slit in her bloomers, and suddenly he was stroking the bare skin of her inner thighs, petting her damp curls. She squeaked in shock and tried to close her thighs, but he stood between her legs.

"It's okay. I won't fuck you." His gentle touch was a stark contrast to his rough language. "I want to, though. Fuck, Marigold, you feel so nice. Hot and wet…" His finger explored her folds, tickling up and down, causing an acute sensation to spark through her.

"Virgil," she gasped and clutched at his shoulders.

"You're so soft. Slippery," he noted as his touch increased in pressure and discovered dampness. He spread it all around in a way that stole her breath.

Ben had sometimes touched her, but it had never felt like this. She had never panted and held still, yearning for more.

Virgil's mouth nuzzled against her neck, sending shivers down her shoulder and into the tips of her breasts. His fingertip probed and she briefly clenched, wary of discomfort, but there was so much lubrication, his finger easily slid in. "Okay?"

She wasn't sure. Well, she was very sure she shouldn't allow this to happen. It felt wicked, but it didn't hurt. It actually felt intriguing, stoking her desire for him to continue.

He kissed her again, moving his finger inside her as though he was making love to her. Sex with Ben had never felt this good. Her sex was heavy and the slide of his finger made the sensations grow more acute the longer he did it. She especially liked the way his thumb was rubbing circles in time with his finger as he moved—

"Oh!"

The most exquisite sensation shot through her. She saw his teeth flash in possibly the first real smile she'd ever seen on him. Maybe there was a hint of cruelty in it, because he withdrew his finger and she sobbed in anguish.

"Can you take two?"

Her breath left her as his two fingers filled her, making her flesh feel taut and full and so sensitized she could only grip fistfuls of his sleeves and try to remember to breathe. When his thumb started up with the circling, she felt swollen and hot, and there was an ache in her loins like she'd never experienced.

"Virgil." She lifted her mouth and sucked at his lips as she kissed him, pleading for something, rocking her hips, aware she was behaving without any inhibition, but in this moment, she truly didn't care. All she wanted in this world was for him to keep pushing his fingers into her like that.

His tongue plunged into her mouth, and she sucked blatantly on it, spreading her thighs for a deeper pleasuring, moaning with delight as the sensations intensified. Her breasts felt hard and her skin was flushing hot and cold. Her entire body was tense with reaching for something she couldn't name. This was the way she had often felt when it was nearly over, when she was wishing for it to go on and on. She clamped down on his touch, silently urging him to keep doing this because it felt so very, very *good*.

"I wish this was my mouth," he groaned against her cheek. "I want to see your pussy. I want to lick you while I do this." He pushed his fingers deep.

That, coupled with his flagrant words, caused something to happen within her. Her muscles clamped down on his fingers of their own accord. Her whole being felt as though it narrowed to a pinprick before expanding. Stars exploded through her, more than the sky could contain.

Dimly she was aware of his hand still working at her while utter euphoria overtook her, making her shudder under the force of it. Sensations crashed and ebbed over her in waves. Her breath broke and she couldn't catch it. Her flesh clasped and quivered where his touch continued sliding in and out of her, playing out the joyous feelings as though stroking an instrument to continue its sweetest notes.

Marigold thought she might be dying. She was equally sure she was happy to.

. . .

Virgil didn't make it to the john. He got as far as the log pile and hoped to hell no one saw him as he yanked open his fly and jerked himself with the hand that was still wet from Marigold's pussy.

"Fuuuck," he groaned as a powerful orgasm nearly ripped out his spine. "Fuck," he panted several more times, bucking his hips into his fist as though he had her bent her over the table before him, the way he'd been aching to have her.

When he'd milked himself dry, he kicked dust across the stain he left in the dirt, as though it was that easy to erase his stupidity. She *worked* for him. He kept his arm braced on the log, needing the support. It took several minutes to gather enough strength to straighten and tuck himself back into his drawers and button up.

On weak legs, he went around the back of the cabin and picked up the water bucket from the porch, taking it down to the stream. There was a well with a pump behind the storehouse that Yeller used for watering the livestock. Gristle and the men used it for cooking, but here at the top of the stream was a small chain pump Bing Sun had built for him so they could have clean water for the cabin.

Virgil washed his hands and face in the bracing water, trying to cool his blood. His heart was still knocking around loose in his chest. His hand was imprinted with the clinging heat and wet hairs of Marigold's pussy.

Don't think about it, he ordered himself, but he couldn't keep from imagining her silky, slippery lips riding his face. How would she taste? If he shoved his cock deep into her tight heat, would she come that same way? Nearly ripping his hair off his scalp while crying out his name?

Fuck, it had been exciting for her to abandon herself to him, but he was such a, "Stupid, fucking *asshole.*" He berated himself aloud, slapping his icy hand on the back of his neck hard enough to sting.

When he carried the water back to the porch and set down the bucket with a clunk and a slosh, he glanced through the open door and saw Marigold sitting on the bench.

She quickly stood, all wide-eyed and wary in the shadowed interior.

"Did I hurt you?" he asked with a flash of concern

at how subdued she seemed.

"No. I don't think so."

She didn't think so? His brain caved in on itself as he tried to make sense of that.

"If I was being too rough, you should have told me to stop." His stomach still ached at the force of his orgasm. Now a sick misgiving crept in. She had been moaning and sucking on his tongue. He thought that meant she was liking it.

"I just…" She folded her arms across her middle and hunched her shoulders toward her ears. "I didn't know women could feel like that. That I could."

His ears rang, he was so dumbfounded.

"Your husband didn't ever…?" He really did want to bash the other man's head in. Bastard cheated on her, stole her house, ruined her reputation, and never even got her off? What a monumental prick.

"Can we not talk about it, please?"

"Marigold, it's okay." He stepped over the threshold.

"No, it's not." She took a step backward, bumping into the bench and glancing behind herself, then looked back at him. She wore a cornered expression.

He gripped the edge of the doorway, growing more angry with himself by the second. He didn't want her to be *afraid* of him.

"It means I'm…what they called me. Loose."

"What? Don't be foolish. You have nothing to be ashamed of." Even as he said it, he heard her scolding him minutes ago about women not being allowed to have their own feelings.

Fact was, he was ready to kick himself into the

next valley for touching her, so he couldn't fault her for having qualms about what they'd done.

Still, she shouldn't be berating herself over it.

Nettie's approaching giggle drew Virgil into taking a step back out the door. He glanced down the path to where Owen was carrying Harley toward the cabin.

Nettie skipped alongside him. When she saw Virgil, she ran toward him.

"Papa, Harley tried to get into Stoney's bunk because he slept there before, and Uncle Owen said Harley is the wee baby bear who tried to get in the big bear's bed. That's not how the story goes, is it? Tell him."

"I'm pretty sure that's exactly how the story goes," Owen teased her, stopping to set Harley on his feet.

"No. Ask Marigold. She'll say it right," Nettie insisted.

"Let's all get on with our chores and save storytelling for bedtime," Virgil said.

Nettie sobered, making him realize how hard his voice had become. He tried to reassure her with a gentle pat on her hair.

"Mick? Peas, Papa?" Harley toddled up to tug at his pantleg.

"I'm fresh out, kid." Virgil showed him his empty hands.

"He wants milk, Papa," Nettie said hesitantly.

"Oh. Look at you with all your new words." Virgil couldn't help but be proud of the little mite, even though he had nothing to do with how quickly he was learning.

"Harley, come with me. I'll give you some milk," Marigold called, still sounding hollow-voiced and unsettled. She bustled around, clattering a can off the shelf and picking up the water pitcher.

It was a stark reminder of her role here. And the fact he was behaving like his father, taking liberties with his employee.

Sickened, Virgil marched away without saying goodbye, hearing Nettie telling Marigold, "Do you know what Uncle Owen said?"

"Everything smoothed over?" Owen asked, falling into step beside him.

"Yes," Virgil lied.

"Why is your collar wet?"

"Because I had to cool off."

"Oh? Why's that?" Owen sent a sideways smirk at him.

"Because I can't tell Marigold to fuck off the way I can with you."

"Yeah, I saw what happened when you tried."

Asshole.

"Nothing makes me more eager to stand in ice water for eleven hours like talking to you, you know that?"

Which was what he did, because he still needed to cool off. The memory of her heat sat like a brand on his skin…and would for the rest of his life.

CHAPTER FOURTEEN

Marigold started the beans, adding a dab of molasses. Then she walked Nettie and Harley to a spot on the far side of the stream.

It was late in the day for an outing, but Harley was filled with milk and peach preserves and mischief. He needed the exercise. Marigold needed something to occupy her thoughts so she wouldn't dwell on what had happened with Virgil. Would one call that lovemaking? Or wanton fornication?

Virgil had said she had nothing to be ashamed of, but men only said that until it was no longer convenient to have a woman of loose morals cluttering up their lives.

She seemed to have an unseemly appetite for relations, Ben had claimed in court.

As newlyweds, were you not trying to start a family? her attorney had argued. *Would that not account for Mrs. Davis showing enthusiasm for the marriage bed? A wife is expected to submit to her husband, is she not?*

To be frank, sir, she wished me *to submit to* her *desires.*

It had been humiliating. Intentionally so.

And had pierced her so keenly because there'd been a grain of truth to it.

Marigold hadn't been sure what she sought when she and Ben were abed, but there'd been a hunger for something. To learn. To discover. Each time they'd joined themselves together, she had felt teased into welcoming him the next time he reached for her. She had wanted his touch and penetration without fully understanding why it was so beguiling.

Now she knew. That culmination Virgil had drawn forth in her was more than disconcerting. It was *knowledge*. It was dangerous because it incited a desire to feel that way again, uncaring that they weren't married. Even though it was sinful and shameful and *wrong*.

"What about bears?" Nettie asked with an anxious look into the brush up the hill.

"Hmm? Oh. We're only going this far." Marigold took stock of where they were. "See? There are men over there making noise." One was using a pickaxe against the bank, and another was rocking a wooden box so water and gravel sloshed. "I don't think we'll be bothered by anything other than mosquitos."

Marigold had walked them a little distance downstream from the abandoned Ute camp. Leyohna had told her to watch for blossoms on a patch of brush to turn into berries here. The leaves looked like currant bushes, and the berries were a glossy red with fine hairs all over them. They were tart, perhaps not ripe enough, but they would make a nice marmalade. They would pick some today and check back over the next week to see if they sweetened up.

They stayed until the mountain shadow was across the whole valley. By then, she had also dug up some dandelion greens while Nettie kept Harley amused with catching grasshoppers. Every time she opened her hands to show one to Harley, it jumped away, startling them into squeals of laughter.

Marigold noticed the men nearby had stopped working to watch and laugh along with them. She waved and offered a weak smile as she gathered up the children for the walk back to the cabin.

She was in the strangest state of melancholy, feeling sensual and aware of everything around her while also insulated from it. There was a slight tenderness in her loins, as if she and Virgil had engaged in congress. She was anxious to see him yet preferred not. She was embarrassed and hating herself while nursing anger toward him and Ben and all men.

She's not the sort of woman who would instill pious values into my children, she could hear Ben saying under oath. *God must have seen it since He chose not to give us any.*

Marigold had already been worrying she was barren, and that declaration hadn't helped.

Now, she did have children in her life and would be heartbroken to lose them. They were demanding, but she was growing to love them—Nettie with her happy, inquisitive chatter, Harley with his cheeky smiles and never-ending cuddles.

And here was Levi, coming up the path as they arrived back at the cabin. He was leaned into the crosspiece of a handcart, pulling the two-wheeled box up the incline, headstrong and determined as his father.

"Are you on your way to Utah? I think you made a wrong turn." Marigold had occasionally seen trains of Mormons starting out with such carts loaded with their meager belongings, women and children walking along behind. Now that she'd made a good portion of the journey herself in a carriage, she was even more in awe of their will and perseverance.

Levi got the cart as far as the flat stretch of dirt near the cabin and dropped the crosspiece. He fell onto the grass with his tongue hanging out, making Nettie giggle. Harley fell on him to wrestle, making Levi chuckle.

"It didn't all fit in the wheelbarrow," Levi said.

"What is it? I thought your father was buying a pair of slates and a fresh tin of saleratus."

"Pa said it's for you to make socks for us."

"That's a lot of socks." She glanced at the case of wool. It would make two pairs for each one of them with enough to make a cardigan for Harley and a few scarves. Nettie would enjoy learning to knit those.

Marigold felt down the side of the cart box, looking for extra pairs of needles, and came up with a quilted bonnet wrapped in a gingham apron.

"That's pretty," Nettie said, then pointed to ask, "What's that?"

"A sewing basket." Marigold lifted out the heavy wicker basket beside the wooden crate. She grunted at the weight.

She knelt in the dirt and set it before her, sensing it had been very valuable to its original owner. The two flaps were decorated in needlepoint vistas of a duck pond and a fancy country house. She spared a moment of prayer for whomever had owned it. Sadly, it was a common enough story for people to die along the trail. She couldn't imagine another reason it would have been sold, since it would provide a means of income for a widow.

"What's in it?" Nettie asked, kneeling down beside her.

Harley copied his sister, crouching to ask, "Wa-nin-it?"

Even Levi sat up with curiosity.

"Let's see." Marigold was ridiculously excited.

When she opened the flap, she discovered the basket was lined with pale blue silk. There were special pockets containing two pair of scissors, one with long blades for fabric, one with very short blades for nipping threads.

There was a soft leather case full of crochet hooks and embroidery needles and a quilted strip holding two dozen dress pins. A pleated pocket on the inside of one lid was meant to store small projects while they were in process. The other side held a pocket with a measuring tape and a tiny leather case with three silver thimbles nested inside it, each with a different flower decorating its rim.

"Oh!" Nettie said reverently.

"Oh," Harley copied with big eyes.

"Aren't they lovely?" Marigold let Nettie try one on her finger. Harley had to try it, too.

Levi inched closer but shook his head when she offered to let him try it on, smirking at the idea, but he continued watching as she explored the rest of the contents.

There were whole spools of thread and ribbons in various colors, full boxes of buttons, snaps, hook-and-eye closures, along with a tin of straight pins. She found three sizes of knitting needles, a swan-shaped pin cushion with a belted band to secure it on her wrist, and in the very bottom, embroidery hoops and precut squares of loosely woven linen for needlepoint.

Did Virgil understand the value in this?

"He really said you should give this to me?" She couldn't believe it.

"And that we should eat without him. Can we please?" Levi clutched his belly. "I'm *so hungry*."

"Me, too," Nettie said, holding her own belly.

"Me," Harley said pitifully, even though he'd filled up on berries an hour ago.

"You are turning into a little parrot," Marigold told the tot, catching at his round tummy.

She went about feeding the children and washing them for bed. At Nettie's insistence, she told them the story of the three bears, being sure to clarify that the wee baby bear was the injured party.

Everything in her would have loved to crawl into bed and not speak to Virgil for a week, she was still so embarrassed, but now she had this extravagant basket to wonder about.

The air was cool, and the last of the evening light was fading when she went outside.

"Oh." She came up short as she realized Virgil had arrived home.

He stood beside the cart, looking down on the contents.

"There's beans and sourdough, but not much left. Levi is eating like a man. I guess he's working like one." She moved across to the fire, trying to think how to act naturally around him when he'd had his hand up her skirt a few hours ago. "I can fetch pickles to fill it out."

"Thanks, but I had your peaches—" He cleared his throat as he lowered onto a log round and didn't bother finishing.

She begged the ground to split open and swallow her. She wished for a bear to leap out of the darkness and knock her dead with one swipe of its paw. Maybe she would simply succumb to the flames of embarrassment roaring like a bonfire through her and be turned into a pile of ash where she stood.

But she had to speak to it and plainly or they'd never get past it. She pressed her palms together and opened her mouth.

"Where did this come from?" Virgil asked.

"What?"

"This." He held up the wooden spoon he was using to scrape beans onto his plate.

"One of the men gave it to me."

"Who?"

"Um…" She had to think. "Jeb? The one with the crooked shoulder, not the Jeb with the thick eyebrows. The Jeb with the eyebrows carved the egg cups."

"Why? Did you ask them to? Did they charge you?"

"No. I gave one of them some of the butter Nettie churned. The other refused to take anything."

Virgil sighed. "I don't think it's wise to accept these courting gifts. It'll only rile the men against each other."

"What? No one is *courting* me." Were they? "They're being friendly."

He dropped the spoon into the pot and set it down. "Are you really that naive? You see anyone carving egg cups for *me*?"

"You're not friendly, are you?"

"Can't argue that," he said flatly.

She folded her arms, growing defensive. "Are you accusing me of flirting or teasing? I only want to feel accepted, Virgil. To have a friend or two." This conversation took on added magnitude as she recalled what had happened between them earlier. "I'm not… I haven't—" She swallowed. Thank goodness it was growing darker since her cheeks ached with a confused blush of hurt and shame. "If what happened today makes you think I've been with some of these men—"

"I know you haven't," he said bluntly and set aside his bowl. He poked at the fire, making sparks lift into the night air.

She watched the light and shadows shift in his face, trying to read his expression as the light flared and faded.

"How?" She moved to sit on one of the log rounds across the fire from him. "I mean, I told you what my husband said. I understand why you might think—"

"You said he lied."

"You believe me?"

"I do."

"Even after the way I acted today?" Smoke must have drifted into her eyes, because they began to water and burn. She had to sniff back a nose that wanted to run.

"Yes. And today proves it." His shoulders came up.

"How?" Her voice was squeezed by the pincers

that had taken hold of her heart.

He buried a curse into his palm, bracing his elbows on his thighs as he rearranged his face with his hand.

"You're not as experienced as I presumed you would be, having been married and all." He lifted his face to hold her stare, even though it was growing dark enough she could only see the glitter of firelight in his eyes. "It's one thing if your husband never got you there, but *no one* has. It's a pretty good bet you've only been with him."

Marigold sat very still, trying to absorb that he believed her while at the same time doubts were swimming inside her, making her wonder if she believed *herself*.

She hid her face in her own hands, tortured enough to confess in a low voice, "I wanted to."

"Wanted to what?" he growled.

"I don't know. Feel like that." She kept her hands over her hot cheeks, toes curled in her shoes, unable to look at him. "I didn't know that was how I wanted to feel, but I realize now that's what I was chasing when I encouraged him to make love to me. He told everyone in the courtroom that I invited him to bed me. He said I was too forward and demanding. That it proved I was a harlot."

After a stunned silence, Virgil spat, "He's the biggest piece of shit alive, isn't he?"

She had to choke a laugh at that. It was either that or cry. She picked up the corner of her apron to dab under her damp eyes.

Virgil rubbed his thighs. "You know, Marigold, I recently learned that women have the right to feel however they want to feel. Men aren't supposed to tell them what to think of themselves, so is there a reason you're still letting that prick tell you who and what you are?"

"You're going to throw my words back in my face like that?" She lifted her wet lashes. The corners of her mouth didn't know if they wanted to go up or down.

"I am," he said gently. "And if you're looking for a man's opinion of you, I'd say you're smart enough to know you're better than that one will ever be. Not that the way we behaved today proves either of us possesses much intelligence," he added drily.

"I thought you would blame me." She scratched at a berry stain on her apron. "Say I wasn't suitable to be around your children."

"Then I shouldn't be around them, either. Should I?"

Oh, why did he have to make her like him so much? She folded her hands. "What are we going to do?"

"Not *that*. Not unless we're planning to marry." He rubbed his thighs again. "I won't be like my father, making children I refuse to recognize."

She nodded, not wanting to raise children without the commitment of their father, but she wasn't sure she wanted to marry and give up this nascent autonomy she was finding here. On the other hand, marrying Virgil wasn't nearly as objectionable a prospect as it had seemed when she had first arrived. Not with today's memory throbbing between her thighs.

"I have to finish this cabin," he continued

absently. "We'll have frost soon, and that'll cost us another batch of men. I should get their help with adding a couple of rooms while they're still here. At least then you and I won't be sleeping on top of each other."

She was aware of him every night, above her. After today, she would speculate even more how it would feel to press her body up against his in the night, to feel his skin brushing hers and his hardness entering her.

She looked away so he wouldn't read the longing in her eyes. Her gaze snagged on the handcart.

"Oh. Um, the sewing basket." She rose and moved toward it. "How much do I owe you?"

"Nothing." He stood and kicked the fire down. "Why would you think I expect you to pay for it?"

"Well, you did just tell me to quit accepting courting gifts. I don't want to give you a wrong impression." She was teasing, trying to defuse the undercurrents still swirling around them.

"It's tools to do your job, Marigold. Same as I give the men who work for me," he said testily. "I thought Nettie would like some of the ribbon on one of her dresses or in her hair. The price was right, so I bought it."

He sounded so surly, she was almost offended, but she heard the defensiveness beneath his purchase of such an extravagant gift. She bit her lips to hide her smile.

"Do you need help carrying it inside?" He came across. "Is that why it's still out here?"

"No, I put it back in the cart so Harley wouldn't get into it. I can't think where I'll store it to keep him out of it."

"The table?" He handed her the basket and took up the crate of wool. "Leave it on my bed when I'm not in it."

"Your bed isn't high enough," she said with exasperation. "He started climbing up there while you were gone. He's so proud once he's there, then he cries because he doesn't know how to get down."

Virgil snorted. "Story of every man who thinks he's onto a good idea until he tries it. I'll ask Emmett to build you a cupboard with doors that latch."

"Thank you." She paused as they stood in the dark. "I mean it, Virgil. Thank you."

"It's just a sewing basket, Marigold."

She wasn't thanking him for that. They both knew it, but she nodded and followed him inside.

CHAPTER FIFTEEN

Virgil had been too young to fully understand why his father had come to the small, barren room he had shared with his mother. She had always sent him outside, coming to get him after some time had passed.

After his father had so publicly and brutally denounced him, Virgil had been sent to bunk and work alongside the enslaved men. He couldn't say whether his mother had welcomed his father to her bed, but she hadn't had a choice, so Virgil knew what that made him. Not just illegitimate, but the product of something dark and wrong.

Most of the time, he could forget how he came to be. Then he did something stupid that made him see his father showing through his better intentions and loathed himself. He didn't want to be anything like that man, pressing his attentions on a woman. He wanted to believe that if Marigold had screamed that first morning he'd woken with her in his arms, he would never have touched her again.

He wanted their tacit agreement *not* to touch one another to be enough to keep his hands and lips and eyes off her. It was damned hard, though. She was not only comely and capable and smart-mouthed enough to keep him on his toes, she had revealed how passionate she was. Not just in her beliefs, but in every way. And erotically receptive to his stoking of those passions—when she wasn't breaking her heart with disgrace over it.

Christ, it hurt him that she'd been humiliated over something so natural. Precious even. It made him want to *show* her how sweet lovemaking ought to be. To discover with her how far they could take their passions.

Instead, he worked himself nearly to death trying to ignore her, but she didn't make it easy. Not when she looked for him when she was walking, which he knew because he was looking for her.

Her face lit up when she saw him, especially when he was coming up the path toward the cabin. Then she would make some idle comment to the children and send them running to greet him, but his eyes would meet hers, and he'd fill up with something bright as sunshine.

Most agonizing of all was when he happened to stand close to her. She would drop her lashes and bite her lip but wouldn't move away. His own feet would root to the ground, and they'd stand for long seconds where he listened to his heartbeat in his ears, holding so still he felt as though he was vibrating, before some noise or other distraction would make him aware of what he was doing.

At night, he lay awake for hours, so aware of her he felt skinless as he fought the temptation to reach down and stroke her calf where her feet were tucked under the overhang of his bunk. His mind was constantly conjuring fantasies of gathering her up and stripping her down, tasting every inch of her and pressing himself deep inside her.

They *really* needed separate bedrooms.

So he asked Emmett to help him peel logs that

should have had a year or two to season, but he didn't have the luxury of time. In fact, he dragged a few more green ones down. They left those for last, taking turns using the spud and the drawknife, enlisting Owen if he showed up, which tended to send him back to the river, checking on the miners instead of jaw-wagging here.

"Looks like hard work for a hot day," Marigold said as she came out with two cups and a pitcher. "I thought you could both use a cool drink."

"Thanks." Virgil drained his in one go, barely tasting the tart berry juice watered down and sweetened with a hint of sugar. He tried not to notice the pretty pink in her cheeks or the button at her throat that was only partially through the hole, as if she had opened it to cool off and closed it before she came out to speak to them.

"Thank you, Marigold," Emmett said, smiling warmly with appreciation.

"If Levi turns up, will you ask him to help us at the clay patch? Unless you need him?" Marigold refilled both cups, emptying the pitcher before lifting her dark lashes.

Virgil held her dark honey gaze and took another gulp to wet his dry throat, feeling the soft burn all the way to his crotch. This craving for her was going to eat him alive, it really was.

"I'll send him to help you." He cleared his throat, trying to shake off his lust so he could talk sense. "Stoney wants to get on with the chimney. We need to fire the rest of the bricks."

She nodded, sent Emmett a friendly smile, gave Virgil one more glimmer of what he felt inside him as longing, and walked away.

Virgil turned back to his work, checking that Emmett wasn't watching her walk away.

Emmett knew exactly what Virgil was trying to catch him at. Maybe he saw what was between them, because he snorted as he picked up the draw knife.

"You know there's deliberation and there's missing a boat? She's thoughtful, she works hard, and she's good with your children. I'm not the only one who's noticed."

"See, this is why I haven't bothered ordering a printing press. We all know what's what without reading about it in a weekly paper."

"That's a long way to tell me to mind my own business."

"You want the short version? It's only two words."

Emmett made a scoffing noise that matched the scrape of the knife as he pulled the blade toward him, lifting a curly cue of inner bark off the log.

"You'd be doing everyone a favor if you'd post your intentions at the cookhouse. The men don't know if they're coming or going." Emmett paused his rowing motion, sending Virgil a sly look.

Did he want a prize for that pun?

"If they're sticking around to see if they have a shot with her, where's the incentive for me to declare myself?"

"The ones who think they've got a shot are taking it," Emmett pointed out.

"That's not front-page news. I've got a wooden bowl that *I* didn't make full of bone buttons and pine cones dressed as owls. They're like barn cats leaving dead mice at the door, but I'm the one giving her that door and the house behind it. I'm not threatened."

"So it doesn't bother you that I made the whistle?"

"That was you?" Virgil dropped the spud and clapped his hands on his hips, dumbfounded. And threatened. His chest nearly puffed up double its size with aggression while his head reminded him that Emmett was better looking and better mannered than he'd ever be. Marigold might prefer him. "You're serious about her?"

"No. Owen said it would be funny. It is." Emmett put his back into drawing the knife, mouth pinned closed while his lips danced as if he was holding something hot on his tongue. Another curl dropped onto the pile on the ground. "Harley like it?"

"You sadistic—" Virgil refused to laugh, even though a hard wave of relief hit him. "I was so fucking glad when he fell asleep and I was able to hide it."

They worked in silence a few minutes with only the scrape of the tools and the distant clatter of the miners.

"I do like her, though," Emmett said. "I'm not saying I plan to get in your way, but… She's trying to make something of herself, same as the rest of us. It's hard to build something on a foundation that's not firm. You should at least let her know where she stands."

"I'll get there when I get there," Virgil grumbled, even though Emmett was right. He and Marigold couldn't go on the way they were.

Emmett pulled the knife. "So if anyone asks, you're still undecided? Because I've been thinking to try my hand at a skin drum."

"I can build this cabin myself, you know. You don't need to be here."

Emmett snickered and kept sweeping the blade across the log, but at least he quit running his mouth, leaving Virgil's mind free to contemplate whether he should ask Marigold to marry him.

How simplistic he'd been, sending away for a wife, thinking he could marry a stranger and live out his years with her, content. His only experience had been with Clara, and they definitely had not been content. He'd started out with a lusty infatuation. She'd been sweet and eager to please. He'd managed to delude himself as well as her that his ambitions were the same as his ability when it came to providing the life they wanted.

Empty pockets put a lot of stress on a union, though. They'd argued plenty and regretted much. They'd both done their best by their children, and Virgil had never had cause to mistrust her, which was why her infidelity had left such a deep mark on him. He hadn't seen it coming. At all.

Maybe that's why he'd been willing to marry a stranger. He hadn't wanted to feel anything toward his wife aside from basic regard. That way any betrayals on her part wouldn't cut so deep. He had anticipated his new wife might want another baby or two, but he'd planned to be cautious about making any. He wanted the sex. God knew he did, but he had figured it would be like it had been with Clara—different times playful or quick and more satisfying than fucking his hand.

Not like something that felt powerful enough to make him cautious. That it had to be with one specific woman and would engage all of him, guts and heart and head.

Would he have wanted Pearl the way he wanted Marigold? He couldn't help wondering what would have happened if he'd married Pearl and Marigold had turned up later. Would he have still felt this hunger for Marigold and wish he'd had the chance to pick her?

If that's what he was thinking, didn't that mean he ought to marry her?

He genuinely believed Marigold would be faithful, but there were those other prevarications and white lies that kept him from fully trusting her. If all he had at risk was his cock and his heart, he probably would marry her, but he had children. A company. Investment shares, a hoard of gold, and soon a house.

"Would you run for office?" Emmett asked. "If we get statehood?"

"Hmm? Oh. I don't know." It was another facet he had to consider. Marigold would make a damned good politician's wife with her pleasant manners and ability to put things in order. Hell, with her education and ability to side-step telling the truth, she was better suited to running for office than he was.

"Why wouldn't you?" Emmett prodded, pausing in his work to frown at Virgil.

"Sounds like there's a lot of paperwork."

"I'm being serious." Emmett peeled another skim of bark. "I keep thinking about what Marigold said about how you can't consent to a government you have no voice in forming."

"Then *you* run."

Emmett snapped his head up with such a look of suppressed fury, Virgil had to drop his gaze in shame.

"I'm not being sarcastic," Virgil muttered, but he knew as well as Emmett that men with skin the color of Emmett's had about as much traction with gaining voting rights as women. Not that having white skin and a cock meant people would line up to elect the bastard son of an indentured servant.

"I'd rather know we had some say," Emmett said, leaning hard into the draw knife. "I trust you to at least try to get me the vote. If it comes up, I want you to run."

Virgil wavered, thinking it was easier to skip trying than to try and fail. *You're nothing. Hear me? Nothing.*

"I'll keep an open mind. Is that good enough?" Virgil asked.

"Guess it has to be, doesn't it?"

Virgil heard Emmett's anger. The most frustrating part was, of the bunch of them, Emmett was probably best suited for politics. He wasn't a hothead and had a natural ability to envision what he wanted to build, then break it down into the steps to make it happen.

"I shouldn't have said it like it was easy," Virgil said with compunction. "I promised Marigold I'd do what I could for women's rights. Of course, I'll do what I can for you, too."

Emmett's stiff shoulder jerked an acknowledgment.

Virgil jabbed the spud under the thick bark, working it away in chunks, angry with himself for disappointing his friend. Maybe he should quit wondering if he should marry Marigold and ask himself whether she would want to marry *him*.

• • •

Marigold was so attuned to Virgil, she felt him approaching before she heard his footsteps as he returned from his evening wash at the stream.

This was her favorite time of day despite it being so excruciating. The children were abed, and she and Virgil would rest by the fire. She sewed while he whittled pegs and wedges to be used in the cabin construction. They would exchange a few words about their day, always too tired to stay awake more than thirty minutes before they found their beds, but it was precious time to her.

She always wished for something more to happen between them. Her whole body *yearned* for more, but she also appreciated how companionable these evenings were.

He set the filled bucket near the fire, something they'd become diligent about because the grass and trees were tinder dry as they edged into the middle of August. She hadn't seen much rain since she had arrived.

Strange to think that tomorrow would mark one month of her being here. In some ways the days had flown, in others, she felt as though she'd lived a lifetime within each one.

"You forgot the cloth," Virgil drawled.

"I have a splinter." Marigold sat as close as she dared to the flame's flicker, tilting her finger into every angle of light, but couldn't seem to get the needle into the right spot. She was right-handed, so that added awkwardness as she tried to remove it with her left.

Virgil moved a log round next to hers and sat. He opened his palm. "Let me see."

She offered her finger and he squeezed the tip, rolling it in the pinch of his finger and thumb. "Needle."

She gave it up, then had to catch her open hand on his hard thigh as he took her off-balance, tugging her hand into the space between his splayed thighs while he leaned closer to the light of the fire. The sharp end of the needle picked at her fingertip.

"Don't hurt me!" She instinctively tried to pull away, but he was too strong.

"Brave smile."

"Virgil." The next poke hurt a little more. She turned her face into the bulk of his upper arm. "Can you really see it? Or are you torturing me for your own entertainment? Because that is... *Stop*."

"Done."

"Really?" She lifted her head.

He showed her the splinter silhouetted on the end of the needle against the firelight. He gently rolled her plumped fingertip again. "Not even bleeding."

He swiped the needle clean on his knee, then picked up the corner of her apron and secured the needle in it, forcing her to quit lolling into him and sit up straight.

She should have made a remark about him having a career in surgery and moved away. She was overheated, sitting so close to the fire, but she stayed where she was, waiting for his big body to brush hers again.

"Splash of whiskey wouldn't hurt," he said gruffly.

"You're not going to kiss it better?" She clenched her eyes shut in remorse at breaking their unspoken rule.

For interminable seconds, there was only the crackle and snap of the fire. She wanted to open her eyes and see how he was reacting, but she couldn't make herself do it. The fact that he didn't move away, however, made her heart pound hard enough she felt it in her throat.

"There's things we should talk about." His voice was rusty, but quiet in a way that sent flutters through her.

She opened her eyes and nodded, not sure what she was agreeing to. Mostly she was watching his lips, thinking how smooth they looked, how she wanted to feel them against her own…

Warm. That's how they felt. He leaned closer and his lips were soft and warm as he brushed his mouth against hers. There was a hint of dampness and those lovely, tickling whiskers against her chin.

She drifted her eyes closed again and tilted closer to create a firmer seal, then brought her hand to his shoulder, touching the heat of his neck, inviting him to kiss her harder.

Oh, she'd been aching for this, the fulsome taste of him as he made a growling noise in his chest and tenderly consumed her, rocking his mouth across hers, stealing her breath and thoughts. Beneath her hand, his thigh was solid as iron.

Her body grew so hot, she actually jerked back to be sure she hadn't caught fire. His hand was in a fist of tension on his knee.

When she looked up at him, his expression was flexing with conflict. "We ought to talk about things, but Christ." His breath left him in a rush. "All I can think about is touching you. Kissing you."

"Me, too," she breathed.

"Come here." He gathered her in his arms as he stood, moving her with such casual strength, her stumbling feet barely touched the ground before she was in the cradle of his arms. He was catching her before she fell.

Maybe she ought to have been scared of such casual power. He could easily defeat any resistance she offered, but there was none in her, and he would stop if she asked him to. She knew that in her soul.

As they melted into the shadows behind the pile of logs, and her feet touched the ground, his mouth found hers again.

She shuddered and reached for him, giving herself up to the sensations that accosted her. His beard caressed her chin, her cheek, the crook of her neck while he licked into the hollow beneath her ear. She brought his mouth back to hers, and he molded his lips to the clinging pull of hers. Her hands kneaded across the layered muscles of his chest and upper arms and shoulders. She didn't understand why that made heat flare in the pit of her belly, but it did and she wanted more. More of him. All of him.

His hands were just as busy, moving with equal

greed as he stroked her back and pressed the layers of her skirt into her bottom. His wide palm stayed against her cheeks, making slow circles that drove her mad and she didn't understand why.

"Virgil," she gasped.

"Stop?"

"No. Keep going…" She twined her arms around his neck so she could lift herself against him, wanting to feel him pressed all over her front, but their clothes were in the way. It was frustrating.

"I want to be inside you. I want that so bad," he groaned into her neck while his fingertips clenched into her hips. He sucked her earlobe, making her shake with need. He was shaking, too. "But we can't."

"I know," she moaned. Her hands wouldn't be still. He was like a muscled beast. A massive wolf that she was allowed to pet and rub and make groan with pleasure. As her hands slid from his back to his chest down to his hips, she hesitantly slid one to the front of his trousers.

When she squeezed his shape through the heavy denim, he drooped his head against her shoulder and hissed, "God, Marigold." His teeth caught her earlobe again, and he breathed heavily as she rubbed and explored.

Ben hadn't been one for a lot of kissing and fondling, but Virgil sure was. Even though he seemed to be helpless under her curious touch, his own hands started to move again, massaging and running his splayed fingers up her sides, thumbs catching beneath her breasts to lift them. Slowly, slowly, his thumbs climbed to press into her nipples.

"Oh," she breathed, startled by the way he seemed to pinch her into a vise of pleasure with that simple pressure on the tips of her breasts.

"Get into my drawers if you want to," he whispered, rolling his thumbs in a way that made words lose meaning.

When he dropped his hand between them and opened his fly buttons, she slid her touch into the warm, loosened layers of denim and cotton and found him thick and hard and heavy in her palm.

He sucked on her lips in a blatant way that made her sex feel aching and hot. Swollen. She was conscious of dampness gathering in her sex. Her body was involuntarily clenching, sending small notes of pleasure through her whole body. She writhed, pushing her tongue into his mouth with a flagrant lack of inhibition.

"That feels really good, but do it harder." He wrapped his hand over hers in a crush, demonstrating how tightly she could grip him.

"That doesn't hurt?" she said in a laugh of wonder.

"It feels so fucking good, Marigold." He guided her into stroking up and down and brought her fingers to the slippery eye. "Rub your thumb here." His voice was low, almost drunken as he taught her how to make him groan.

"What about…" She trailed her hands down to explore his testicles. They were fuzzed with hair and drawn tight. "Does that feel good, too?"

His reply was an unintelligible moan. His hands cupped her face while he kissed her deeply, tongue stroking against hers, lips wide.

She was so lost in their kiss and the feel of him pushing into her hand, she didn't realize he had burrowed under her apron to release the buttons down the front of her dress. His tickling touch crept in, gentle and hot as he cupped her breast through her chemise.

She gasped, startled by how sensitive she was to such a light caress, how it made prickling tingles race across her shoulders and into her spine.

"Can we get some of this out of the way?" He picked up the neck ruffle of her apron. "I want to suck your nipples."

She drew back slightly. "Why?"

He froze. "He didn't even give you that?"

She was beginning to realize Ben had been a terrible lover. Frankly, that other woman was welcome to him if it meant she could have Virgil. Marigold dipped her head as he tugged her apron over it.

He brushed away the muslin of her underthings, sending swirls of cool air across her chest.

"I wish I could see you," he whispered, whiskers teasing her collarbone so her nipples stung more than ever. He bent his knees and angled so she could continue to fondle him as he nuzzled his lips down the swell of her breast. When his mouth found her nipple, his tongue swept out to lick, sharpening the sensation of cool night air. Then he closed his mouth over the tip and a tugging heat speared into her sex. Such a needy ache arrived there, she moaned.

Marigold set her free arm across his shoulders, trying to balance while stroking him with her fist. His hips thrust into her touch, and he sucked harder on her, making her clench on emptiness and wish fervently for this thickness to invade her yearning flesh.

Suddenly, his arm locked around her waist and he buried a strangled moan against her breast. His erection pulsed and throbbed while heat poured into her palm and scorched her wrist. He seemed to shake uncontrollably before he exhaled and relaxed.

He stood and gathered her in, holding her close while pressing her into the logs as though he was drunk and needed help standing.

"Did you—?" It was so dark, she could only guess what had just happened, but she had a very good idea. Ridiculously, she was disappointed at not being able to see. She'd always wondered what happened during a man's moment of crisis.

Virgil's heart was pounding hard enough she could feel it against her breast. His skin was damp, his breaths still uneven.

"Yeah. Took me by surprise. Damn, that felt good, Marigold." He drew back and guided her hand into his own. He had what she presumed was the tail of his shirt over his splayed fingers. He dried her hand and wrist, then wrapped his arms around her and pulled her into a lazy kiss that amplified all the twinges and tickles and yearnings in her.

She was happy she'd given him that, she was. If this was Ben, she would have thought this was how she was supposed to feel, all sensitive and needing to cling. Thankfully, the dark hid how her hot cheeks must be flushed with desire and embarrassment at how hungry she was for more kissing and fondling and, yes, *fucking*.

"You want me to make you come, too?" he asked

in a murmured voice that was indulgent and accompanied by a fondle of her breast.

"Yes, please."

She felt his smile against her throat. "So polite. You can tell me what you like, you know. What you want me to do."

She wanted him to make love to her, but she couldn't ask him to do that. They couldn't. He had said they should talk, not that he wanted to marry her.

"Do you want to touch me the way you did before?" she asked into the space between them, voice thin with pained shyness.

She seemed to have an unseemly appetite for relations. She wished me *to submit to* her *desires.*

"I can definitely do that." Virgil was gathering up the short skirt of her gown, sliding his hand along the drawstring of her bloomers, searching out the slit. "Or I can do what I wanted to the other day. Will you let me?"

"W-what?" She remembered exactly what he'd said. It sounded positively sinful.

"I want to lick your pussy." His fingertips invaded past the overlapped cotton and muslin, finding the fine hairs that she knew were wet because she could feel how she'd dampened the edges of the fabric.

He groaned as his fingers pressed into her swollen folds. He worked his fingers all over, spreading the juices, making her weak with wanton desire.

"Rub your nipples while I do it," he suggested, lowering his head to suck at one while he pushed a thick finger inside her. "Move any way you like that feels good."

The dual points of erotic sensation had her releasing a shuddering moan, unable to form proper words.

He made a satisfied noise, adding drily, "Try not to wake the children."

Then he was on his knees, head going under the drape of her skirt. Her clothing was pushed aside while his face burrowed in. His whiskers played against her inner thighs, increasing the plumped sensation in her folds.

Her inner muscles clenched to keep the finger he removed. Two came back, plunging satisfyingly deep. She was full. Stretched in the most delicious way. His other hand spread her lips, increasing the tension right before a tickling caress swept across the exposed tissues.

"Virgil," she gasped. Her hand went to the back of his head of its own volition, pressing to encourage him. It took all her strength to stifle her moan.

His tongue was hot and thorough, exploring and laying claim, tasting where his fingers were moving with luxurious care in and out of her, then licking up to toy *there*. The spot that made her navel pull in and her legs weaken.

She didn't realize she was lifting her hips into his mouth until she faltered in the rhythm she'd set, and he kept going. In the next moment, they were in perfect harmony again, her thrusting into his face as his fingers plunged deep while all of her sang with tense, glorious need.

She wanted to tell him it was going to happen. She was nearly there, but suddenly it was happening. She was losing all her substance as she tipped her head back against the wall of logs and shivered in exquisite clenches of pleasure before riding the sweet tail of release.

Her whole body wanted to melt, but Virgil did something. Sucked and kept sliding his fingers in and out of her. Her body clamped down, and she was suddenly thrust back into the tension of near crisis.

She closed her hand against her skirt where it draped over his head and pushed her hips into his mouth more roughly. He kept moving his fingers inside her. She had to push the back of her free hand against her mouth to keep from crying out at how good it felt to balance between intense pleasure and wanting the release.

Some distant part of her was thinking, *Look at yourself, Marigold*, but she didn't care. Her body felt like one live nerve. Nothing was more important than the filthy thing he was doing to her. When her climax struck, it was ten times as powerful as the first. The rolling waves were hard contractions in her middle that hurt, they were so intense, but they were so sweet and satisfying, she could have cried.

She was making sobbing noises, unable to stifle them. Her muscles had become twitching, useless things that could barely hold her upright.

Now he was tenderly sweeping his tongue over her quivering folds one last time, gently extricating his fingers, emerging to let her skirt fall and rising to draw her shaking body into his strong embrace. He held her up when she was utterly weak with gratification.

"We have to stop before they hear you clear across the valley," he teased. "But that's gotta be the best meal you've served me. Bear included."

She choked on a laugh of outrage and gave him a light shove. They wound up kissing, and that, too, was a little bit filthy, given her scent and flavor was all over his lips and beard. It didn't seem to bother either of them.

When they drew back, both sighing, he smoothed his hand over her hair and said, "You need to get to bed or I'll keep you here all night."

Yes, please.

She nodded, though, and slipped away, fixing her clothes as best she could. She paused at the bucket to splash her hands and face clean before drying them with her apron. Then she stumbled into the cabin for the deepest sleep of her entire life.

CHAPTER SIXTEEN

Virgil's head was still up Marigold's skirt as he went about his morning. It was bad, so bad what they'd done. But so fucking good. If that was a taste—pun intended—of the sex they could have once they were married, he was definitely marrying her at his first opportunity. Should they make a special trip to town? Or wait until the referendum in Septem—

"Fuck." He stumbled as he walked across the stream bed. He tried to catch himself on the sluice box and wound up knocking it over. It cracked and spilled the gravel the men had been shoveling into it. This section had been paying out really well, too. "Shit!"

The men grumbled under their breath while Owen teased, "You drinking already, Virge?"

A fair question when the stream was reduced to a trickle by the lateness of the season and the dry weather. The rocks weren't even wet and slippery. His own distraction had caused him to be so clumsy.

Since Owen had walked his horse over to stand next to him, Virgil braced his hand on Owen's saddle horn as he rocked his foot up and down, back and forth. Not sprained. He was lucky in that respect.

Absently, he pushed his hand into his pocket, fingers searching out his good luck charm, but the nugget wasn't there.

"Oh, fuck," he muttered again. He always changed into his clean clothes before he went to bed. Last night, he'd been so drunk on pussy, he'd forgotten to move his nugget from the pocket of the dirty ones into the clean ones. That's why he was knocking over sluice boxes and jeopardizing their fortunes. He didn't have his lucky nugget.

"What's wrong?"

"Nothing." Shit. Now all he could think was that Marigold would take his clothes down to the stream and lose it. "I have to run back to the cabin. Lemme take the horse."

"I'll go. What do you need?"

"You want me to sign a requisition form? Give me the damned horse. I'll be back in a quarter hour."

Owen dismounted with a sour look on his face, and Virgil urged the horse to pick his way out of the stream, then cantered up the path toward the cabin.

The laundry wasn't on the line, but it was still early. He'd left Marigold sleeping serene as an angel. He'd had a smug swagger in his step when he walked to work, knowing why she'd slept so soundly.

Levi was already gone to release the livestock. Nettie and Harley were dressed and sitting outside next to the fire, each with a bowl of oatmeal in their laps. Marigold wore the prettiest smile of pleased surprise when he dismounted.

"We don't usually see you back here midday. Is anything wrong?"

"I forgot something."

"Oh?" She slid her gaze to the little ones, then trailed him toward the cabin door.

He would love a stolen kiss, but, "Owen's expecting me right back. Are you doing laundry today?"

"Yes— No, Harley. Don't eat that." She hurried back to the fire.

Virgil walked into the cabin to see she'd already gathered his clothes into the net she'd made of twine to carry laundry down to the stream and back. He pulled it apart, withdrew his heavy denim trousers, and checked all the pockets including the seat pockets where he never kept the nugget.

It wasn't here. Huh.

He stood and looked around on the floor, leaning to open the door more fully, letting in as much light as possible. He pulled his dirty shirt out of the bundle and checked the chest pockets and shook out all the clothes, watching and listening for the drop of a solid gold nugget.

"What are you doing?" She arrived in the open door again. She frowned at the way he'd strewn the laundry onto the bench and was now shaking out all the bedding.

"I've lost my nugget."

"What nugget?"

"The gold nugget I keep in my pocket."

"You keep a gold nugget in your pocket?" She started to come in and bent to look, but he waved her off. "Why?"

"It's my lucky nugget. The first one I found when we got here." They'd all been disheartened by the journey, wondering what they would do if this venture failed to pay out. Wondering if they were going to die here, tired and hungry.

Virgil had been searching for a sign it was worth staying here and pursuing their plan when he'd spotted the nugget sitting in a couple of inches of water, shiny as a new penny in a wishing well.

"How big is it?"

"Size of a hummingbird egg." It wasn't even half an ounce.

"How much is it worth?"

"Ten dollars." Maybe. He sighed shortly as he got the beds stripped and the mattresses shaken and still found nothing. He threw all the bedding onto the lower bunk and got down to look under it.

"You've found bigger ones, haven't you? Yeller told me you sometimes let the men buy a nugget if they want to keep something they've found."

"That's not the point, Marigold." He ran his hand into the dark space, finding nothing but a desiccated berry and a dead spider. He stood, annoyed. "Where is it?"

Marigold snapped her head around from checking on the children. "Are you asking me if I have it? I've just told you, I didn't even know you had a lucky nugget."

He wasn't accusing her, but he was hearing her say again, *How much is it worth*?

And there was the ledger book he'd bought her with her neat little figures shaving down her debt with her haircuts and other services. He didn't blame her for wanting money and wanting to clear her debt.

"Men know not to take gold out of this valley unless they can prove they earned or paid for it," he blurted.

"Yes, you shoot the ones who do. Good thing I'm not a man. And that I haven't touched your precious nugget." She was glaring at him, but the double-entendre hit both their ears at the same time. She went red, and he felt his own face grow hot with a mix of embarrassment and anger.

Because now there was this poisonous thought creeping in that they'd been intimate last night and this morning one of his most valuable possessions was missing.

"Nettie, have you seen your father's gold nugget?" Marigold called. "You have?"

Virgil stepped onto the stoop, damned near bowling Marigold over, but she didn't let him steady her. She brushed off his hands as she stumbled and found her feet by herself.

"Where?" Virgil barked.

Nettie shrank into her hunched shoulders, eyes wide. "When you showed me and Levi that time."

That had been months ago, when they had first arrived and he was trying to help them understand why he lived here.

Fuck. He pushed his hand into his hair and glanced back into the cabin, now in disarray after he'd searched it. He looked to Marigold and saw resentment. Hurt.

"I have to get back to work," he muttered. "Let me know when you find it."

She didn't say anything, but she didn't even blink as she kept her malevolent gaze on him while he mounted the horse.

He looked away first, not wanting to accuse her, but *it wasn't here*.

• • •

He thought she had stolen from him. That was as clear as today's bright blue sky. All the deliciousness of last night turned sour and ugly. His mistrust hurt her so badly, Marigold could hardly see through the stinging tears that sheened her eyes. She could hardly speak past the lump in her throat.

It took all her might to conjure a smile for Nettie and Harley and pretend their day was the same as every other one. They washed the breakfast dishes in the bucket before they doused the fire. Then they took the laundry to the stream, but not before conducting a second, thorough search of the cabin.

"You're sure you didn't see it?" Marigold asked Nettie several times. "Your papa thinks it fell out of his pocket while he was changing last night."

It would have been dark, but there were no floorboards for it to fall through. The dirt floor would have dulled any thump it made. Still, the cabin was small, the furniture sparse. There simply weren't that many places for a nugget to roll into or get lodged. Marigold turned everything upside down that she could but came up empty-handed.

Virgil thought she was light-fingered. She was positively suffocated by that thought.

She spent a distressing day wondering what would happen if they didn't find it. When Levi came home as she was preparing dinner, she asked him if he'd seen it when he rose this morning.

"Pa already asked me. I didn't see it anywhere."

With a despairing sigh, Marigold went about her work, hoping Virgil would have cooled off enough by the time he returned home. She wouldn't steal anything from anyone, least of all him. Surely after what they'd done last night, he trusted her a little?

He arrived home more sullen than she'd ever seen him. He was civil to the children but only asked her, "Find it?"

"No." She had even searched near the logs where they had trysted.

His mouth tightened, and the air in her chest grew thin and hot. Acrid.

They didn't exchange another word until the children were in bed. Marigold hesitated to go back out to sit with him, she was so wounded and angry. And frightened.

All she could think of was that moment she'd sat with her attorney after the court granted her divorce. She'd been staying with her uncle, sleeping with her sister in her sister's bed, counting on proving Ben was the one who had turned his back on their marriage. At the very least, she believed she should receive back the money she'd put into the house purchase.

You abandoned your husband and property. You have been found at fault, Mrs. Davis. You are not entitled to anything.

But where will I live?

Her attorney had shrugged. He had done all he could. She had lost.

Before she had become a "ruined" woman, Marigold had always seen soiled doves as unfortunate souls who had made wrong choices and got themselves into their own predicament. Even Pearl had made remarks about how Marigold was "too assertive" and had put Ben off, driving him to that other woman who was more amenable.

Now Marigold understood she and women like her were birds that flew into a window, believing the mirrored reflection they were shown, blind to the very real barrier until it knocked them flat.

She'd still been trying to pick herself up from her fall when her uncle had suggested they "start fresh" and "make a difference" by moving to Topeka. Marigold had wanted to support the free-state movement, but she had also latched onto the means of fleeing her own embarrassment. Her naivety. She'd received another harsh slap in the face once they arrived there.

Given how many slaps she'd had, she ought to be immune to delusions of safety and security, but she had relaxed her guard after arriving here. She had started to think she had a chance here, a real chance to make a life.

Virgil had allowed her to believe that.

Now he was pulling the rug, toppling her once again.

She had been trying to think all day where she would go, how she would survive. His partners wouldn't help her, not if Virgil said she was a thief. She would have to walk to Denver, she supposed. Perhaps one of the miners would take her, but no one would leave before payday. Even if one took her, would she be reduced to sharing his tent? At what cost? And she still owed Virgil a hundred and three dollars and twenty-five cents. How would she ever square things with him?

She clenched her hot, dry eyes, then blinked to see through the shadows as she stepped outside and started toward the dying fire. Her leather slippers felt heavy as blocks of ice.

As she lowered onto the log round and looked across at him, she saw only grim shadows in his face, no sign of the man who had held her so tenderly last night. The one who had said they had things to talk about.

She had believed he wanted to talk about their future. Stupid, stupid Marigold. She had started to believe Virgil was different, but he was the same as all men, saying one thing to ply her into granting liberties, then treating her like trash when he no longer had use for her.

Her fingers were so numb where she clasped them, it could have been the frostbitten middle of January. She was terrified of his answer, but she made herself ask the question.

"Are you going to turn me out?"

"I can't, can I?"

His answer punched the air clean out of her. She sat reeling from the resentment in his tone. The frustration that she was his only option to mind his children when he clearly wanted to be rid of her.

"You really think I stole it?" This ache of false accusation was so familiar, it ought to be something she could bear by now, but it was as fierce and fresh as it had been when she'd heard those ugly things in court while Ben had refused to look at her.

Virgil wasn't looking at her. He was roughly scratching his hair and grumbling, "I don't know what to think. You keep taking things from all these men here—"

She stood, so offended she blurted, "And what did you take, Virgil? The little self-respect I had left."

He lifted his face, and they glared at one another. The memory of last night was sullied and tawdry. *She* was.

"Ask me if that's why I took it," she said in a voice that scraped its way up from the depths of her chest. "If that's what you really think of me, you damned well say it."

She thought that scar on his cheek might be pulsing and ticking, but her vision was so glazed by her anguish, she couldn't be sure.

As the silence stretched, the tears pressed behind her eyes and filled her nose and clogged her throat. She whirled and started into the cabin, refusing to let him hear her cry over hurting her this way.

"Are you going to leave?" he asked in a low rumble.

She halted and looked up at the stars, arms shooting straight at her sides as she turned.

"I can't. Can I?"

• • •

"Maybe it's just lost," Stoney said when Virgil came to see him at the quartz crush.

How did everyone know his business? Emmett had overheard Virgil ask Levi about the nugget yesterday, but somehow it had gotten around that Virgil was suspecting Marigold and everyone seemed to be taking her side.

"Maybe," Virgil said flatly. He'd searched and searched everywhere he could think, including near the logs where they'd… Fuck. He couldn't think of it without feeling both horny and remorseful.

What did you take, Virgil? The little self-respect I had left.

He'd heard her crying below him when he came to bed. She'd been trying to keep it quiet, but he'd heard her catching small breaths and sniffling.

He rubbed his hand down his face, trying to erase the jumble of memories and the equally tangled emotions attached to them, wanting none of it reflected on his face.

"I came to ask what happened to Rufus," he said to Stoney.

"Stuck his hand where he shouldn't. First thing I tell the boys is, 'Never put your hand here.'" Stoney pointed at where the pair of granite wheels rolled in the circled track of granite, crushing the gold from the quartz so it could be retrieved with mercury. "How bad is it?"

"His fingertip is crushed. Could be worse, but Ira said he should go to town, see a doctor. Two of the men are going with him, so we're losing three."

Stoney swore under his breath, but if those men hadn't left now, they would have found another reason to leave soon enough.

"Men shouldn't be in here at the wheel anyway," Stoney said with a scowl. "Throw the rocks on the pile, I tell them." He nodded at where a load of boulders had been tumbled from a wooden wheelbarrow off the edge of a gulley onto the pile. "Break them up over there."

Virgil grunted, thinking there wasn't anything to be done now.

"Is she going with them?" Stoney asked.

"Who? Marigold? No. She's staying here to mind

my children." He hoped. It was sitting heavy in his mind that if he trusted her with his children, he ought to trust her not to steal a gold nugget.

"She can't sell it here," Stoney noted. "What are the men going to do? Buy gold with gold? It's no use to her, so why would she take it unless she's planning to leave?"

"I know. All right? I know." Virgil's mind had been going around and around, trying to absolve her.

He didn't want to believe she would steal from him, he really didn't, but he'd been around long enough, encountered the dark side of humanity enough, to know there wasn't one person alive who wouldn't jump on an opportunity if the right one presented itself. That's why he was here, tearing up a pretty little valley for his own gain, giving a perfectly healthy boy like Rufus a chance to lose his hand.

Marigold had been struck some low blows herself. She had arrived here with a pair of drawers and a hairbrush. He didn't blame her for taking the gifts the men offered her, but that nugget wasn't a gift. And hell if losing it wasn't causing him to have all manner of shit luck.

Yesterday, on his way to getting the horse back to Owen, the animal had thrown a shoe. Not long after, there'd been a small brush fire that had forced all the men to leave their posts while they put it out. Now there'd been an injury that was taking three men.

Virgil wasn't a superstitious man, and God knew he hadn't prayed since he was a child, but he couldn't help thinking the missing nugget was bringing him bad luck.

Sure enough, by nightfall, two men had been fired for throwing fists, Levi had been sprayed by a skunk, and a cracking great thunderstorm rolled in to scare the shit out of all of them before it dumped a year's worth of rain in an hour.

Levi washed himself top to toe in the rain, trying not to cry because he was so cold and frustrated. Marigold set his clothes to boil with vinegar, but the stench filled the cabin once they all went to bed, making for a restless, noxious sleep.

They all woke grumpy and cold. Marigold hadn't finished the children's winter wear, so they all wore something half stitched. She was shivering, but damned if she would put on the warm bonnet or the apron he'd given her. She did loop a lopsided scarf around her neck that Nettie had made.

The laundry she'd washed had been caught in the deluge, so Virgil had to wear his muddy ones to work. He slipped on his way back from the stream and spilled all the water, so he had to go back again.

He returned in time to find her trying to start a fire with wet wood in a wet pit.

"I'll do it," he said, starting to crouch down beside her.

"I can do it," she hissed. If she'd been a cat, he would have had four more claw marks to go along with the scar on his cheek.

He decided right then and there that he would give up the goddamned nugget if it meant they could go back to the way things had been, but he was pretty sure that would never happen. He stalked away.

There were washouts all through the diverted

stream, sluice boxes knocked over, and men trying
to dry out their clothes and tents and whatever else
had been soaked in the downpour.

"Could have been worse. Could have been snow,"
Owen said.

True, but it was a reminder that cold weather was
on its way and they would soon be trapped indoors.

Virgil didn't want to think about being trapped in
a cabin with three restless children and a woman he
couldn't trust, so he did what always cleared his
mind. He waded into the cold stream and put his
back into shoveling gravel into the sluice box.

· · ·

This was her life now, Marigold kept thinking. She
could handle hardship. Wringing out clothes and
trying to put up with the musk of skunk in Levi's
bedding and discovering a roof leak that threatened
all her drying herbs was one thing. The coldness of
her employer was another.

She and Virgil hadn't spoken at all yesterday.
Maybe she should have let him light the fire this
morning, because it had taken her until the little
ones were up to get it going, but she was still so *mad*.
Not just that Virgil had accused her and that they
were no longer friends, but because she felt as
though she no longer had any friends at all. The ones
she'd thought she had were his partners and employ-
ees. They would all side with him.

She couldn't summon the courage to go see
Yeller or Gristle, worried they would ask her uncomfortable questions or look at her with mistrust.

"Oh, that skunk," she groaned as she came in from setting Levi's bedding in the come-and-go sunshine and hit a fresh wall of stink.

Nettie giggled. "Harley pooped."

"Oh. Thank goodness. That can go down the john." Marigold set aside the board with the hole in it and picked up the chamber pot.

If there hadn't been a soft clink of tin on tin as his little turds rolled, she might have thrown the works down the hole and forever lived with her reputation as a thief.

As it was, she gave the contents another jiggle and the turd rolled over. There was a gleaming spot of gold.

CHAPTER SEVENTEEN

Virgil stood to stretch out the crick in his back. His head swam. He'd only had a cup of coffee for breakfast, he realized. His feet were so cold they'd long gone numb. The rest of him was sweating, making the cool breeze on this cloudy day get under his clothes.

"Boss?" There was such a tone of foreboding in Buster's voice, Virgil snapped his head around. Buster nodded. "Tornado comin'."

"Tor—" Virgil shifted to see over the edge of the ditch. The "tornado" was Marigold.

She was stalking up the lane the way one did when they had a score to settle. Her knees were swishing her short skirt this way and that. Her feet were kicking back the dirt.

Behind her, in the open door of the office, Ira stood with Tom.

Tom's back, was a fleeting thought, but much as Virgil wanted to know what news their partner had brought, he was also taking in the fact Ira was holding Nettie's hand. Tom held Harley. Emmett had stopped his work with Levi in the field near the storehouse. They had moved to the fence and were staring in Virgil's direction. So was Yeller. Owen whistled to get Bing Sun's attention, thumbing toward where Virgil stood.

The whole damned valley was stopping to see why the hell Marigold was charging through the camp like a stung bull, carrying— Was that his chamber pot?

"Oh, fuck." Virgil closed his eyes. He knew what was coming, and it was going to hit him like a train. Or rather, like a chamber pot upside the head. How had the kid swallowed it without any of them hearing him nearly choke to death?

Marigold reached the edge of the ditch and looked back and forth along it.

"Trail's there, Missus Davis," Buster pointed out helpfully. He was smiling a greeting and taking off his hat.

Virgil shot him a glare while Marigold scampered down, then lost height on her air of superiority while she negotiated the loose gravel, skittering her way across to Virgil.

"I'm guessing the nugget turned up?" he said.

"When I asked you how big it was, you might have said it was the size of a lemon drop." She dumped three turds at his feet. "Take the shortest road to Hades, sir. And take that nugget with you."

She spun to walk away with twice as much resentment as had carried her here.

Fuck, fuck, fuck. Virgil stepped on the biggest poop, scraped his foot across the gravel, and yup, there it was. Funny, he didn't feel near so excited to see that glint of yellow as he had the first time.

"Marigold," he called.

She was up on the path and swung around to say with loud wrath, "Don't you dare punish that baby for eating it. I will slit your throat in your sleep if you say one cross thing to him." She sailed away with her nose in the air.

He supposed he deserved that slander after throwing groundless accusations at her, but it stung to have her even suggest he would lift a finger against any child, especially his own.

"You didn't think she took it, did you, boss?" Buster's voice was squeaky with hurt on Marigold's behalf. "Missus Davis would never."

Virgil ignored him and used his shovel to throw the shit-covered nugget onto a screen. He moved to run it in the stream, rubbing it with sand until it was clean. When every crevice was gleaming, he dropped it back into his pocket where it belonged.

Somehow, though, he didn't think it would turn his luck around. In fact, he suspected his luck would be bad for a while.

• • •

Marigold was still shaking, still incensed. Now, she was also deeply embarrassed for staging a Shakespearean play for every pair of eyes in this valley.

Emmett and Levi had joined Tom and Ira outside the office. Owen was trotting toward their group with a wide smile of enjoyment on his face.

"Are you going to leave?" Levi asked with a wary look.

Nettie stood close to him, holding his hand in both of hers. Her mouth was trembling.

"No." What sort of monster could abandon these innocents? Besides, she still had nowhere to go. All she'd done was lift the cloud of suspicion Virgil had placed on her. It didn't mean another wouldn't descend tomorrow.

"That was the best thing I've seen in years," Owen said as he arrived.

"Shut up, Owen," Emmett said out of the side of his mouth.

"She dropped shi—I mean poop on Virgil's boots." Owen eyed the kids.

"Did you?" Nettie asked with a solemn blink.

"I dropped it in front of his boots," Marigold stated. "Which wasn't appropriate. Being angry with someone doesn't mean you're allowed to be rude to them."

"You're angry with Papa?" Nettie asked.

"Yes. I will be angry with him for some time. That doesn't mean I'm angry with you." She cupped Nettie's little face and searched up the closest thing she had to a reassuring smile. "You and I are still friends, and we'll see each other every day."

Marigold wanted to hug this little girl until her nerves had calmed down and her tears weren't pressing against the backs of her eyes. She made herself lift her head and scan all the men's faces, though. A spike seemed to be lodged in her chest, one she couldn't swallow past.

"But I won't sleep at the cabin any longer. Tom, would it be all right if I occupied one of the wickiups that are still standing in your family's encampment?"

"I—" His jaw hung open. He looked to his partners' faces. Every single one of them looked at Tom as though he'd just been handed his own hot turd.

"Come on, Levi. Back to work," Emmett said, nudging the boy's shoulder.

Levi didn't move. "You're not going to stay with us in the cabin?"

"I'll come across in the morning the way Leyohna did. And I'll read a story before bed, same as always."

"So you're going to sleep with Tom?" Owen prodded with a sly grin.

"Shut *up*, Owen," Ira said through his teeth.

"There are at least three empty structures," Marigold pressed Tom.

"Built for summer, Mrs. Davis. And with it being so quiet over there, I don't know that you'd be safe. Wolves…" He looked to the other men.

"Oh, yeah. Lynx," Emmett said.

"Raccoons." Ira nodded.

"With all the noise we make?" Owen scoffed. "We barely get squirrels."

"*Owen*," Tom said, practically spitting his name. "I saw a coyote as I was riding in."

"I'll come sleep with you there." Levi nodded in the same decisive way Virgil did. "I'll bring my slingshot."

"Me, too," Nettie said. "So you don't get cold at night."

"Me," Harley said, twisting around in Tom's hold. It was always hard to tell if Harley fully understood what was being said, but he knew his siblings were up to something, and he would never be left behind if he could help it.

"Virgil's going to be so glad you're back," Owen said to Tom, mouth still dancing with a grin.

"Here comes Virgil," Tom said, looking past her. "You should ask him."

"I've said all I need to say to Mr. Gardner for the moment. He's my employer, not my husband. I can sleep where I like. Unless you expressly forbid it, I will move into one of the wickiups today."

Tom's mouth was opening and closing like a landed fish, helpless gaze fixed beyond her. As Virgil's steps came up behind her, Marigold said, "Children, you are welcome anytime, but stay here with the men while I move my things. I'll come back for the little ones in a while."

"You want any help?" Owen called as she started toward the cabin.

"Yes," Marigold said tartly. "Since you seem so determined to stir the contents of one of these, take charge of it." She handed him the chamber pot and walked away.

• • •

Virgil found her pouring beans into the stew pot, something he supposed she always did midday so the children had something to eat later. So *he* did, when his workday was done.

"Shall I find some crow to go in there?"

She shot him one dour look, sniffed, and used her cuff to dry her cheek, staying silent as she gave the pot a stir.

"You have a right to be angry. I owe you an apology." He folded his arms across his tight chest. "I didn't want to believe you'd taken it, but I didn't know how else it could have disappeared. I accused you, and that was wrong. I won't do it again."

She tapped the spoon on the edge of the pot, set

the lid on it, and brought it to him where he stood in the open door. She shoved the cold stew pot into his hands.

He stooped to set it at his feet and said, "Come on, Marigold. I don't let things fester. Say whatever you need to say and let's get past this."

She pulled her carpetbag from the hook on the wall beneath his bunk and started thrusting her meagre possessions into it.

"It's fine that you're packing. I told the men that first thing tomorrow I want all hands to report here to build out this cabin for winter. We'll all camp out across the way while the roof's off."

She paused at that news, then gathered her writing supplies from the shelf.

"Emmett reckons it'll take ten days if the weather holds, so long as we don't lose any more men. Then you'll have your own room."

She took her hairbrush off the small washstand she'd fashioned from a crate. She left the hand mirror hung by its handle above it, the one that had been a gift from one of the men. That little wash area was one of the small but welcome improvements she'd made to their living conditions here. Everything was better now she was here.

"For Christ's sake, Marigold. Refusing to speak to me is childish."

"I don't have anything to say."

"Like hell you don't. Call me an asshole and get it over with."

"What's the point in that?"

"You'll feel better."

"No," she said with a faint shake of her head,

sounding baffled. "I knew that's what you were the day we met. All men are."

He snorted. As far as insults went, comparing him to her ex-husband and his attorney was about as mean as it got.

"I'm not angry with you," she continued in that lost little voice. "I'm angry with myself for wanting to believe you were different. I hate myself so much for that."

"Marigold." He gripped the edge of the door, trying to withstand the knives turning in his guts.

"And running away hasn't really worked out for me in the past, but I would walk all the way to Oregon to get away from how I behaved with you, it's so humiliating." She was talking to the wall, not even looking at him.

"Stop it. You're not going anywhere." He lurched into the cabin on instinct.

His foot hit something. The stew pot went clattering across to hit the table leg. Beans and water and chopped onion tops spilled across the dirt floor.

"Fuck!" he shouted at the ceiling.

She hunched her arms into her body, shoulders protective up around her ears.

"It's all going to be fine," he insisted. Maybe he was still yelling because she was staring at him with apprehension. "The men will bring crates and the handcart so we can pack up and move across the way. I'll sleep with Tom and you can sleep with the children, and it will all be fine. Just quit talking about leaving and give me a chance to make this right."

He left before she could say anything, heart pounding so hard he thought it would burst. As he strode away, a heavy weight settled over him. How the hell was he going to follow through on his promise?

• • •

She missed him, damn him, not that she had much time for pining over Virgil. He and the men worked dawn 'til dusk on the cabin. Levi helped them between his other chores, but Marigold kept the little ones out of the way by working with Gristle in the cookhouse. They ensured the men had good meals each day and jugged the hare that Levi had learned to snare. He was bringing in one or two a day along with the occasional grouse or wild turkey.

In the evenings, Marigold took the children back to her wickiup. She read to them by firelight, then slept in the snug shelter. One night it rained, and the children cuddled in closer to her, mostly to avoid a drip through the leaves and branches that formed the cupped roof, but otherwise their nights were uneventful.

Stoney had finished the chimney on the second day of work. When Marigold heard he was headed to Denver, she asked him to post another letter to her sister. She hadn't given away the intimacies she and Virgil had shared, but she had needed to cry to someone about her hurt and disappointment.

I thought briefly that our arrangement might progress to marriage. Virgil is a good provider and a good father, but after an incident in which he accused me of theft, I have realized my past will always color how people see me. He will never truly trust me, and for that reason I am better off regarding him as my employer and only my employer.

I miss you dreadfully every single day. I wish often that I could hop on a wagon to come see you, but I would be heartbroken to leave the children. They are the sweetest things you would ever want to meet, Pearl. In that way, my situation is ideal. I feel very blessed.

Stoney returned within the week. The wagon was loaded with lumber. By then, the exterior walls of split logs were in place and the roof shakes ready. The roof went on at a rapid pace, and a hoopla of cheers erupted one afternoon.

"I think you have yourself a house, Missus Davis," Gristle said, shading his eyes to look up toward the cabin.

"You mean the children do, John," she corrected gently. "It's not mine."

Nettie paused in turning the coffee grinder handle. "Can we go see?"

"Yes, of course." Marigold had barely spoken to Virgil and preferred it that way. Once she did, she would have to decide how long she could cling to her principles and weather the elements in that shelter made of saplings and branches that were dropping their needles. Joining him in the comfort of his new home sounded like the depth of capitulation. It would also be pure torture come winter, when they wouldn't have the luxury of stepping outside to get away from one another.

"Harley?" Marigold dried her hands. "Do you want to go see your papa?"

He dropped the rattle Emmett had made him

and ran out of the cookhouse in the direction of the office.

"Not that way, Harley," Nettie called. "Papa's at home." She held out her hand for him. He quickly caught up to her and clasped her hand with his. Nettie's face was bright with excitement.

Harley wrinkled his nose as he smiled up at her, sensing her anticipation. "Papa home."

"Yes. He's at our *new* home," Nettie told him.

"New."

"Mmm-hmm." Nettie nodded.

Oh, they were so endearing, Marigold could have spent all day with her arms wrapped around the three of them, absorbing the love that emanated from those children like warmth from sun-soaked blankets.

Buster was coming down the track toward them and halted when he saw them.

"I was coming to fetch you, Missus Davis." He took off his hat. "There's still some mudding to finish, but Boss wants to see if you approve."

She blushed and practically shoved the children ahead of her. "Go on, Nettie. Your papa wants to know if you like it."

It was a cool day, but most of the men were standing around, swiping their foreheads and holding out mugs for the berry juice that Marigold prepared every morning. Ira nodded a greeting while he poured it. Owen smiled and started to step forward. Emmett slapped a hand into the middle of his chest and said, "Nope."

As they noticed her, the men stood straighter, all watching her with eagerness for their hard work to be recognized.

"Goodness," she was compelled to say. "What a fine house! And built in record time. Well done, gentlemen. Nettie, Harley, say thank you to everyone for building such a warm and sturdy home for you."

"Thank you," Nettie said shyly, backing into Marigold.

"Ta-too," Harley said.

Virgil came out the door, and Harley ran toward him. Virgil stooped to catch him up, and Harley grabbed his nose, saying, "No."

Virgil caught Harley's hand and lowered it, keeping hold of it as he said absently, "We'll play that game another time."

Virgil wore his dirty work clothes. His hair had grown shaggy since his last cut, and his expression was stiff and remote, but he always looked irresistibly attractive when he was being soft with his children.

Marigold's heart was trying to pound itself out of her chest after that little climb up the path that she'd made a thousand times. Maybe it was all the attention. She refused to attribute it to the man, but—

"Can I see, Papa?" Nettie asked.

"Sure thing, little bug." He waved her in but stayed on the small, covered porch, waiting for Marigold with a "ladies first" nod.

She bit her lip, wanting to see inside and definitely wanting to take any conversation on whether she would move in here away from the listening ears of the men.

The porch was large enough all three children

could divest of their muddy boots before entering. As she met Virgil's gaze, she saw his eyes were silver as a pond under a stormy-gray sky, silently asking a question she wasn't prepared to answer.

With a flicker of a smile, she stepped over the threshold.

The inside was much brighter now it held a window on three sides of the original cabin. The fourth wall had two doors cut into it, leading into the rooms added to the east side.

There was now something closer to a kitchen with shelves and a cabinet with doors. A waist-high bench held a recess for a basin and water jug. Above it, the window looked up the valley away from the work site, affording a pretty view of the mountains in the distance.

The floor was solid wood planks, and the space where Levi's bed used to fold down now held the wood stove. Where the original sleeping bunks had been, the table and benches stood. The children could do their schoolwork where it was warm near the stove and still have light from the window that looked up the hillside behind the house. There was a door behind the table, but they were all distracted by Levi's voice above them.

"Nettie. Come see!" Levi was in the fenced loft, grinning ear to ear.

The ladder-stairs next to the entrance door went up about four feet to a small landing. A window there caught the southern light. A second ladder went from the landing to the loft at a different angle over the door beneath it. It had a small catch rail on it.

"Emmett thought this would be a safer configuration for—"

"Me!" Harley demanded as Nettie scampered up to Levi.

"You watch him close," Virgil warned Levi as Harley went up the ladder after his sister. "Don't let him come down until I can watch and see that he can do it by himself. If he can't, he'll sleep with me until he learns."

Levi nodded. There was only room for the children to move on their hands and knees up there, but that seemed to be its charm.

"Come on, Harley. Come see my bed," Levi said.

"Harley, our toys are here!" Nettie was breathless with excitement.

"I'll turn that leftover lumber into shelving this winter." Virgil pointed at the scraps stored beneath the landing. "This is my room."

Marigold hung back at the door, glancing in warily. Someone had made a sizable bedframe from sturdy log rounds and thick, skinned branches. Floor planks were braced across the frame as a sleeping surface, and Virgil's old, skinny mattress was on it.

"I need to string the ropes. I had Stoney place an order for cotton-stuffed mattresses for the bunch of us while he was picking up the lumber. They should be ready when supplies are picked up next. View isn't much to speak of." He looked out, and his profile flexed with some odd reaction she couldn't interpret.

She glanced out the window. Now the logs were gone, she easily saw down the track toward the torn-up riverbed. It wasn't pretty, but once the snow came, it might be.

"You'll want to check on things when you rise and again before you sleep. It's perfect for you." She realized the men's voices outside were fading because they were being ushered down to the cookhouse by Emmett.

"Emmett says there's not much to see when you're lying in the dark with your eyes closed anyway," Virgil said drily.

Alone? Or…? Guilt flushed heat into her cheeks. She flashed a look up at him, hoping he couldn't read her mind.

He was staring at her so hard, he was practically boring holes through her skull. His cheeks might have pinkened, but she looked away so quickly, she probably imagined it.

She hugged herself and hurried back to the main room, glancing up to see the children were busy negotiating the arrangement of toys and blankets. She smiled faintly at how happy they sounded.

"Everyone seems to have worked very hard. The men should be congratulated on their excellent craftsmanship."

"This is your room." Virgil moved along to the door she had been ignoring, the one behind the table and benches. There was a shadow of admonishment in his gaze as if he knew she was trying to find a reason not to stay here with him.

She swallowed, genuinely unsure what to do. Looking around the main room, she saw potential. She was itching to sew curtains and put a rag rug there and fill those shelves with the jars of preserves she'd been working so hard to put up.

She couldn't do any of those things in that branch hut across the way. Tom had pointed out that it hadn't been built to hold a fire. One spark would ignite it, especially since it had been drying all summer.

At best, Marigold could hold out for a few more weeks if she wanted to continue nursing her pride. Eventually, she would have to seek a sturdier shelter if she planned to winter here.

Apprehensively, she slipped past Virgil into the tiny room next to his. It was only big enough to hold the old bunk she had shared with Nettie and Harley. Drawers beneath it were unfinished, but they would be tremendously handy when completed.

The small window looked mostly at the john, but she supposed there wasn't much to see when lying in the dark, asleep.

The washstand was wedged between the bed and the window, the hand mirror hung from a nail above it. Next to it hung a tarnished brass picture frame holding—

"Is that *Pearl*?" She scooted around the bed and along the narrow passage to look closer.

"She sent me that portrait when she wrote to accept my, uh, proposal. I forgot I had it until I was moving things around for construction. That frame isn't the right size. It's all Yeller had. That's why the glass is cracked."

It was still such a thoughtful gift, it brought tears to her eyes. Pearl with her angelic smile, the one that got her out of the trouble her inquisitive nature got her into. She was sweet at heart, but too pretty for her own good, convinced her looks were a commodity that ought to buy her things. Too often it did. That smile earned her an extra sweet roll from the baker or a silk scarf that had been ordered in for another customer.

Pearl hadn't suffered the same wrath from slavery-supporters as Marigold because she was not one to kick up a fuss or confront people or sign her name to suffrage petitions. *You get more flies with honey*, she would often tell Marigold.

Sometimes Marigold was so infuriated with her sweet, oblivious, spoiled behavior, she wanted to shout herself blue.

But she missed her sister. She missed how they made each other laugh and shared secrets and how Pearl expected life to work out for her, and thus it always seemed to.

Marigold lifted the portrait off the nail and pressed it to her heart, touched beyond measure. Why couldn't Virgil stay grumpy and blockheaded so she could continue to despise him? Why did he have to give her a piece of her old home, as if he knew she was missing her family, when she doubted he'd ever had a sentimental moment in his life?

"Look…" He paused to glance upward to where the children's voices and movements were penetrating through the ceiling. "I can't have you sleeping in the open like a trapper. I brought you here with the understanding you'd be given room and board if you looked after my children. Can we go back to that?"

Because they'd managed that so well so far?

"You can't work through winter," she pointed out. "You'll be here, able to look after them yourself." She'd been thinking about that a lot, how she was not as necessary now as she had been two months ago. Leaving felt wrong, nonetheless. She didn't want to abandon the children. She still owed him a lot of money, but he didn't need her.

"Not true. The weather will get in the way of mining, but we can skid logs when it's icy. Emmett has milling equipment coming. We'll cut timber for walling the cookhouse and build a bunkhouse for next year. Men will stay through the winter if we can keep them warm and dry, but someone's gotta hunt and trap to feed the bunch of us. I'll be out doing that, too. If I could cook anything worth eating, I'd already be doing it. I'm never going to learn to sew—"

"Goodness," she muttered, holding up a hand. "You'll turn my head, making me feel so important to operations here."

"The children need you, Marigold." He folded his arms. "I need you as an employee. That's *all*."

She bit the inside of her lip as she looked out the window, nodding an acknowledgment of the boundary he was putting in place around her position here. She understood it was meant to reassure her, but it hurt. Everything about this arrangement hurt.

How nice it must be to be a man and not feel anything.

"Is that a nod yes? You'll move back in here?" he pressed.

Above them, the children suddenly went silent.

As the sense of anticipation thickened, Marigold broke the skin on the inside of her lip and tasted blood. She made herself smile through the pain and nodded more deliberately.

"How could I refuse?"

Upstairs there was a small squeal and a fervent, "Yes!"

She sent a rueful look toward Virgil. He wore a somber expression. He nodded and turned away, saying, "Good," but something in his demeanor told her he was disappointed on some level.

What had he expected? Unbridled enthusiasm?

Maybe she had imagined his dour reaction, because she heard him encouraging the older children to show Harley how to come down the ladder.

Marigold looked down at her sister's portrait still tilted against her chest.

Pearl smiled up as if to say, *See? I fixed it for you*.

Nothing was fixed, of course. This was exactly the sort of fix that Pearl was famous for, one that had all sorts of flaws that were plain as tarnished brass and cracked glass, but there was that undeniable vision of optimism radiating from within it.

Oh, to be that unmarred by life.

She kissed her sister's image and put the frame back on its nail. Time to get to work on making this a home.

CHAPTER EIGHTEEN

In the next week, two other men failed to come back from their payday trip to town. Bing Sun packed up with his crew, intending to winter in San Francisco. Virgil hated to see Bing Sun leave, but one of the reasons he'd invited Bing Sun into this partnership was the valuable manpower he brought. The retreat to San Francisco was an important recruitment step for next spring.

Emmett and Stoney left a few days later to spend some time in Denver. They were picking up mill equipment and wanted to show Levi how it would all come together by visiting a sawmill there.

Virgil was proud as hell of how much talent and interest Levi was showing in woodwork. He had encouraged him to go with Emmett and Stoney for many reasons, not least that it was good for a young man to step beyond his father's shadow, but Virgil was surprised how deeply it affected him to have his son out of his sight. Through the day, he typically only saw Levi from a distance, up on the hills with the animals or he might hear a casual, "Howdy, Pa," if Levi happened to be helping Emmett or Yeller at the storehouse.

The cabin ought to have been more comfortable now there was more room for all of them, but it felt empty. Nettie had decided the loft was spooky without her big brother to protect her, so she and Harley were back in Marigold's bed.

"They can sleep with me. My bed is bigger," Virgil told Marigold when she'd tucked them into her bed and come back to take up her sewing by candlelight.

"I don't mind." She barely looked at him these days if she could help it. She was always polite, never sassy. If she happened to be laughing with the children, her smile would fall away when she noticed him watching.

She wasn't trying to make him feel like a shit heel, but he sure did feel like one.

"You can buy enough wool for a long gown," he muttered when he noticed she was measuring out a dull gray plaid against the short one she usually wore. "You'll need something warmer for winter."

She blinked. "I find the shorter length is more convenient. I'm making a warm pair of bloomers as well."

"Oh." He kept tying the knots for the netting that would hold his mattress, but the next time he was down at the storehouse, he resolved to have Yeller order in more bolts of wool so she would have something to work with if she changed her mind.

He kept telling himself her reticence was for the best. There were plenty of times he had wished she had kept her opinions to herself, hadn't he? Why the hell would he want to marry someone who offered nothing but cheek? Especially when he knew from experience that marrying because a woman kept a good home and was receptive to sex didn't guarantee a happy future.

But the evenings were damned quiet once the little ones were asleep. He wished they could go back to at least a sense of camaraderie.

"Are you still getting gifts?" he asked her.

She straightened from laying out her fabric on the table. "Pardon?"

"I noticed the, uh…" He pointed at the skinned branch over the window with misshapen metal rings strung along it. If it was supposed to be a wind chime, it was ugly as hell, but Virgil had enough sense to keep that to himself.

"Oh. No. Nettie and I made it so I could get an idea whether it would work to hold curtains. I cut a tin can to make those rings, but they lost their shape. Yeller said he has a tool that will cut them more cleanly."

"That's a good idea." He saw it in a new light and admired her ingenuity.

"I stole it from a former neighbor."

Was that meant to land on target and sting? Because it did. She turned away, so he couldn't be sure of her motive.

He resolved to keep an eye out for smooth branch wood the next time he got to chopping. It was time he stacked more than what Marigold needed for cooking, anyway. It was only mid-September, but the days were shorter and cooler. He started the fire in the stove when he rose the next morning, as much to warm himself as readying it to cook oatmeal.

"Papa?" Nettie peeked out Marigold's bedroom door.

He touched his lips and motioned for her to come out. He shook out Marigold's shawl from where she'd left it on the bench and held it up for his daughter.

She let him swaddle her into it and giggled when he picked her up and squeezed her.

"What's up, little bug?" he asked quietly. "You should stay in bed where it's warm."

"Is Levi coming home today?"

Ah. "Today or tomorrow. If he's late, don't you worry. The bears are looking for a place to sleep for winter. They aren't interested in chewy boys."

"How do you know he's chewy? Did you bite him?"

"Ha. You got me. I never have. Maybe I should bite you? See if you're chewy?" He clacked his teeth.

She giggled and wiggled inside the snug shawl, then let her head tip onto his shoulder. "I miss him," she said wistfully.

"If he comes home today, they'll arrive in the afternoon. Do you want to come down to the office later and wait with us?"

She nodded.

"You tell Marigold when she wakes up that I said you could."

"Okay. Thank you." Nettie pecked his cheek. "I love you."

He nearly dropped her, he was so shocked. "I—"

He'd never said those words to anyone except Clara. Even then, he hadn't been sure he'd meant them, not with anything more than the superficial infatuation of a young man. Not like this, where he would lay down his life to protect this earnest face and wiry but delicate body.

"I love you, too, little bug." The tangled knot in the depths of his chest felt pulled so taut, its threads threatened to snap, but the ache of that tension felt strangely good. Terrifying, but the fact those knots held strong was reassuring in its odd way.

He cleared his throat, feeling foolish for how moved he was. He set her on her feet.

"Do you want me to show you how to make the oatmeal?"

"I know how, but the pot is too heavy. I need help lifting it."

He moved the pot onto the floor near the cupboard where Marigold kept the oats. He handed Nettie a tin cup. Then he picked up the shawl she had let fall to the floor. He folded it and put it back on the bench.

As he glanced up, he saw Marigold watching them through the cracked door.

How long had she been there? Long enough to hear him turn himself inside out to his daughter?

"If you're up to help Nettie, I'll fetch the water." He was practically strangling on his tongue. He hurried out.

• • •

Marigold had heard, "tell Marigold," and had quickly risen, thinking she was needed. She cracked the door in time to hear Virgil tell his daughter he loved her. It was a poignant moment of realizing that he did, in fact, possess a heart.

He wasn't about to let Marigold anywhere near it, though.

He brought the pail back, filled with water, but didn't come in. "I told Nettie she could wait at the office with me later, to see if Levi comes home today."

"I was planning some baking at the cookhouse. We'll come down when the dough is ready." She could only boil and fry on the top of their new stove, which was better than cooking over an open fire, but bread and rolls still needed an oven. The covered cast-iron pot set in the coals of the outside firepit worked in a pinch, but it wasn't big enough to feed a family of five and it was usually full of stew.

He nodded and left.

Marigold slipped into his bedroom, ostensibly to "make" his bed, which was still his old pallet on the newly strung ropes. Straightening his blanket took two seconds, but she was really watching him walk away down the path.

She stifled a sigh. Everything felt awkward between them. She was so sensitive these days, any little thing he said hit like a criticism. When he had asked last night whether she was still accepting gifts, she'd taken it as a reproach and responded with a retort that she still regretted. She wanted things to be easier between them, but it wouldn't happen if she was defensive and tossing out provocations.

Nothing smoothed a man's mood better than food, so she made extra dough for rolls, intending to leave a batch in the office with a little of the rose hip syrup she'd made. She and Nettie had been picking them whenever they saw them and spread them on paper in the loft for drying, seeing as the children weren't sleeping up there right now. She would use the dried hips for a tonic that eased winter coughs, and they made a nice tea when paired with pine needles.

Nettie was nearly two feet off the ground as they

walked to the office. Marigold dreaded the fall if Levi failed to turn up. The wagon could easily be delayed considering the blustering rain, but she was on her way from the cookhouse with her first batch of cooling rolls when she heard the noise of the mules and the wagon.

Smiling, she stepped into the office where the well-stoked stove made it cozy enough that Nettie was playing a game on the floor with Harley. Virgil was at the table with Ira, studying the ledger books.

Tom had disappeared again, perhaps with a shipment of gold. Marigold imagined Bing Sun had taken some to San Francisco. There was every likelihood that Emmett and Stoney had used gold to pay for the equipment they were bringing in. Owen and a small crew were still eking a little of the ore from the ground, but only a handful of men remained. Owen was rarely on horseback these days, more often standing in the river alongside the men.

"They're coming," Marigold said.

Nettie leaped to her feet and shot her hands in the air. "Yay!"

Harley quickly copied her. "Yay!"

"No, wait." Marigold caught Nettie. "It's cold outside. Stand at the window until they're closer." She left the basket of rolls on the table, where Virgil and Ira pounced on them.

Ten minutes later, the wagon ambled to a stop in front of the storehouse. Levi was hunched between the two men on the bench, seemingly for warmth despite his new winter coat. It was meant for a young man, not a boy headed that direction. He had the front doubled over across his chest and wore a new wool cap pulled down to his squinted eyes.

He smiled and waved when Yeller greeted him. He was already looking toward the cabin as he climbed off the wagon behind Stoney.

Marigold opened the door, and Nettie ran out. "Levi!"

His face lit up. He caught her in a big hug. Harley joined them, and Levi hugged him along with his sister. When he noticed everyone smiling at them, he grew self-conscious and rolled his eyes.

"I guess they missed me."

Yes. *They* had missed *him*. Marigold bit her lips at how transparent they were. Dear Lord, she loved them so much.

Levi pulled away and said, "Guess what I brought you?" He pushed his hand into his pocket and came up with paper-wrapped lemon drops.

Nettie gasped. "Yes, please!"

"Ess, peas!" Harley waited patiently while his big brother unwrapped one and gave it a crunch exactly the way Virgil did.

Marigold had to cover her heart before it expired and went straight to heaven. Could they be any more endearing?

Levi held out his hand to her. "Would you like one, Marigold?"

"Oh, you!" She couldn't help it. She ignored the candy and pulled him into a big hug, hearing a little, "Gack," as she squeezed him. "I missed you."

"It was only a few days," he mumbled into her shoulder, seeming to have grown in that short time. His arms closed around her in a quick return of her embrace. He was blushing with pleasure when he drew back. "You want a lemon drop, Pa? I used the pocket money you gave me."

"You save it for yourself, but it was nice of you to think of your sister and brother. It's good to have you back." He yanked him close and hugged him.

Hugged him.

It was awkward and quick, and she caught a glimpse of Levi's shocked face. They both stepped back almost before it happened and looked anywhere but at each other.

Levi's cap was crooked. He lifted it and smoothed his hair before he replaced it.

Virgil looked to Stoney and Emmett. "Good trip? All went well?"

"It did, but…" Emmett's expression darkened. "We got a copy of the proposed constitution for the State of Jefferson. Vote is September twenty-fourth."

Marigold took from his dismayed tone that voting rights were limited to white men. She stifled a sigh.

"You'll help us read it?" Stoney asked Marigold.

"Of course. I have to check my baking at the cookhouse, though, and I want the children out of the cold." Nettie was pressed to Marigold's side, using her as a windbreak. Harley had gone to Virgil, who had him tucked beneath the open edge of his jacket. "Levi, are you staying to help the men unload?"

"Yes, but wait, Marigold. You got a parcel!"

"Oh?"

He hurried up to the front of the wagon and retrieved her carpetbag from beneath the bench. She'd loaned it to him, and the sides were swollen with more than his spare set of clothes. It looked like a snake that had swallowed a shipping tin. "I put it in here so it wouldn't get lost."

"Thank you." Marigold accepted the bag. "Goodness, it's heavy."

"It's from Pearl. It says 'Happy Birthday,'" Levi informed her.

"It's your birthday?" Nettie looked up with wonder.

"Two weeks ago," Marigold dismissed. "Long past."

Virgil turned from looking into the back of the wagon. "Why didn't you say something?"

He had to ask? They hadn't been speaking.

"It's not worth fussing over." Not when it was such a stark reminder that she wasn't anywhere near where she had imagined she would be at twenty-seven. "Yeller, may I have two tins of milk and a jar of peaches? We'll have a treat later to celebrate Levi arriving home safe and sound."

CHAPTER NINETEEN

Virgil tried telling himself that a new mattress was a hell of a birthday present, but since everyone in the house got one, it didn't really count.

"You gave me my sister's portrait," Marigold said when he brought it up. "That was very thoughtful."

It had been an emotional bribe. A grovel. They both knew that. Virgil wanted to give her something that made her smile the way she did when she opened the tin box her sister had sent her. There were three colored bookplates showing poisonous and edible mushrooms, a book of home remedies with illustrated descriptions of medicinal plants, and sheets of cheesecloth wrapped around packets of seeds. So many seeds.

"I can't imagine how she collected such a variety. Asked for donations at church, perhaps."

There were more than two dozen folded envelopes, each neatly labeled. She handled them with great care so they didn't spill. They ran the gamut from lavender and thyme to onions, beets, and peas to violets and foxglove. There were even a few strawberry runners and some gnarled roots with wilted raspberry leaves clinging to them.

"I need to find a sheltered place to plant those where they might survive the winter." She looked to the window. A sharp wind was buffeting the glass behind the curtain she'd hung.

"There's a hot pool up on the plateau. Ground

stays warmer there. I could plant them and fetch them in the spring," he suggested.

"Levi told me about that." Her expression brightened with curiosity. "You wouldn't mind walking all that way?"

"I'll ride," he said drily. "But no. It won't take any time at all." After a moment of hesitation, he asked, "Do you want to come with me?"

"With the children?"

He winced. "That's a full day's outing, best left for when there's not so much work waiting. I can be up and back in an hour if I go alone."

"That's probably best, then," she said with a faltering nod. He heard her disappointment, though.

Ah, screw it.

When he arrived at the office the next morning, he said to Emmett, "Levi can't help you today. I'm leaving the children for a few hours while I take Marigold to the hot pool."

All the men paused what they were doing to give him looks of speculation, suspicion, and affront.

"I'll turn my back," he growled. "It's a birthday treat."

"I wish she had told us about that." Ira squared the promissory notes he'd been recording and set them under a quartz rock they used as a paperweight. "I can sit with the little ones if you want to finish that gate with Levi," he said to Emmett.

"I promised I'd show him how to make a pegboard puzzle," Emmett said. "Maybe we could make it for her. Let's both go and keep them amused, help them make some gifts for her."

"Stoney and I will operate the rock crush by

ourselves, then?" Owen griped.

"I'll make her a bread oven," Stoney said, drying the face he'd just washed. "Then she can make us bread without walking so far."

"You're going to do that today, are you?" Virgil asked with a skeptically cocked brow.

"I can start. I'll find a good site, measure it out, calculate how many bricks it will need." Stoney nodded with satisfaction.

"Then you'll come help me at the rock crush?" Owen asked.

"You'll be here minding the vault," Stoney said.

"I hate being here by myself." Owen scowled with annoyance. "I'd rather play with the children."

"Then speak up sooner next time," Ira suggested. "Sweep and wash the windows, since there's nothing else that needs doing around here."

"Fuck that," Owen said without heat.

Virgil left them bickering while he saddled one of the horses.

Ira and Emmett walked up to the cabin with him. Neither said a word, but he could feel their smug sense of having won a sure-thing bet.

Not true, he wanted to say. It was all Marigold could do to speak to him in a civil tone, and all he could do to keep his wayward thoughts in check.

I need you as an employee. That's all, he had told her, but it wasn't true. She was under his roof every night, he saw her every day, yet he missed her. He wanted to go back to their easy friendship. If that meant literally softening her up in a warm bath, so be it.

Marigold was visibly taken aback when he told

her the plan.

"I can't leave the children to…sit and do nothing."

"Have you tried it?" Ira asked with a smirk. "It's pretty easy."

"I don't have a bathing costume," she added with a discomfited look toward Virgil.

"Drawers will do. Or your nightdress."

"Go on," Emmett coaxed her. "You won't catch Virgil being agreeable very often. Take advantage." He waved his hands as though shooing a chicken from the garden.

With a waver of indecision and an anxious *tsk*, Marigold slipped into her room and came back with her shawl rolled around something. She set it in a basket with two leftover rolls, a chunk of cheese, and a jar of pickles.

"I nearly forgot the berry roots," she said, flustered as she hurried about.

Virgil couldn't tell if she was nervous about the outing itself or being with him.

A short time later, he secured everything to the saddle and mounted. Stoney boosted Marigold up behind him, tipped his cap, then went back to the spot where he had measuring chains staked out.

"It's terrible weather for an outing." Marigold retied her bonnet. "Are you sure about this?"

"I hate to break it to you, Marigold, but this is fine fall weather. 'Terrible' weather doesn't let you out the door to use the john. Hang on."

She wrapped her arms around his waist and hunched into his back, face between his shoulder blades.

He waited until he was facing away from the cabin to let himself smile.

...

They dismounted where tall grass stood brown and brittle around a wickiup that seemed to have withstood several seasons of winds and rain. A stream burbled nearby, and a squirrel with fat cheeks scampered from a fallen pine cone up the trunk of a tree.

Marigold turned to look back on their valley. This elevation afforded a view westward as well. Through the sleet, the mountains plaited one into another into the distance. Some wore red and gold skirts in their lower valleys. All wore white crowns and a powder of sugar.

"What a beautiful view."

"'Tis." Virgil removed their things from the saddle and led the horse into a crude barn that she imagined had been the home for whichever animals they'd brought from California. "I think of building a house up here sometimes," he said when he emerged and stood next to her, surveying the world. "Mostly it's a pipe dream to get me through a shitty day," he said with a self-deprecating quirk of his mouth.

She almost said, *Like this one?* The spitting rain was more like ice pellets that stung her cheeks. *Not* terrible weather, he claimed, but it felt pretty abysmal.

"This spot loses sunshine for a few weeks in the winter. The streams make up for it, though. That one's cold." He nodded to the thin trickle moving down a line of rocks, then picked up the shovel and the paper-wrapped raspberry roots. He led her to where steam rose from a thicket of cattails that were turning to fluff.

As she followed, Marigold hugged the shawl she had rolled around her nightdress and her small towel. "Hot and cold running water? Where are we? New York City?"

He snorted. "The cold water is sweet, but this warm stuff makes coffee taste like the south end of a goat. We made ourselves drink it because the Arapahoe say its medicinal. Tom knew of it and brought us here. We dammed it, then lived in that wickiup." He thumbed back at it. "We would have rather stayed down in the valley to protect against claim jumpers, but we would have died if we hadn't had this bath to warm up in."

The cattails hid a pool that had been dug into the embankment and was surrounded by stones. The water was deep enough in the center that she couldn't see the bottom. She could hardly imagine a half-dozen men jammed into such a small space, but with frost biting at them, they probably hadn't minded rubbing shoulders.

"Did you want to change in the wickiup?" He looked back at its barely there walls. "We always stripped here and, well, we were all men so we didn't wear anything at all." He cleared his throat. "I'll scout a spot for your raspberries while you—" He abruptly brushed past her, leaving her standing on the muddy shoreline.

Marigold hesitated, but the biting wind had been trying to cut her in half for the better part of an hour. She glanced to the water, then looked for Virgil. He was gone.

She crouched to touch the water. It felt too heavenly and inviting to stand on modesty. She had brought her nightdress but decided her chemise would do.

She left her outer clothes and drawers under a small lean-to she suspected had been built for this very purpose, to keep snow and rain off one's clothes while bathing. She carefully entered the pool, inching her feet along the slippery rocks as she slowly submerged into water that was so warm it was almost uncomfortable.

As she grew used to it, she slithered farther along the edge. The water gradually grew deeper. She had never learned to swim, but she and Pearl had often waded into the neighbor's pond on hot summer days. This was better. Marigold found a flat rock near the embankment and settled onto it.

The water covered her chest and met over her shoulders. She sighed, listening to the hiss of the wind in the drying vegetation around her. Sleet continued to peck her cheeks, but she turned her face into it, feeling invincible against it. She had a fleeting thought that she ought to look for watercress or any other plant tricked into believing it was spring because of the warm water here, but she closed her eyes, mind drifting to other things.

As birthday gifts went, this might be the best one she had ever received. She was thrilled with all that Pearl had sent her, but every single thing meant work—planting and harvesting, instructions for foraging and preserving, preparing tonics and poultices.

Having a break from thinking and working and minding the children was invaluable.

Not that she resented them. They were well-springs of love, providing affection and a sense of value that had been missing from her life for far too long, but the younger two were demanding. Harley had to be watched closely, and Nettie never ran out of questions. She reminded Marigold of herself at that age. Marigold spared a moment of pity for her parents, the headmistress at Miss Linnington's Academy for Young Ladies, and poor, beleaguered Uncle Felix.

She hadn't thought of her parents in a long time. In many ways, she had only been able to think of survival since they'd died in a carriage accident. She and Pearl had been caked in grief when Uncle Felix had told them they would have to leave Bedford and go to boarding school. Marigold had thought she couldn't feel so abandoned as when they arrived there and were forced into separate rooms.

The academy had been a constant test, full of snobbish girls who had families to go home to on summer and Christmas break. She and Pearl had struggled to find their place, Pearl less so because she was naturally warm and compliant. Marigold was more assertive and competitive with her grades. She had wanted to become a teacher, but the pressure to marry had been enormous. Everyone had said she was doing the right thing marrying Ben. She had thought it would give her the stable, fulfilling life she had longed for since her parents had passed. That had been the dream that had got her through her own shitty days.

She hadn't had any sort of fantasy to get her through her days in court, though. Her character had been publicly assassinated, and friends began crossing the street to avoid her. When Uncle Felix suggested moving to Kansas Territory, she had thought it couldn't be any harder than what she'd been through. At least the daily struggle would be for a good cause, she had reasoned.

There had been a heartening promise in homesteading. At first, she had made a few friends through the suffragists. They had supported her decision to rid herself of her no-good husband and had loaned her books to read, then engaged in stimulating conversation about the texts.

There had been that other element, however. The angry, denigrating people who knew what she stood for—not just a free state, but voting rights for all and abolishing slavery. She believed women should be allowed to own property and pursue an education—professional employment, even! What a scandal! But if she had been allowed to obtain a law degree, perhaps she would have kept her house in her divorce.

For those radical views, she'd become a pariah, so much so that Pearl had often tried to hush her in public. *Don't say anything. Don't embarrass me.*

Uncle Felix had been equally vocal, but men were allowed to have opinions. As they had stood outside their burning house, Pearl hadn't sent baleful looks at Uncle Felix as the reason for the arson. She had asked Marigold, *Why couldn't you let things be?*

Marigold liked to think she knew better, she supposed. That she could *make* things better. If she didn't try, who would? That's why she had interfered with Hiram, nudging him toward Pearl.

Her sense that she *did* know better had been re-inforced on that bleak morning when they had found themselves homeless. Hiram's mother had extended an invitation to Pearl. Marigold had yet to receive a letter announcing their engagement, but she was sure it was only a matter of time. She took a lot of comfort knowing Pearl was in a good situation, and yes, perhaps she was a little smug about it, too.

It struck her that she missed her sister sorely, but she had stopped wishing that she could have stayed in Topeka. Uncle Felix had been offered a room at a men's boarding house, but the one for women was only for spinsters and widows. *I'm sorry, Mrs. Davis, but you seem to attract the wrong sort of attention.* Even the church had been hard-pressed to find someone willing to let her sleep on their screened porch for a few days.

So she'd come here.

Against the odds, she had begun to feel as though she had a place in this world, until things with Virgil had become so complicated. Lately, they walked around the small cabin like a pair of horseshoe magnets aligned on the same poles, pushing against one another with invisible force. She kept trying to let go of the silly pipe dreams she'd had about him, but now he had done this incredibly nice thing for her, bringing her up to this pool and leaving her to—

Wait. Had he *left* her here? Completely alone?

"Virgil?" she called, fighting sudden panic.

Even if he was nearby, what if he was attacked by a wolf or a mountain lion? Her heart began to race as she realized how vulnerable she was, like a new-born baby helpless in the wilderness. She could die trying to find her way back to the cabin.

"Virgil!" she shouted.

A tromping crash sounded. He waded through the patch of cattails and looked around, then scowled at her with confusion. "What's wrong?"

"Nothing." She sank back to her chin, feeling silly. "I didn't know where you went."

"To plant your raspberries."

"You found a suitable place?"

"Yes. They're in the ground."

"Oh. Thank you."

"You're welcome." His gaze met hers, then quickly shot off into the distance. "Are you enjoying the soak?"

It struck her that she was in her chemise and the lace-edged calico would be hiding little now that it was soaked through.

He didn't leer, though. His profile only held a sense of listening closely, as though it mattered to him whether she was pleased.

"Very much. Thank you," she said shyly.

"Good." He nodded and— Was that a smile?

No. Not really. Maybe? His scar pulled his mouth offside when he smiled, making him look more threatening than he was. He wasn't cruel at all, just thoughtless sometimes. Protective of himself. People struck out when they were defensive. She knew that because she did it herself.

"Well, I'll—" He started to move away.

"Would you—" They had spoken at the same time.

He paused. "Would I what?" he prompted.

"I only wondered if you would be willing to tell me how you got your scar?" She bit her lip, wishing she hadn't asked. They weren't so close anymore that he would confide personal details just because she asked.

He shrugged. "Saloon brawl. Owen thinks he's funny. Not everyone agrees."

"You protected him?" Why didn't that surprise her?

"He did it for me once." He took hold of a bursting cattail, and a puff of fluff scattered on the wind. "More than once, but that's how we met, when we were boys. My mother sent me to school. I have no idea how she got my father to agree to it. I didn't go half the time because no one wanted me there. Everyone knew who my father was, but they also knew he didn't claim me, so they made me a target without any consequence.

"One day a group of older boys thought they'd put me in my place. Owen stepped in and took a beating beside me, but we got our own licks in. We were schoolmates for the next year or so, but he didn't like it any more than I did. Then I was set to work in the field. We lost touch, and I didn't see him again until we were in the army."

"How long were you in the army?"

"Three years." His expression darkened.

"You didn't like it."

"Funny thing about life is you don't know how good you've got it until you're facing worse," he said with grim irony. "Things we were ordered to do…" He grimaced and shook his head. "We left as soon as we could. Neither of us wanted to go back to Virginia, so we trapped, found our way to Missouri where I met Clara, and got on with the steamboats. Then Owen talked me into California. This happened shortly after we got there." He pointed at his cheek.

His scar had turned white against his cold-flushed cheeks. His fur hat was jammed down tight on his head, his coat buttoned up to his chin. His body held the tension of bracing against the wind.

"Do you want to come in and warm up?" she asked impulsively.

"Marigold."

"Not for—"

"I know that's not an invitation." He gave his beard a rub. "What I *want* is to be friends again. I don't know how to do that. And I don't want to screw up now that you're actually talking to me again. So no, I'll stand here in the cold and answer questions I'd rather not."

"You don't have to answer them. This isn't a trial." She drew her knees up and hugged them, trying to get more comfortable on the hard rock, but she couldn't resist asking one more. "Is that what we were? Friends?"

He pushed his hands into the pockets of his coat and frowned into the gusting wind.

"Yes," he decided after a weighty pause. "The men who are my friends know things about me that no one else does. They aren't afraid to tell me the truth even when they know I don't want to hear it. We stand by each other despite wanting to tell each other to go to hell."

"I did say that to you, didn't I?" she said ruefully.

He nodded. "Then you stayed to mind my children." He blew out a frustrated breath. "This isn't something I'm used to, you know, wanting friendship with a woman. I've always been surrounded by men. Women are migratory creatures that move through sometimes, but I don't know much about them. When I married, I wanted to be a good husband and a good father. I didn't know what that meant, only that I expected Clara to abide by our vows and welcome me into our bed. I didn't think much about whether we liked each other, which isn't to say I disliked her, but I didn't know her enough to like her."

Marigold picked up her head. Her jaw went slack with shock. "You want me to *like* you?"

"Well, I don't want you to hate me," he asserted. "I don't want you to think I'm like your ex-husband. I don't want anyone to treat you the way he did, and I want to kill him when I think of it, I really do. I'm furious that *I* made you feel used and under-appreciated." He rubbed his beard against his shoulder. "Because you're a good person, Marigold. Believe me when I say I've met the shitty ones. I know the value of the good ones."

She drew her knees in tighter. "I was really hurt that you thought I would steal from you."

"I know." His voice thickened with self-loathing.

"I thought you'd make me leave, and aside from being terrified because I have nowhere to go, I love your children, Virgil. So much." Latent tears gathered in her eyes, and she couldn't help the pang that made her voice crack. Her mouth wobbled.

"I know." His voice was even heavier.

"I like it here. I like *you*. Even though you're harder than this rock I'm sitting on." She shifted, uncomfortably aware that she more than liked him. That's why he was able to hurt her so deeply. She was deeply saddened at losing something that hadn't even manifested fully. It left her desolate and feeling stupid for thinking he could be hers.

"Life made me hard," he acknowledged somberly. "I forgot that you've had hard knocks yourself because you've still got kindness in you. I don't know how, but you do. That's why I wanted to marry you."

Wanted. Not want. She nearly buried her burning eyes against her kneecaps.

"I thought you just wanted sex," she mumbled, thinking of what he'd said the day they met. *Having been married, you understand a man needs more than a hot meal and a mended shirt.*

"'Course I want sex. I mean, I was hoping you wanted sex, too," he added in a self-conscious mutter. "And that you'd marry me so we could do that. You shouldn't feel ashamed if you want that," he added with more heat. "It's natural, but it wasn't just that I wanted sex. You're putting so much work into making my house a home it ought to *be* your home, and wearing my name would be protection for you. That's what you said you wanted when you came here, right? If we were married and something happened to me, you would have income from my share of the company and could support my children. Otherwise, the men will hold it in trust for them, but you'd have nothing. I'm sure they'd pay you to look after them, but it wouldn't be the same. Christ, if nothing else, take my name so the men will quit calling you Mrs. *Davis*."

She blinked as she tried to assimilate that he'd put a lot more thought into this than she'd given him credit for. And emotion. It was animosity, sure, but it was kind of endearing.

"You really hate him," she said of her former husband.

"I hate him so fucking much."

She bit her lip to hide her smile, recognizing this as the moment that she fell in love with him. Unequivocally and irreversibly. She had never loved anyone this way. It was a strange, new type of love. When she'd married Ben, she'd been steeped in a combination of flattered ego and romantic ideals. She'd been enamored with achieving what she'd been told to achieve. She'd been admired for it, which had reinforced to her that what she felt must be what she had been told it was: love.

This was love, though. It was a much more complex emotion that dug far deeper than anything she had ever experienced. It held the same affection and acceptance of flaws that she held in her heart for Pearl and Uncle Felix, the sort of love that would put their interests above her own because they were important to her.

It was broader than that, though. She could feel her heart stretching as it tried to accommodate all the ways she wanted to let Virgil into it. She wanted to know what was in his head and how she could bring him comfort. She wanted to tell him her secret yearnings and laugh with him and be brazen and wicked and unguarded.

She wanted him to love her back.

"I worry that if I marry, I'll wind up trapped again, stuck with a man who doesn't really care about me," she confided.

"Tender feelings aren't my strong suit, you know that." His voice held regret, but his expression was pensive. His gaze held hers, asking for something. "I do care about you, Marigold. When I married Clara, I thought— Hell, I don't know what I thought. My cock wanted a wife, so I found one. It was a disaster. This is different. I don't want a wife. I want *you*. In my home. In my bed. Throwing shit on my shoes." He pushed his hat more firmly onto his head. "I sound like an idiot."

"No. That is quite possibly *the* most romantic proposal any woman has ever received." She was speaking facetiously, but she was also blinking dampness from her lashes that had nothing to do with the wisps of steam condensing on her face. Her throat was clogged with laughter that held every other soaring emotion attached to it.

He swore under his breath and looked away. "I just told you I'm not one for sentiment. If you want a husband who will bring you flowers, Gristle is still available."

"I had one. A husband who gave me flowers, I mean."

"'Course he did," he said with disgust.

"But he only did it to impress other people. He brought them to me at the academy. He would show up with flowers so the headmistress and my fellow students would flutter around saying what a romantic suitor he was." She swirled her arms through the water, wondering who that girl was who had believed that illusion. "The first day we came to court, he brought a bouquet and tried to give it to me. He made it seem as though he was trying to reconcile and I was at fault for refusing. It worked."

"Can we make a pact?" He crouched and dangled his fingers in the water. "Can we never talk about him again? Because I get to planning murders. It's not healthy."

"One last thing." She winced because it was still a very tender topic. "I tried to start a family with Ben. It didn't happen. I might be barren." She braced herself as she lifted her gaze. "If you want more children, we should stop talking of marriage."

She held her breath as inscrutable reaction flickered across his face.

"I have my hands full with the three I've got," he pointed out, but his expression grew concerned. "I would want to give you a baby if you wanted one. Does it upset you that it might not happen?"

"It used to upset me a great deal." She'd been devastated each time her menses had arrived. "With the divorce and everything, I came to see it as having been for the best, but I've always wanted a family. When I decided to come here, I made my peace with being a stepmother or a governess, never realizing I would come to love your children as if they were my own." He'd shown her with his own actions that you didn't have to make a child to love them with your whole heart. "If I had your baby, it would be more goodness, but I wouldn't feel so empty if it didn't happen."

He nodded somberly. "I would welcome more babies if they came along, but I won't feel cheated if they don't. I'm not shopping for a mare, Marigold."

"*So* romantic," she groaned at the sky. "Are you shopping for a herd dog? Is that what you're going to say next?"

He abruptly lifted his hand to send a spattering of water at her. "Have I mentioned lately what a pain in my ass you are?"

"I understand the water is medicinal. Sit in it. See if it helps." She lifted her brows, ridiculously pleased to be back to throwing harmless barbs.

"You better mean that, because I'm coming in." He stood and started to unbutton his coat. "I bathe naked."

"Am I supposed to be frightened?" She was giddy with excitement.

"You're supposed to politely turn your head. You know how modest I am."

She sputtered a laugh and twisted around. "From what I recall, you're not built modestly. More like branch wood— Hey!" Another splash hit the back of her head.

"Smart-ass. If I come in there, we're getting married. You know that, don't you?"

She twisted around to see him stripping without ceremony, balling up his cloths and stuffing them next to her own. His coat was draped over his boots.

"Then you should stand there naked—" Whew.

He stood unabashedly nude, radiating confidence and power with his broad shoulders and muscled chest. His body hair was the same dark brown as his beard. Short, wiry wisps grew from his breastbone toward his tight, beige nipples. His torso wore a fading tan, and his hips and thighs were pale and planted firm.

She'd never actually seen Ben's penis, only Harley's little dangler when she bathed him. Virgil's was—

"This is what happens when I'm cold. All right? Now you've seen me naked, you have to marry me." He came in with a lot more grace than she'd managed, seeming well-practiced in where to brace his hand and where to step his feet.

He pushed off and bobbed into the middle with a *sploosh*, submerging before his head reappeared. He gave his hair and beard a scrub. Another rinse and he skimmed the water off his face, releasing a long gust of breath that clouded the air.

He turned his head, and his silver eyes seemed to pierce straight into her soul, snagging her heart like a barbed fish hook.

"Come here."

CHAPTER TWENTY

What had she done?

Even though the water had loosened her joints and made her bones feel like pudding, tension invaded her belly. Her skin seemed to have shrunk.

"I can't swim."

"Can you stand?" He rose and water sluiced off his torso down to where the surface lapped at his navel.

"Oh. I couldn't see the bottom. I thought it was over my head in the middle."

"Muck settles on the rocks so you can't see them. Makes it slippery, too." He lowered to submerge his shoulders again and drifted closer. His hand searched for hers beneath the water. "You want to kiss and seal the deal? Or do you need more time to think on it?"

He looked strange with his hair slicked back. More open. His scar was turning bright red, but his expression was relaxed. Perhaps he'd dropped his guard this once. For her.

She was still trying to form sensible thoughts, but her hand went into his of its own volition. The offset smile touched his mouth again as he drew her toward him. In a brief panic, her feet tried to find purchase and her hands sought the solidity of his shoulders, but she didn't fall under the water. He manipulated her so she floated into a seat across his thighs as he found a rock to settle on.

She scrambled to be sure her chemise was pulled all the way down, but as her bottom came to rest on his thighs, the firm swell of his erection prodded her cheek.

"Oh."

"I'm warming up," he said drily.

She cupped his beard, aligning her thumb along his scar. "Did you bring me up here to make love to me?"

"I thought about it. I can't help thinking about it. It happens even when I sleep, but I was only trying to make up with you. Give you a treat and maybe talk without the children eavesdropping. I want lovemaking to happen, but I don't expect it." His hands shifted on her, making the calico feel like an obstruction. His heavy-lidded gaze held hers, and his voice roughened. "*Is* it going to happen?"

"It feels like it is happening," she said with a rueful husk of a laugh.

"Does it?" He lowered his head, lips almost touching hers. Beneath the water, his hand shifted so his thumb slid beneath the swell of her breast, then brushed over the tip.

She caught her breath.

His lips formed a wicked smile. His mouth brushed damply against hers while he caressed her nipple again, circling and sending lightning strikes into her loins.

"That's why I can't stop thinking about you," he confided in a graveled whisper. "You act like my touching you is the best thing you've ever felt."

"It is," she said, nudging her mouth against his in invitation.

"Me, too," he said against her lips, then pressed his wet mouth over hers.

His whiskers were cold and damp, and his hair was the same when she ran her hand to the back of his head, but the rest of her was so hot, she liked it. She loved the way he plundered and consumed and slid his tongue against hers. It really was the best thing she'd ever felt.

His hand massaged her breast until she began to feel lightheaded, as though she was under the water and drowning. She broke away from their kiss to catch her breath, and he dropped his gaze to the button in the middle of her neckline.

She bit her lip and opened it, struggling to coax wet cotton to give up the three little buttons. When he would have nudged the cap sleeve off her shoulder, she held his gaze and started gathering her chemise up to her waist.

He helped her, balancing her to keep her head above water as she pulled it from between the press of their bodies. Her bottom felt the naked brush of his thigh and the steely shape of his erection. Her stomach dipped with excitement. He shifted her so she straddled his thighs, knees pressed wide where they braced on the hard rock he sat upon. Slowly, he gathered the weighted cotton to her waist, then dragged it upward.

She lifted her arms and her chemise landed in a plop against a nearby rock. Her shoulders and arms pimpled at the cold. Her nipples tightened to stung points. She wanted to sink back into the warmth, but Virgil made a noise of protest.

"Let me see," he said in a rumble, hands

skimming over her back and waist, firming on her hips to keep her chest above the water. "You're so pretty, Marigold."

He dipped his head, and his mouth encompassed her nipple. The sensation was such a contrast, it sent shivery pleasure up to her scalp. As he suckled and pulled, her thighs tried to close, but she discovered his were in the way.

He moved to taste the other one while his hands drew flat circles on her bottom, clasping handfuls of her cheeks and squeezing, stroking down the backs of her thighs and inward.

Hot water was rushing against her intimate flesh, and Virgil's touch was an even bolder caress in the same place. His long fingers reached to circle and nudge at her entrance, both daring and teasingly insufficient.

She couldn't help herself, she arched to invite his prodding touch while hugging his head into her chest, fairly begging for more of his torture of her nipple. Maybe it was the silky water, maybe it was the freedom of bathing naked in the woods, maybe it was his delight in her most libidinous behavior, but she had never felt so wondrously natural.

With a gratified noise, he wrapped his arm around her waist and shifted, slouching and opening his thighs, spreading hers open farther. *Now* he was touching her. Probing. Pressing his thick finger into her sheath while he licked all the way up her neck.

She dropped her mouth over his, dancing with the slow thrust of his touch, sucking on his tongue and stroking her hands all over the straining muscles of his shoulders and flexed tendons in his neck.

She did whatever felt good, and it all felt inordinately good, but it wasn't enough. Her inner muscles were squeezing tight around his finger, searching fruitlessly for that more piercing, intense sensation.

"I want—" She reached between them, squeezing the thick shape she found.

"Take it. It's yours." He withdrew his finger and guided her hip with one hand, held his erection with the other.

As the swollen head of his penis rubbed against her engorged folds, she moaned with need. *There.* She cupped his velvety crown against the sweet spot, and they thrust against one another a few times, both releasing ragged noises.

Their movements grew more blatant, rubbing and rocking. His tip caught behind her pubic bone, found her entrance, and he steadied her. Hard hands pressed at her hip. In the next heartbeat, he was forging steadily into her.

Their gazes locked. This wasn't perfect. There was an uncomfortable friction that she remembered from her marriage. A rough rock scraped her knee. She was still half fearful they would somehow plunge under the water and drown together, but there was something deeply gratifying in being joined with Virgil in this deeply intimate way.

His arm slowly clamped across her lower back as he settled in the final inch and sealed them tight. His thick hardness was buried deep inside her, pulsing like a second heartbeat. They were nose to nose, uneven breaths clouding, gazes locked in wonder and earthy pleasure.

He didn't thrust. Instead, he held her tight as he shifted slightly, as though he couldn't get close enough or deep enough. They ground together while they kissed, moaning and rubbing their naked chests. She was caressed everywhere—by the movement of the water and his hands sliding over her, playing with her breasts and tickling her spine, stroking her thighs and cradling her nape while he kissed her neck. He sucked her earlobe and said, "You're going to make me come, squeezing me so tight."

"I think I'm going to come," she gasped with startled realization.

"Do it," he commanded.

She wanted to, so badly. His taut skin and his hairy chest abraded her nipples. His thick sex was lodged hard and deep inside her. She rubbed her pubis against his and licked flagrantly into his mouth, squeezed her knees against his waist, seeking the pinnacle, but it eluded her.

In a swooping move, he shifted so he was over her. His arm braced on a rock behind her head, providing her a pillow with the back of his wrist. His other hand stayed firm at her tailbone, holding her for the pulsing thrusts he gave her.

The edge of a rock dug into the middle of her back, but she had the freedom to strap her arms across his back and dig her heels into his flexing buttocks. As she arched and writhed, the angle changed. His plunging hardness touched a place inside her that felt incredible. She worked herself on him, moaning as the fire in her roared into a ferocious blaze. Her pussy clamped down and glorious release rolled through her.

The waves of pleasure intensified as he withdrew slightly and began to thrust with more vigor. His intrusion rubbed and stimulated and caused the expanding ripples within her to strengthen and continue. To shatter throughout her body, creating a shivery joy that returned again and again as he moved within her. She was completely at sea, losing herself in a floating fog of pure, hedonistic joy. She let all of it sing out of her in moans of agonized delight.

His body tensed. He gave a few deeper, more powerful thrusts, then held himself inside her, gritting his teeth. A feral shout fought its way out of his throat and his sex gave powerful throbs within her. He bucked and clenched and said, "Fuck! Marigold."

Then there were no discernible words, just them clinging to one another, moaning with ecstasy.

· · ·

Slowly, their ragged catches of breath mingled and their convulsions settled to twitches. As their tension bled away, Virgil kissed the corner of her mouth, feeling the most tender he ever had. He was still shaking as he withdrew and glided them into a nook where he cradled her while they both waited for their heartbeats to settle.

Between the lethargy of their long soak and the stupor of sex, they climbed from the water like a pair of drunks exiting a bordello.

Virgil was still shirtless when he noticed Marigold was shivering and struggling to button her bloomers. He couldn't tell if she was hurrying because she was shy or upset or cold. He shook out her gown and helped her into it.

"Thank you. I shouldn't have wet my hair. I'm going to catch my death, but it felt so good." She angled her body as she twisted the length and wrung a few more drops out of it. She coiled it onto her crown and wrapped her shawl tightly around her wet head.

He pulled on his undershirt and shirt. "It was better than good."

She glanced up from kicking into her moccasins, giving him the most potently sensual, heavy-lidded smile he'd ever seen.

His concern eased. He had wanted to make her smile, and he had. It was a heady, powerful triumph that made his heart thud in his chest.

He belatedly realized she hadn't actually agreed to marry him, though. Not in so many words.

I worry that if I marry, I'll wind up trapped again, stuck with a man who doesn't really care about me.

He did care. More than he knew how to deal with or express. It was hooks and barbs that pulled and tugged at the knots inside him, reminding him he was more vulnerable now. He had more responsibility. More to protect.

"You *are* going to marry me, aren't you?"

"I saw you naked. I don't have a choice, do I?"

"You do not," he assured her and pulled her close, liking the way she melted into him. God, it felt good to touch her all over like this. He didn't think he'd ever get enough of her batting her lashes at him, either.

"I think we'll have to keep to our own rooms, though," she said somberly. "Even after we're married."

His heart lurched. "Why?"

"I don't know how we'll keep from waking the children when—"

He covered her laughing mouth with his own.

• • •

"They're going to tease me, aren't they?" Marigold said.

"The men?" Virgil kicked free of a stirrup so she could set her foot in it, then he held her arm to help her slide down to the ground. "Not if they want to live."

She had to chuckle and, yes, fall a little more in love with him, but they both wore damp hair and smug expressions. It was obvious they had made love. She hoped Emmett and Ira only teased her and didn't outright lose respect for her.

"Any remarks they make will be aimed at me." He dismounted and hitched the horse to the porch post. "They like you."

"They don't like you?"

"They put up with me."

She shook her head with exasperation but collected herself and entered the cabin.

"Marigold! Look what we made for you!" Nettie pointed to the windowsill over the basin. "It's for your birthday."

"Meego. Yook," Harley repeated, standing on the bench to point. He quickly scrambled down and ran to his papa.

"Aw, one went out," Levi said, frowning over his shoulder.

"They're still very pretty." Marigold moved closer to the three lanterns made from empty tin cans, each pierced with a dotted snowflake pattern. Candlelight shone through two of them, but one had sputtered. "I'm very touched. Thank you." She tentatively glanced at Ira and Emmett. "Thank you for helping the children make them."

"Our pleasure," Ira said. He and Emmett weren't looking at her. They were sending such pointed looks at Virgil, he ought to be glowing with a snowflake pattern himself, possibly turning to melted wax and ash.

"We made this, too," Levi said proudly. "It's a game."

"Oh, yes." Marigold looked at the board of holes and pegs in a cross pattern. "I've played that. You jump the pegs and try to remove all of them?"

Levi nodded and pushed it toward her. "Do you want to try?"

"I will, but I need to hang my wet things and comb out my hair. I should start something for our dinner, too. Ira, Emmett, will you eat with us? I want to thank you for today. It was very…um." Her thoughts ground to a halt, incapable of finding appropriate words. Relaxing? A special treat? "Well, you know," she said with a perturbed wave. "You've been to the spring."

"We have," Ira said, still glaring at Virgil, who was letting Harley try his hat.

"Levi, have you checked your snares today?" Marigold asked. "Perhaps there's something for our stew pot."

"Not yet."

"I'll take you, since the horse is saddled," Virgil offered. "We'll check them on the way to the barn. But Marigold, wait." Virgil held out his hand to beckon her closer.

"Oh, um…" She came to stand beside him, feeling very self-conscious as he took her hand and squeezed it.

"We've decided to tie the knot," Virgil announced. "We'll go to Denver for the vote on the twenty-fourth and see Woodrow."

Ira and Emmett lost their tense expressions, and big smiles took over their faces.

Nettie asked worriedly, "Where are you going?"

"To Denver, sweetie." Marigold stepped closer to smooth the girl's hair. "To get married."

"Really?" Levi snapped his head around. "Then you'll be our mother? Forever?"

"Would you?" Nettie's eyes widened with such cautious hope, she nearly broke Marigold's heart in two.

"Yes, if you would like that?"

Nettie threw her arms around her waist so exuberantly, Marigold's breath was squeezed out of her. Happiness flowered in her chest. She bent to gather Nettie closer while she kissed her hair.

Levi rose to hover behind his sister, offering a lopsided grin.

Marigold reached for him, giving him a hug across his shoulders.

"Me," Harley said, trying to get out of Virgil's arms.

"Oh, yes, I'll be your mama, too." She straightened to take him, so pleased by this reception, she was growing teary. She cherished the hugs from all the Gardners and wondered how she had become so lucky as to earn this bright and wonderful future.

CHAPTER TWENTY-ONE

If they'd managed to retain more men, Virgil would have been a delegate for more than his partners and a handful of miners willing to winter in Quail's Creek. As it was, he carried fourteen votes against becoming the State of Jefferson. Most were objecting because the constitution didn't include the right for Emmett, Tom, Bing Sun, or Marigold to vote, but their stance might not be noted one way or another. The prevailing winds were against statehood because of the tax burden.

Virgil would have tapped the ferryman for the latest gossip on the subject, but he wound up supporting Marigold as she hung her head over the stern of the raft.

They'd made good time in the near-empty mule cart. Even with their late start and the need to stop for Marigold to overcome her nausea, they had arrived at the ferry before the moon rose. They could have pushed into Denver but had camped with a handful of prospectors who were heading into the mountains despite the lateness of the season. Virgil had taken the opportunity to tell them there was work in Quail's Creek if they didn't find their own gold.

This morning, they'd risen early and skipped breakfast in favor of buying flapjacks in Denver. They were nearly there, but here she was, retching despite her empty stomach.

"Are you sure—?" They hadn't found time or privacy to make love again, but she'd been downright emotional when they'd said goodbye to the children.

"I'm sure. That's why I needed my bag yesterday." She'd been very red-faced, and he hadn't wanted to ask what she'd retrieved before she had disappeared behind a tree for the second time in as many minutes.

He'd been thinking of taking a room for their wedding night, but it was just as well that they hurry back to camp. He trusted his partners to keep his children alive for a day or two, but it was a lot to ask when there was so much work to be done. If he and Marigold finished their business quickly, they might be home before dark.

The ferry landed, and Virgil said, "You walk off ahead."

"Thank you. I'll be fine in a moment." She took a cleansing breath, adjusted her bonnet, and smoothed the front of her blue coat.

The ferryman gave Virgil an odd look as he drove off, the kind that had Virgil's neck prickling with warning. Shit. Rumors would be flying from this performance, suggesting he had an urgent reason for seeking out Woodrow's matrimonial services.

He didn't say anything to Marigold. Thankfully, her color was better as she climbed up to the bench next to him for the last short leg of their journey.

"I'll head straight to Dudley's Saloon to get the voting out of the way," he said. "With any luck, Woodrow will be there. I expect half the town will be. Once we're hitched, we'll see about spending your wedding money. What are you thinking you'd like to buy?"

"Bolts of wool to make the children some warm clothes for winter and something for heavier bedding."

"Marigold," he chided. "I'll buy what my children need. That money is for you." His partners had each put a twenty-dollar promissory note in an envelope, urging her to, "Get something you've been missing."

She leaned toward him to ask, "Have I got sick on me? People are staring."

He had noticed himself that they were attracting attention. The pregnancy rumor couldn't have made it off the ferry faster than they had, could it?

"They're probably amazed you've survived this long and look no worse for wear."

The noise she made was more despair than humor. She looked to the gloved hands she was twisting in her lap. "I know those looks. I've become notorious for some reason."

He hated to bring it up but, "The lost nugget? Plenty of men were there when—"

"No!" She covered her face, peeking through the web of her fingers. "Do you think so?"

"I wouldn't be surprised. At least a few of the men would have come through here on their way to somewhere else. A good story will buy you a whiskey in the saloons." Which didn't explain why men were halting in their tracks when they spotted them. Every single one spun and followed their same route toward Dudley's.

Irked, Virgil hurried the mules to the saloon and drew them to a halt on the grassy verge next to it.

Not to be outdone by the tallest building in Auraria, Dudley had added a second floor onto his original wood-framed saloon. The upstairs had yet to be framed in with rooms so he could call himself a tavern, but the open space was useful for meetings, and Virgil had heard that a few traveling entertainments had performed up there, too.

Today, it was the site of the referendum on the state's constitution. Cecil was doing a steady business below, and pockets of men stood around outside, smoking and wagging their jaws.

They all stared as Virgil helped Marigold from the cart.

"What are you gawking at?" Virgil asked crossly but didn't wait for an answer. "Woodrow," he called as he spotted the man. "Don't go anywhere. Soon as I cast my votes, I'm getting hitched."

That ought to answer the question these men weren't asking.

Woodrow scraped his hat off his head and gave his bald patch a scratch. "To who?"

"What the hell do you mean, 'to who'?" His intended was right here.

Suddenly, a woman broke past a wall of men and cried, "Marigold?"

• • •

Marigold knew that voice better than her own. Even so, she grabbed Virgil's sleeve to steady herself, unable to believe her eyes.

"Pearl?" Could it be true?

Yes. There was her sister rushing toward her with

her wide, bright smile. Her red curls poked from her
bonnet to frame her angelic face. Her yellow coat
over her green calico gown brought out the gold in
her teary brown eyes.

"Oh, Pearl!" Marigold's heart nearly burst from
her chest. She hurried forward to snatch her close,
soaking in the warm, familiar scent of lavender and
sun-dried cotton and that special, familiar smell that
told her she was with family. *Home.*

"I've been waiting for days." Pearl hugged her
with all her strength. "Everyone said he would come
here today, but I didn't know *you* would. It's so good
to see you." Her voice was choked with tears.

So was Marigold's. Happy ones. "How did you
get here? Did Hiram bring you? Are you married?"
She drew back to look around, still in shock, but
smiling so widely her cheeks hurt.

"No. No." Pearl shook her head. "Hiram— I'll
explain somewhere private." Her lashes quivered as
she realized ears were cocked in an effort to eaves-
drop. "But, oh, I've missed you." Pearl gave her
another exuberant hug, rubbing Marigold's back.
"Your last letter sounded so discouraged. I was worried. That's why I convinced Uncle Felix I had to
come. I must say, things aren't nearly as primitive as
you made them sound. I've been very comfortable."
She drew back.

Marigold had already noted how much Denver
had grown through the summer, but— "How did
you get here? By stagecoach?" Impossible. Uncle
Felix had been destitute after the fire.

"We found a family coming to homestead. When
I arrived, I was directed to the Dudleys' to wait for

Mr. Gardner to come vote. They were kind enough to put me up in one of their rooms." Pearl waved vaguely toward a row of shacks behind the saloon.

"Good heavens, you're not serving here, are you?" In a saloon? Marigold was appalled, but she couldn't imagine Uncle Felix had given Pearl more than a little pin money.

"No!" Pearl laughed with outraged amusement. "But…" She leaned in to confide, "I have been helping Mrs. Dudley make corn whiskey."

"For heaven's sake, Pearl."

"I wanted to help. They're being so kind, not even charging me for the room." She leaned in again. "I think they see it as currying favor with my intended." Her brows lifted in amusement.

"Your—" Marigold's heart juddered to a halt in her chest.

Pearl's big eyes grew wider as gravel crunched behind Marigold. Someone's shadow fell onto her sister's face.

Pearl swallowed, then adopted her most charming expression, the one that always had men tipping their hats and rushing to pick up something she'd dropped.

"Mr. Gardner?" She pitched her voice in a way that suggested she had been waiting her whole life to meet him. "I was assured you would turn up here for the vote today. I'm Pearl Martin." She offered her hand. "I'm so glad to meet you at last."

"But he's m-m…" *Marrying* me. *He's mine.*

Marigold had to press her lips together to steady them. Her stomach was purged dry by her travel sickness, but it managed a final death clench that nearly sliced her in half. Such acute jealousy arose in her, she wanted to slap her sister's hand for daring to touch him.

"Miss Martin." Virgil shook Pearl's gloved hand while wearing a frown of confusion. "Marigold told me you were staying in Topeka to marry someone else."

"No," Pearl said firmly. "An acquaintance from church took me in when we lost our home and her son was… Well, I didn't have feelings for him and"—her gaze struck Marigold's with a hint of censure—"his interest in me was not as romantic as I was led to believe."

Virgil's brows became a single, disgruntled line as he shot Marigold a look that asked, *What the hell is going on?*

You'll find me to be a fair, respectful man to all but liars, cheats, and thieves.

Marigold's heart gave a disconcerting jolt as she heard suspicions seeping back into his mind, bricking a wall between himself and any tenderness he might have felt toward her.

"Since Marigold's letters assured me you're a good man and a good father, I was encouraged to pursue the offer of marriage you had extended." Pearl wore her most earnest and engaging smile. "You haven't written me to retract it."

Virgil's gaze traveled over Pearl in a more detailed study, the way a lot of men did, as though he hadn't known women came in such pretty colors and styles. He shot Marigold another look of confusion.

"But *you've* agreed to marry me," he said.

"What?" Pearl's outrage was lost in the collective

gasp of their audience.

As an awkward silence took hold between the three of them, voices in the crowd carried clear as a bell.

"They're sisters?" someone asked.

"Yes. That plain one's been living with him at Quail's Creek. Now the pretty one has turned up."

"*Shhh.*"

"Pearl," Marigold strangled on her own voice. "I was going to send you a letter today. It's in my bag…" She glanced back at the cart, thinking the rushed words were horribly inadequate when her sister was right here, believing she still had a chance with Virgil.

Did she?

Virgil wore his most thunderous expression.

"No, she's not a widow," one of those infernal spectators was saying. "Missus Davis is divorced."

This was worse than being slandered in court. By stepping into her sister's arrangement with Virgil, after *engaging in congress* with him, Marigold had earned her label of adulteress. She was everything Ben's lawyer had accused her of being.

"And a suffragist," another helpful voice provided. "That's why Virgil is voting against statehood."

"Is that true, Virgil?"

Virgil sent a glare across the crowd. "I'm voting against this constitution because every person ought to have the right to vote and that's not written into this one."

"See? She's already influencing him."

"I wonder how she does that," a sly voice said.

"Hey!" Virgil's hands closed into fists. "Button

your mouth or I'll do it for you." With an impatient look at Marigold, he said, "Let me get these votes cast. Then we'll" — he flashed another look at Pearl — "sort this out."

He strode into the saloon.

CHAPTER TWENTY-TWO

"First you stole the ticket, now you're stealing him?" Pearl hissed.

"I haven't stolen anything! This happened very suddenly."

"You always *do* this, Marigold." Pearl stamped her foot. "You go ahead of me and stir things up, ruining it before I get there. It doesn't matter how sweet I am, you've already salted the fields. Why can't you let things happen as they're supposed to?"

"That is very unfair." She drew Pearl back toward the cart where they were less likely to be overheard.

"You said yourself that your past colors how people see you. It also colors how they see *me*," Pearl insisted. "It happened at school, when you were always so outspoken. Then you left your husband when I was trying to find one. I couldn't stay in Philadelphia after that, could I? Hiram was the only man in Topeka who looked twice at me—"

"I knew I was getting in your way," Marigold cut in with remorse. "That's why I told him—"

"He thought I was loose," Pearl said with a humiliated, furious pang in her voice. "When you told him I had feelings for him, he took it to mean he could take advantage of me. He didn't want to *marry* me. His mother caught him pressing up on me and kicked me out!"

"Oh no." Marigold was sickened. Why were men such snakes? She hated Hiram for treating Pearl so horribly, but she hated herself more for interfering and putting Pearl in the path of such an unscrupulous man. She was no better than Uncle Felix when it came to dragging family into strife.

"That's why I wanted to find a husband for myself, one who didn't know anything about you and your past." Pearl waved toward the entrance to the saloon where Virgil had disappeared. "I would have sent for you once we were settled. Why couldn't you be patient?"

Because she'd had so little. She'd had no place or sense of acceptance in Topeka even before the fire. When her sister talked of leaving to marry a stranger, Marigold had fixed it so she wouldn't. Then, mere days later, they had lost their home and she'd had no other option than to take her sister's place on the stage.

She had only ever wanted a good life for herself. Why was it so hard to make one?

"You really came here to marry him?" Marigold asked, fighting the way her chin wanted to crinkle.

"Is there a reason I shouldn't? Why did *you* agree to marry him? Did you know he's running for marshal?" Pearl asked, making it almost an accusation.

Marigold lurched her gaze back to Pearl, understanding what she was really saying.

"Statehood has to pass before he could run," Marigold protested. "That isn't likely." Not according to Virgil. All the votes he'd brought were against.

"A territory is, though. Maybe not today, but soon. Even in Topeka, they know this side of Kansas Territory won't remain Kansas much longer. Not with all the gold here." Pearl had sat through as many meetings as Marigold had, serving refreshments to their uncle's fellow agitators. Pearl might have less interest in pushing for women's suffrage, but she wasn't ignorant. She knew how all of this worked and perhaps had a better grasp on the game of politics.

In fact, if Virgil wanted to run for marshal, Pearl was definitely the sort of wife he would need, with her warm, compassionate temperament. She was rarely this strident. Only when she thought Marigold was overstepping.

Marigold crossed her arms over the stabbing sensation residing behind her navel. It was hitting her exactly what a detriment she was to Virgil's ambitions. Any sort of politics invited dirty laundry to be aired. Hers would always be hung out. Always.

"I— He needs a mother for his children," Marigold offered a weak, not wholly truthful reason for why she'd agreed to marry him.

"You wrote that your arrangement with him wouldn't progress to marriage. That he'll always see you as a thief. I wouldn't have come and made a fool of myself if I knew you were taking him. What am I supposed to do now?" Pearl asked plaintively.

Marigold's throat locked up, refusing to allow her voice to emerge.

Pearl was looking anxiously toward those massive mountains, perhaps feeling as stymied and helpless as Marigold had felt when she'd arrived.

Marigold loved Virgil, but she also loved her sister. The very last thing she wanted to do was hurt either of them.

She was also heart-wrenchingly aware that at no

point had Virgil declared feeling anything more than friendship toward her. He might have been willing to marry her when she'd been all he could get, but here was Pearl. She was everything Marigold was: bright and capable, skilled at keeping house and good with children, but kinder, prettier, and she didn't wear the tarnish of divorce.

Marigold had had relations with him, but she wasn't pregnant. She still owed him money, but he didn't owe her a damned thing. If she stepped out of the way, Virgil and Pearl could have a chance at making a good life together.

Why did it have to hurt so much to even think it? She ought to be happy for them.

What would become of her sister if Marigold married Virgil, though? Pearl didn't deserve to become a spinster aunt. She could easily find a husband of her own, of course. The men here weren't nearly as choosy as the ones out east, but most were hardscrabble miners offering a hardscrabble life. If Marigold hadn't ruined Pearl's chances in Philadelphia, she would be welcoming a baby to a lawyer by now, or a doctor. She would be making their home on a proper street with gas lights and would have everything she needed a short walk away.

If Pearl couldn't have that, a marshal with a mining company was the next best thing.

Virgil was the husband Pearl had chosen for herself, and he had agreed to marry her. Marigold couldn't ruin her sister's future *again*. She had to give him up.

• • •

Virgil's mind was still numb with disbelief that Miss Pearl Martin had shown up out of the blue.

"Nothing like a catfight to make a man feel good about himself, am I right, Virgil?" P.J. asked as he came up the stairs to where Virgil was registering the names of the men whose proxy votes he was casting.

Virgil glared him into silence and watched that Ed was recording everything correctly.

They weren't fighting over him. Were they? It didn't matter. He'd already chosen Marigold.

Well— He scratched his brow. *Damn it.*

Since Marigold's letters assured me you're a good man and a good father, I was encouraged to pursue the offer of marriage you extended. You haven't written to retract it.

He hadn't. It had seemed moot when Marigold had made it sound as though her sister was engaged to someone else. He was embarrassed to have left things open-ended, though. He was a man who cleaned up after himself, so it was his own fault that his private business was being bantered about like an amendment to an amendment. It still annoyed the hell out of him that it was happening.

He kept seeing Marigold looking that sickly green, too. *I know those looks. I've become notorious.*

Pearl seemed as cheerful as promised, and she was definitely as pretty as the portrait she'd sent. He couldn't deny he'd noticed. Maybe she wasn't quite so delicate as Marigold had implied, either, since she seemed to have made her way here in a late wagon and fared well enough in Denver for several days alone.

Of course, it sounded as though she had traded on his name with the Dudleys. Virgil couldn't blame anyone but himself for that. He had a distinct memory of telling Cecil to look after those who said they belonged to him, and he had made an offer to that woman, one that she had accurately pointed out he had failed to revoke.

He'd have to compensate her for his broken promise, at the very least.

"There you are, Virgil. Fourteen." Ed handed him the ballots. "Cast them in the Yay or Nay cigar boxes as you see fit."

"Thanks, Ed." Virgil opened the Nay and dropped them in.

He came outside to find Marigold and Pearl over by his cart. Someone was loading a bedroll and a trunk into it.

"Rufus?" Virgil asked as he recognized the young man.

"Mr. Gardner. Howdy." Rufus touched his hat and flashed his chipped tooth in a wide grin.

"How's the finger?" Virgil asked.

"Lost the tip, but the doc says it'll grow back." He held up the shortened, bandaged digit. His smile faded. "That was a joke, sir. I know it won't grow back."

Virgil must have looked as cheerful as a cornered porcupine, but he'd just noticed that Marigold's carpetbag was out of the wagon and sitting at her *feet*.

"There's still work in Quail's Creek if you want

it," Virgil told Rufus. "We're looking for hands to help build the bunkhouse and furnish it. You'll have a roof and meals through winter until we start mining again in spring."

"I'll think about that, sir. Thank you, but for now I'll stay in town…" He trailed off and glanced with speculation toward Marigold.

Pearl was chewing the corner of her mouth as she stared at Marigold.

Marigold avoided his gaze and wore red flags of war in her cheeks. Her chin was thrust out with the stubbornness of having made up her mind. It was a look he'd come to know a little too well.

"Rufus was kind enough to fetch Pearl's things from the room where she was staying," Marigold said in a high, thin voice. "I've had a word with Mrs. Dudley. She's agreed to let me continue to use it—"

Marigold's voice almost disappeared as she bent to pick up her bag.

Virgil heard her but couldn't believe he'd heard right.

As she straightened, he caught her elbow and marched her in the direction of the "rooms." They were shacks made of rough-hewn lumber set out in a row behind the saloon. They were sturdy enough against a brisk wind and snow, but they had dirt floors, no windows, and little else to recommend them except being a dry place to sleep.

"What the hell, Marigold? I was gone five minutes. What happened?"

She dropped her bag and folded her arms, pulling her elbow free of his grip so she could clasp onto it herself.

"You have to take Pearl."

"Take her where?" His growing suspicion caused his teeth to clench.

"Home with you."

"No, I don't." He was a grown man who made up his own mind.

"Pearl was the one you wanted first, Virgil. You *should* want her. She's much easier to get along with than I am, and she won't cause you all this talk." She waved toward the front of the saloon.

"People will always find something to talk about. Ignore it."

"I *can't*." Her eyes grew glossy with tears, but she only pressed her lips a moment before she continued in an unsteady voice. "You owe it to her to at least give her the chance you gave me. Take her home and see how you two get on."

"Just like that?" His whole chest felt carved out. "You're backing out on me?" He couldn't find words for how betrayed he felt. How rejected.

Was what he offered her not good enough? Was that it? He was prepared to give her his home and a right to his share in the company. He wanted her to be the mother of his children. If that wasn't enough, he didn't know what was.

You're nothing. Hear me?

"You really want me to marry your sister. That's really what you want?" He simply couldn't believe it. "You promised my children that you would be their mother."

"You promised my sister that you would be her husband," she snapped back. "And I don't want a husband. I told you that the day we met."

Virgil rocked back on his heels, nearly bowled onto his ass by that kick in the gut.

"If you marry Pearl, I would still be an auntie to your children. I could come back to camp to help her with them if that was something you wanted, but you have to give her a chance, Virgil." Her arms were crossed so tight, her hands were about to meet in front. "It's not as if you and I…" She swallowed. "Fell in love… Is it?"

Her question hung in the air so long, he thought time itself had stopped. He couldn't speak. He could only stand there immovable as the mountains. He was cold to the bone, as though glaciers weighed in all his joints.

You're nothing.

"No." He took no satisfaction in the way she reacted as if he'd struck her.

"Wait," she said as he started to turn away. She offered him a handful of the company's promissory notes. "Take this back to the men. I can't accept it now."

It was her wedding gift from his partners. He stared so hard at it the papers should have caught fire in her hands.

"What the hell will you live on?"

"Rufus has agreed to loan me twenty dollars until—"

"Rufus!" That claim-jumping little fuck.

"I know I still owe you for the stagecoach ticket," she said with agitation, shaking the notes at him. "As soon as I find a job, I'll continue to pay down my debt to you."

"My bride is here. Your debt for the ticket no

longer needs to be repaid. I'll settle up with the men. Keep that as payment for minding my children all summer." He pivoted and walked away.

CHAPTER TWENTY-THREE

Marigold had already said her goodbye to Pearl, insisting that she visit the camp and make a decision for herself as to whether to marry Virgil.

"I can't marry him," she had said. "I would always wonder if he would have preferred you. I'm sure he will." Marigold waved them off with a brave smile.

Once the cart had pulled away—without a backward look from Virgil—Marigold turned into her drafty box of a room, locked the door, and fell to the dirt to cry her heart out.

She had never felt so abandoned! Or betrayed. She didn't know which one of them she resented more, Virgil for taking Pearl or the other way around. Or herself, for all her past mistakes, making her an impossible choice for Virgil.

She *didn't* want a husband. Not once she realized her past was always going to cause him strife, too. Of course, if he had said he loved her—

But he hadn't. Because he *didn't* love her, which was the real source of her heartbreak. She had hoped right up to the last second that he would say, *I can't marry Pearl. You're the one I want. I love you.*

He had only turned into the hard, practical man life had made him and took her at her word, throwing money at her as though…

She turned her face into her bent elbow, sobbing

with humiliation, never been made to feel so cheap. He had already paid her to mind his children. They had agreed on her wage before she left for Quail's Creek with him. For him to give her so much money *now*, after she'd given him her body and her heart and her sister… It felt as though he was paying for something else entirely.

If only she had thrown it back at him! But she didn't have that luxury, did she? No, she was truly starting over now.

All she had ever wanted, from the time her parents had died, was a sense of permanence again. Security. A home. *Love.*

Every time she tried to achieve any of those things, she wound up discarded and bereft. It was beyond disheartening. How would she carry on? What sort of life was she to have *now*?

"Missus Davis?" Rufus's voice called out right before a light knock sounded on her door.

"I—" Her voice was a garbled choke. She fought back her convulsive sobs as she searched out her handkerchief and blew her nose, trying to regain her composure. "I don't need a loan after all, Rufus," she called, voice high and thin. "But thank you."

"Oh." He sounded disappointed. "Well, that's fine, but there are a couple of fellas here. I told them you write letters for men who can't. They wondered if you'd be willing?"

Marigold shifted to set her back against the wall and took a few shaken breaths as she continued mopping her face. The last thing she wished to do right now was take dictation, but sitting in the dirt wasn't likely to improve her situation, was it? She had brought her writing things in case she wanted to add a few lines before posting her letter to Pearl.

Oh, Pearl. Her letter had proudly announced, *By the time you receive this, I'll be Mrs. Gardner.*

She found a dry edge on her sleeve and pressed that under her leaking eyes but didn't let her emotions collapse again. Self-pity was another luxury she couldn't afford. It was time to take stock and think.

Writing letters was hardly a living, not for twenty-five cents a page, but it was a foothold toward supporting herself. Perhaps the barber would let her sweep hair and learn how to trim. Perhaps there was a woman in town who needed help with her children. Was there a schoolhouse that needed a teacher? She could teach miners to read and write if she was deemed too disreputable to teach children.

With the tiniest spark of resilience coming to life in her breast, she called, "Will you give me a minute, please, Rufus? I need to wash my face."

• • •

Virgil wanted to despise Pearl Martin, he really did. If she hadn't turned up—

If he had only written one stupid letter…

Damn it, it had happened. Marigold had rejected him, but he was still getting what he needed, wasn't he? He had someone to mind his children.

Would she be up to that task?

She was proving to be an amiable companion, especially to someone who was as sour as a green apple. There had been no fussing for new shoes or flashing of underwear, no stroppy dickering or purchasing of cushions. When they passed the tree where he'd first wondered if Marigold was pregnant, he thought to ask Pearl if she felt all right—which was also when he realized they'd barely spoken since leaving the saloon.

"Am I traveling too fast? You'll tell me if it's too much for your stomach."

"Oh, I'm not like Marigold. She's always been a poor traveler," she said with a pity-filled shake of her head. "No, this is a lovely change after the horse and wagon to Denver. That felt endless. This is pretty country, too. It's nice to see so much of it so quickly."

He couldn't tell if she was being sincere or cheeky. She turned her face up to admire the bright glaciers hanging in their valleys.

The resemblance of her profile to Marigold's was so strong, a slashing sensation scored into his chest.

"Marigold's letters spoke highly of you and your company," she continued. "I'm looking forward to meeting everyone, especially your children."

"They're still missing their mother." Now he would have to explain Harley to her and explain her to them. His heart sank. "Bringing you home instead of Marigold will be difficult." Nettie would disown him. He couldn't blame her for it, either.

"I tried to persuade Marigold to come with us. She said we need a chance to get to know one another without her there." Her tone was flat and pensive before it lifted to something more optimistic. "But I'll assure the children that she'll be back with us in no time. We could manage that, couldn't we? I understood Marigold to have her own room, so once…" She cut herself off and blushed, pretty with it, especially when she dropped her long, thick lashes.

He looked to where the mules were heading while his brain tried to imagine sleeping next to this woman while Marigold was in the room beside theirs. Ever. It wouldn't conjure.

"I'm not likely to run for marshal. You should know that."

"Oh? I'm sure you'd make a fine one, but it sounds like a dangerous occupation, so that's probably for the best."

She wasn't disappointed?

"Are you a suffragist like Marigold?" he asked.

"I'd certainly like the vote, but watching Marigold and our uncle put themselves through wringers over politics has always been agonizing. They scold me for not being as supportive as I could be, but I hate watching them get hurt. There's no avoiding it in those sorts of blood sports. It was the same with Marigold's divorce—"

She cut herself off, glancing guiltily at him.

"I won't gossip about her, but I was glad when she found this situation as your housekeeper and governess. She's said many times that she didn't want to marry again. That's why it was a shock when you said she had accepted your proposal."

Why *had* she accepted it? His children? Embarrassment after he seduced her at the pool? He brooded on that for the rest of their journey.

He was glad he wasn't pulling a big, loaded cart with the oxen, the way he had with Marigold. They would have had to stop overnight. The weather held and the moon came up big and bright, so he could see to push on the last few miles. They reached Quail's Creek under a sea of stars so thick, they streaked the sky like milk.

As Virgil drew the cart right up to the cabin, everyone poured out, children included. But their cheer of welcome abruptly ceased. Their faces blanked with confusion as they saw that Pearl, not Marigold, was with him.

"Marriage really does change a person," Owen said.

"You must be Owen." Pearl stepped down from the cart and held out her hand to him. "I'm Pearl Martin, Marigold's sister."

"Ohhh," Emmett and Ira said under their breath.

"Emmett? It's good to meet you. And you must be Stoney. Ira? Hello. And you're Tom?"

"Levi, ma'am. Tom's minding the office." Like everyone else, Levi was looking between her and Virgil with confusion.

"But you're not the size of a boy. I thought you must be one of the men." Pearl's smile told Levi she was teasing him.

He smiled with flattered humor and ducked his head.

"Hello, Nettie! Goodness, Marigold has told me what a good friend you've been to her. She stayed in Denver for a few days, but I hope you'll be my guiding light here, the way you have been for her. And here's Harley. Well, you are a button, aren't you? Will you come see me?"

Harley went straight from Ira into her arms. No one asked Virgil for lemon drops. They all stared in awe at Pearl.

That ought to have made Virgil happy or relieved or something, but it left him feeling hollow and terrible.

"What...?" Emmett scratched under his chin.

"This is what Marigold wanted," he muttered, not in a mood to explain how things had gone so far off track he didn't know where he was. "Help me with Pearl's things."

That's when he realized Marigold hadn't even taken her bedroll. She had likely left it on purpose for her sister, but now she would be sleeping on a cold, dirt floor in Denver. Damn it.

At least he'd left her with some money. He'd been furious when he had walked away and probably not kind about it, but he hadn't been able to leave her as destitute as she'd been the day they'd met.

Within a few minutes, he'd kicked out the men, asking Owen to put away the cart and mules for him. He stood awkwardly by the door as Pearl examined his modest house.

"This is very cozy and— Is that my portrait?" She moved into the small bedroom. "Marigold found a frame for it."

"Papa did," Nettie said helpfully. "So she would feel at home here."

"Oh?"

Virgil didn't try to interpret her tone.

"Have you children eaten?" he asked as he poked his nose into the stew pot on the stove. He and Pearl hadn't eaten since midday.

"At the cookhouse, Pa. Ira brought that for you and M—Miss Martin."

"Please call me Pearl, Levi." She emerged

without her gloves and coat. "It smells good. Shall I serve it?"

After they ate and washed up, Pearl helped the children ready themselves for bed.

"I'm bushed," she said as the children filed up to the loft. "I'll turn in, too, if you don't mind. Good night, Virgil."

"Good night, Pearl." He stepped outside to walk the bucket to the stream, filling it for morning. He was also bushed, but restless. Tense. Not in the way that Marigold made him tense, either. This was the tension of having screwed up. Of wanting to walk off his mistakes while knowing he couldn't walk far enough to get away from them. This was the kind that couldn't be fixed.

Which didn't make sense because things were actually fine. Pearl was exactly what he had wanted when he had advertised for a wife. She was kind and the children were taking to her. Marigold didn't want him, but Pearl did.

Accept it.

As he undressed for bed, he heard Nettie upstairs in the loft, sniffling as she told Harley, "M-meego isn't h-here."

Ah, shit.

He stepped outside his door and whispered, "Nettie!"

Her teary face peered over the rail.

"Do you want to sleep in here with me tonight?"

She nodded, and Harley said, "Me."

"Yes, bring him, too."

Levi poked his head over the rail.

Virgil was really fucking standing in it, wasn't he?

"You, too." He jerked his head.

Minutes later, his children were arranged around him like a litter of puppies, all drifting off while he lay awake, throat hot and eyes salty behind his closed lids.

CHAPTER TWENTY-FOUR

"What did you do?" Stoney demanded.

"*Nothing*. Her sister showed up, and Marigold said I ought to at least bring Pearl back here with me to see if it will work." Virgil shoveled gravel into the sluice box as he spoke.

He was standing ankle deep in bitterly cold water, trying to freeze out the ache that had taken hold in his chest. He was working alongside Emmett and Stoney and Owen, just like their days in California. If they'd still been working for someone else, Virgil would have driven a pickaxe through his own skull, but they were doing this for themselves. It didn't make it any easier, but it made it less an exercise in resentment.

The part where his partners got their noses into his business was deeply unwelcome, though. He was plenty twisted up in recriminations and questions without their mining for more.

He put his back into his work, trying to drown them out with the scrape and slough of the shovel into wet gravel.

"So are you going to marry her?" Emmett asked.

"Pearl? My children need a mother, don't they?" His back was screaming, and his arms were wilted as onion tops. His palms were blistering, but he stayed on the shovel.

"What's Marigold going to do in Denver?" Emmett pressed. "You shouldn't have left her there by herself."

"She wanted to stay."

"Marigold has never been short of suitors." Owen shook the box. "She'll find herself a husband soon enough."

"She doesn't want one!" Virgil shouted.

All three men straightened from what they were doing to look at him.

"Say it louder, Virge. I don't think the rest of the camp heard you," Owen said mildly.

Sometimes Virgil wanted to smack a shovel across Owen's smirk, he really did.

"She had a rough end to her marriage and changed her mind about getting into another one. Maybe she was already having doubts, and when Pearl turned up, she saw her chance to back out. I don't know what made her stay there, but I didn't walk away from her. *She* turned her back on *me*." Figuratively. He had actually done the physical walking away.

He hadn't walked away from her, though. He'd needed distance from that sensation inside him that had said, *Please don't reject me. Recognize me. Want me.*

He knew what that painful longing was. A desire to be loved. There was no forcing such a thing, either. That only begot rejection. Even if you did earn the love of someone, it didn't mean you wouldn't fail and disappoint them. He'd never saved his mother from his father's wrath, had he? And Clara had been so disillusioned, she'd taken up with another man.

Look at his children, crawling into his bed for solace last night. No matter how hard he tried, he always let down the people he cared about.

"How will she live if she doesn't marry?" Emmett asked.

"Is she going to work in a saloon, do you think?" Owen asked. "She'd be good at that."

Virgil jabbed his shovel into the stream bed so he wouldn't run it through his friend. "I'm warning you, Owen."

"I mean—" Owen held up a hand. "She'd be good at running a business. She has a head for ledgers and counts your pennies like they're her own. If I ever get away from here for more than a day, I'm going to open a saloon of my own. I'd trust Marigold to take charge of it."

"You want to give her a roomful of unruly drunks to manage?" Virgil's ire climbed several more notches.

"I'd teach her to shoot first."

Virgil swore under his breath while the rest of them started bantering about how dangerous she was with a chamber pot.

He was dog tired and discouraged to the bone when he limped home in the heavy rain that had cut their workday short. There was a warm glow of a candle in the window, and he was looking forward to seeing his children, but his steps were heavy and slow. Marigold wasn't there.

"The children said they usually eat without you." Pearl paused in serving their dinner when he entered.

"We were all soaked through, so we called it a day." He moved into his room to change into dry clothes. When he came out, he said, "The days are getting shorter, too, so I'll be home for dinner more anyway. How was your day?"

"Good." She smiled but avoided his eyes. "Nettie and Harley walked me down to meet Mr. Gristle and Mr. Yeller. They're both full of stories."

"That they are." Did he detect something in her tone? If he did, he had to wait while the children had monopolized the conversation with the day's trappings and a new knitting stitch and additions to Harley's growing vocabulary.

When the children were finally ready for bed, Nettie hesitated at the bottom of the ladder to the loft. Harley stood next to her, holding her hand and looking at her expectantly. Levi scratched his elbow and pretended he was interested in the underside of the loft.

"My bed?" Virgil guessed.

Nettie nodded.

"One more night." He was turning into the biggest duck-down pillow. "I'll tuck you in, but no giggling or you go straight upstairs."

"Yes, Papa." They all beamed and hurried into his room.

He was tired and sore and could have used a good night's sleep, not a wrassle through the night while they all wriggled and kicked and hogged up the covers, but he liked the feel of their limbs across his and the warmth of their bodies curled into him. He liked knowing they were safe.

Was Marigold safe? He didn't know, and he couldn't stand the not knowing.

He gave them each a pat and kiss on the forehead, trying to ignore the yawning chasm that opened inside him. Marigold had given him this, he acknowledged. He could hug and kiss his children and tell them he loved them. Instead of fearing him, they looked to him as their protector.

But he'd upended their world again by not bringing her home. Why the hell hadn't she come home? Because, as nice as Pearl seemed, he didn't want her. He didn't know what the hell he was going to do, but he knew he couldn't marry Pearl. She wasn't Marigold, and Marigold was the only one he wanted.

"Straight to sleep now," he warned the children in a voice that was thick with emotion.

He closed the door and glanced to where Marigold had always sat to do her sewing.

Pearl was there now, turning over the wishing stone in her hands.

"Nettie told me one of the men gave this to Marigold. It sounds as though everyone here is very fond of her."

"They are." He lowered to the bench across from her, thinking he ought to say, *I'm sure they'll warm to you, too*, but his chest felt as though a wishing stone the size of this house sat on it.

"I forgot what it was like to see her happy," she said wistfully. "When I saw her yesterday morning, that was my first thought. *Look how happy she is!* I thought it was because she was glad to see me, but it wasn't just me. She's been happy here, hasn't she?"

He grimaced slightly and rubbed his hands on his thigh. "I guess. On and off?"

She made a faint noise of amusement. "Mr. Gristle and Mr. Yeller told me about some of her misadventures. The bear?" She gave a little shudder.

"But that's so like Marigold to give no sense to what danger she's in." Her smile turned unutterably sad. "I said I wouldn't gossip about her, but has she told you about her divorce?"

"Some," he said gravely. "It sounds as though she was treated very unfairly."

"Very." She nodded. "But she was hurt and angry and wouldn't settle for anything but being right, which was absolutely to her detriment."

"Marigold?" he asked with feigned surprise.

"Mmm." Her smile kept turning itself upside down. "Ben wanted to reconcile. It wasn't fair for me to say she ought to do that, but I could see what fighting him was costing her. She was digging her own grave, risking everything. It didn't make sense to me that she refused to forgive him, but now…" She swallowed. "Now I understand how scorned she felt. How unwanted." Her lashes lifted over solemn eyes.

Oh, shit. His stomach tensed, anticipating a blow.

"I can't marry you, Virgil. Not when you're in love with my sister."

Her words stung sharp as that whip of his father's. The thoughts that followed were each their own lash. He did love Marigold. She had rejected him. He was nothing to her. Pearl knew it. Everyone did. He was nothing.

"I think she loves you, too."

He negated that with a shake of his head. "She said she didn't."

"Exactly like that? She said she didn't love you?"

"She said *we* didn't love *each other*. I'm not talking about this anymore." He rose and turned to the door.

"Virgil!"

Her voice was so like Marigold's when she was cross, it stopped him in his tracks.

"Did you tell her that you love her?" she asked.

"No." He was still swallowing the shame of being rejected.

"She thought she was in love once before, you know. Her husband threw her over for another woman and took the home she had made with him. The house our father's money had paid for. She was broken right in half after that. Do you honestly think she would bare her heart to you before she knew how *you* really felt?"

He had to push the heel of his palm into his chest bone, such a splitting sensation arrived there.

"You maligned her character to this whole valley—"

"That was a misunderstanding." He spun back around. "I owned up to my mistake and apologized. And that's why I wanted to marry her. So no one could say she was anything but my wife. I wanted her to have my name and—" Everything. He had wanted to give her *everything* he had, but he had withheld his heart. Because he'd been scared.

"All these men courting her…" She set down the wishing stone and linked her fingers together. "She had plenty to choose from. She had a job, and she had sworn not to marry. So why would she agree to marry anyone at all, least of all a man who had hurt her, unless she trusted and loved him with her whole heart?"

Well, *fuck*.

His own heart tore right open as he saw the

mistake he'd made. He'd been so blinded by his anger and hurt, he hadn't seen that Marigold was as fearful of rejection as he was, so she'd gone and done it first.

"I should have seen how she felt about you." Pearl's brow pleated, and tears came into her eyes. "I was thinking of myself. Thinking…" She used her finger to turn the wishing stone in a circle. "She's just so infuriating, sometimes. Especially when she thinks she's right."

He could have laughed at that if he wasn't suffocating in the tragedy of his own wrongness.

"I was angry with her for pushing Hiram on me. I couldn't stay in Topeka, either. She made you sound like such a good prospect." She looked up, mouth quivering. "I thought I could be like her. Brave enough to come here and start over on my own terms. I thought I could marry you and look after *her* for a change. But she's ahead of me here, too. She turned this into a home I could love, but I can't stop feeling as though I'm taking what's hers. And she deserves good things, Virgil. She does."

She used the inside of her wrist to swipe away a tear, so pretty in her sorrow, he thought someday, some hapless man was going to be completely undone by her. Not him, though. His heart belonged to another. He only felt kinship because they were both miserable and angry with themselves for hurting the one person they loved most.

"Will you please go get my sister?" she implored.

"I will." He didn't know how he would make up with Marigold and bring her home, but he would. Because he loved her and he couldn't live without her.

• • •

Virgil got underway at first light, tempted to ride on horseback for speed, but settling on the mules and the little wagon so he wouldn't have to double Marigold all the way back here.

It was still raining, but he ignored the discomfort. He deserved to suffer for leaving her in Denver, enduring whatever gossip he'd stirred up with his stupidity. It must have looked like he had cast her off in favor of her sister, which was about the worst thing he could do to her, given all she'd been through.

God, he was sorry for that. He would have to find a way to fix it. He wasn't a man for making public speeches, but he wanted people to know she wasn't second-best or a convenient arrangement for the sake of his children. She was a remarkable woman who would make him the luckiest man alive if she would be his wife.

He needed to get to her and say that. Make her believe it. Make *everyone* believe it.

He realized that rushing noise in his ears was actually the roar of the swollen creek as he approached the bridge he'd built. The mules halted a few feet in front of it, refusing to cross, danged stubborn things.

Virgil clucked his tongue and snapped the reins.

They didn't move.

"Damn it, I have a woman to win back." He got down from the wagon and walked out in front of the animals, drawing the reins with him as he stepped onto the bridge, trying to tug them across.

They stayed exactly where they were.

"I am not fucking arguing with you two. She's hurting. Do you understand that? And I can't bear it." It tore him apart, filling him with urgency to *get there*. "Take your mule asses across this bridge—"

The bank gave way beneath his feet.

He somehow kept a slippery grip on the reins as he slid onto his ass against the soggy embankment.

Flopping onto his stomach, he clasped the wet leather in both hands and shouted, "Back, back!"

The mules backed up, pulling him up the broken edge of the creek onto solid ground.

He was covered in mud, shaking, and trying to catch his breath, but all he could think as he stared at the broken bridge and rushing water was that he still had to get to Marigold.

But how?

CHAPTER TWENTY-FIVE

Writing letters for the men in Quail's Creek had been hard enough. They'd often been homesick and disillusioned by the difficulty of a goldminer's life. Here in Denver, they were destitute and begging for money so they could go home. Rather than turn anyone away, Marigold had started accepting a potato or a cup of cornmeal or even an empty cup, reasoning that she needed dishes as badly as she needed something to put in them.

Once the Dudleys realized her service could bring in customers—some broke, but also curiosity-seekers who were so starved for entertainment they would watch a woman write a letter—the saloon-keepers had allowed her to work at one of their gambling tables so long as it wasn't needed by anyone who wanted to play cards.

Marigold's promise to give the house 10 percent of her fee had also greased the way to their acceptance of her working here. Not that the forty cents she'd given them yesterday went very far, but she happened to know Mrs. Dudley liked china cups. She would give her the one with the floral design that she had just accepted in payment for a very morose tale about an infected leg and a dead horse.

Good thing she was equally morose, or this story would have made her cry.

Marigold shed plenty of tears as it was, all through the night. She kept dwelling on her conversation with Virgil three days ago. Should she have admitted she loved him? Should she have gone back with them and let him choose between her and Pearl? Maybe they could move to Utah and practice polygamy. Ira had said his mother was one of seven sister wives.

Of course, that would mean Marigold had to share Virgil, and she didn't want to. That was the truth of it. She loved him and wanted to be his wife, and he had chosen to take her sister home without hardly any argument at all. Because he didn't love her.

Rufus had been perplexed at the way they'd left so summarily without her. *Mr. Gardner seemed so sweet on you. He was always easier to talk to when you two were getting along.*

She had always felt sweet when they were getting along. He'd had a way of making her feel important and respected and needed. Not just for his children, but by him. He'd made her sexual feelings seem natural, too. He had never berated her for enjoying his attentions. He'd reveled in it. Her eyes still stung at how welcome and healing his attitude had been.

But that was another reason she'd had to send him home without her. Every time she thought of being there with him, she knew she would covet her sister's husband. She might even lure him into adultery with her.

No. She had made the right choice.

"With love, from your son, Benson Hedley," Marigold repeated as she finished up the letter with a final dot of ink.

She folded the letter and tucked the upper

triangle into the pocket she had made at the bottom, then wrote the direction the miner gave her onto the front.

"Good luck," she said as she handed it off to him. "Goodness," she exclaimed as she noticed there were several men standing about, many with drinks in their hands. Word was getting out. "Who's next? You, sir?"

She set out a clean sheet of paper and waved at the chair set far enough away she wasn't asphyxiated by anyone who happened to have noxious breath, which was sadly most of them.

"Let me put this cup away." She leaned down to tuck the cup and saucer safely into her bag.

When she straightened, there was a rock on her blank sheet of paper. It was about the size of a lemon drop, one that had been crunched and suckled until it was pocked and misshapen, yet also smooth. She recognized it exactly as her body recognized the belt and the wet, mud-caked trousers and filthy boots of the man who had come to stand beside her.

She couldn't seem to make herself lift her eyes to him, though. He would see the instant wetness in hers. The despair and the longing and, if he looked hard enough, the *hope* that was trying to flicker to life inside her.

"Hey! No cutting in line," a voice called from further back.

"It's Gardner," someone else said with resigned disgust.

"From Quail's Creek? Those fellas always think they can do that. What do you need a letter for, Virgil? Can't you write your own?"

"I'm here to propose marriage," he said, voice so strong and deep and clear it made Marigold's heart lurch. Had she heard him correctly?

"You should definitely get in line, then," someone muttered.

He didn't. He flicked his hand at the man who'd taken the seat across from her. The man dove out of the way, and Virgil sat so he was eye to eye with her, making it impossible for her to look anywhere but at him.

There was a streak of mud on his cheek above his beard and his hair was wet when he removed his hat to set it on the table. Even his shirt was soaked, she saw, as he removed his dirty jacket and let it flop against the chair back. His brow was heavy and grave, his mouth tight, but he was still so handsome, her throat closed up with helplessness.

For a few seconds, they only sat with their gazes locked while she tried to absorb what he had said. Why? Why her and not Pearl?

"Wh—Where's Pearl?" she asked, throat so dry she could only rasp out a whisper.

"Pearl's at home, safe and sound. So are the children. But you're not. That's not sitting well with any of us. It's killing me." His scar was a bright white line in a face that was frowning with concern.

The line of men had shifted to crowd around them, so everyone could see and hear, but he wasn't scowling at any of them for witnessing him in this state. He was looking on her as if she was the only person in the room and he was worried about her.

She bit her lip and looked to where she was nearly twisting her fingers off her hands in her lap.

"Is it really marriage you don't want? Or marriage to a man who doesn't love you?" he asked gravely. "Because I do love you, Marigold. I should have said it before I left."

A fiery jolt shot through her, as though she'd been struck by lightning. Was that really true?

There was a murmur through the gathered crowd that made her cringe, reminding her she was making a spectacle of both of them. Her eyes were so hot and blurred she couldn't see him when she looked up. But Virgil wasn't letting the public nature of his declaration bother him. In fact, he stood up tall and repeated, loudly for all to hear, "I love you, Marigold. You're the *only* woman I want to marry."

"I don't see why." Her insides were scraped hollow, her composure hanging by a thread, but the tiniest spark of hope was glinting inside her. "Pearl is b-better."

"Pearl is sweet enough to make my teeth ache, but she isn't *you*, is she?" He put his hand on the table, palm up. "Will you please come home with me, where you belong?"

"Virgil," she choked in protest. Her eyes were leaking so much, she couldn't see.

"Here you are, ma'am. That's clean." Someone offered a handkerchief. "I was going to see if you'd take that for a letter."

"Oh, for heaven's sake." She took it and tried to dry her streaming eyes and jammed the rough cotton against her running nose. "I'm trying to—" She lowered the balled handkerchief into her lap. "I can't be the woman who steals her sister's husband." Her voice rang with the agony of her impossible position.

"No one would respect me, least of all you. I remember what you said when you wrote to Pearl to ask her to marry you. You said you don't abide liars, cheats, and thieves, and I—"

"You're all of those things," he cut in flatly.

She dragged in a gasp that felt like fire and sat back in her chair, stung to her bones.

"You lied when you said we didn't love each other. You cheated me out of three days of marriage we could have already had. And you've stolen my heart." The hard line of his mouth slowly softened into a wry smile, one that dawned wide across his face and seemed to reach straight into her heart like sunshine, filling her with his love. "Now, how do you plan to make that up to me?"

Oh, this man.

She was still fighting the tears that wanted to leak from her eyes, but they were turning from desolation into something more hopeful.

She couldn't believe he was doing this, declaring himself so publicly. Part of her was saying, *Be careful. You've been here before*, but he wasn't trying to manipulate her. He was trying to convince her.

He was making it clear to all and sundry that she was someone worth loving. Someone he would fight for. Because he loved her. Really *loved* her.

Her throat held a huge lump that wouldn't allow her to speak.

"You're not any of those things anyway." He used one bent knuckle to brush away the tear tracking down her cheek. "Not deep down. Not when it counts. You could prove it by being truthful about whether you love me," he added in a low rumble.

"I do." Her heart shuddered as she let her love break through the log jam inside her. Her love for him poured out in fresh tears and a shaken declaration of, "I love you so much I thought I would die without you."

A look flashed on his face that mirrored her own agonized joy.

He pulled her onto her feet and into his arms, holding her close and hard. His hand cupped the back of her head, and his mouth pressed to her temple, her cheek. She lifted her mouth, and his lips were on hers, urgent and fervent and cherishing.

Dimly she was aware of sound around them, but in this second, Virgil's kiss was her whole world. *Virgil* was. Her heart was thudding, and her insides were quaking as she let her love for him suffuse her whole being.

More crucially, she allowed the belief that he loved her back to pour through her. He'd had thousands of paths and choices he could have made that wouldn't have led him here to her today. He wanted *her*, and the knowledge of that had her clinging to the back of his shirt as they kissed for long enough that the whoops grew to a volume they couldn't ignore.

He lifted his head, and she ducked her face into his chest, embarrassed by their public display.

"Serve a round on me, Cecil," he called out.

There was another whoop, and the men disbursed from gawking at them.

"Damned Peeping Toms," Virgil muttered, still holding her close and rubbing her back. He touched his mouth to her ear, asking, "You'll marry me?"

"Are you sure, Virgil? What about running for marshal?"

"I don't want to be a marshal." He huffed an exasperated breath. "Once I won, I'd have to arrest myself for the murder of everyone who had brought up your name during elections."

She snorted and petted the front of his shirt. "That is a conundrum."

"One I could avoid by not running at all."

"And Pearl?" she asked with concern.

"She can stay with us until she finds her own husband." He sounded unbothered. "She won't want for offers."

"You wouldn't mind?"

"You'll be happier if she's close by, won't you? I want you to be happy."

"I am happy." Such a jubilant feeling was dawning through her she could hardly contain it. She was in love with a good, caring man who loved her back. It was truly the most wonderous moment in her life because it was real. This time it was real. She slid possessive arms up around his neck and leaned her body into his in a most unseemly way, considering they were in public.

He still didn't seem to mind. He kept one arm around her back while his other hand cupped the side of her neck. He looked on her with eyes that were polished silver, glittering with humor and something bright and admiring and hot. It filled her with confidence and worth and such optimism her heart was liable to burst.

"Let's go find Woodrow and make this official." His thumb caressed her throat. "We'll spend the night at the hotel, then I need to scare up tack for the mules before we can leave for home. I rode in bareback for you, you know."

"Here I thought you shouting at everyone that you loved me was the most romantic thing you'd done for me today," she teased and pulled away to gather her things. When she picked up the gnarled nugget and tried to hand it to him, he shook his head.

"I want you to keep it."

"No," she protested. "It's your lucky nugget. You always keep it with you." She wouldn't mess with his superstition.

"Exactly. You keep it, and I'll keep you. I'll still have all the luck it's brought to me."

"Virgil." She couldn't help but fold her fist around it and hold it against her heart. He really was a romantic.

"Ma'am? Are you ready to write my letter now?" a young man approached to ask.

"Oh, for Christ's sake. Come work at Quail's Creek, and I'll pay Marigold myself to write your damned letters. Man can't even get a minute of peace on his wedding day." Virgil started to put on his wet hat, then gave his hair a smooth. "Think I need a haircut first?"

Marigold bit back a smile.

"What's that face for?"

"Nothing." He was such an adorable grump. "Shall I trim it?"

"*No*." He scowled, then said more gently, "I like the cutting, I don't like the cut. Is this all you have?" He went back to frowning as he took her bag. "We'll have to stop at the trading post before we leave. See if we can find you something warm so I don't lose you at the first frost. Buffalo-skin bloomers, maybe."

"Hold up there, Virgil!" Mr. Dudley called as they started through the doors.

"Come on, Cecil," Virgil groused. "I'll settle up after we marry. You know I'm good for it."

"I only wanted to say…" He lifted his full glass and nodded at everyone to do the same. "Best wishes to you. May your love be true."

The men cheered and shot and tapped their empty glasses.

"Thank you." Virgil nodded and touched his hat, then looked at Marigold with all his love for her reflected in his expression, there for everyone to see, especially her. "It is true," he assured her.

And she believed him.

EPILOGUE

TWO WEEKS LATER…

Marigold woke to the press of her husband's firm erection against her bottom. His palm cupped her breast. She stretched, enjoying the caress of his warm strength against her back and legs.

He stretched at the same time. "I thought you'd never wake up," he whispered very softly against her ear. "Do you want—"

"Yes," she breathed, rolling onto her back while he shifted over her.

They both moved as quietly as possible, conscious of the children above and her sister in the next room.

As he pulled her nightdress up, Virgil slid beneath the covers. She had taken him in her mouth a few times, but he nearly always "wanted a taste" before he pressed into her.

She bit her lip as his tongue parted her folds, and he rocked his mouth against her sleepy lips. A shiver of arousal swept over her skin. She spread her legs for more, gasping as quietly as she could when she wanted to groan lustily.

Her excitement pooled as liquid heat, and she was soon pushing against his mouth in encouragement. He climbed to kiss her stomach, pushing her nightdress up and up, causing another flood of heat into her loins when he sucked on her nipples.

She was panting with desire, shakily measuring her breaths so she didn't make any audible noise. Eventually, their struggle to keep their lovemaking silent might grow old, but for now it made it all the more intense. There was something wickedly sneaky in these trysts, not to mention the eroticism of fighting their most animalistic urges, keeping their movements abbreviated and soft when they were dying to tear into each other.

Virgil emerged from beneath the covers, gasping for air. He pressed his smiling mouth to hers. Beneath the covers, she guided his swollen, slippery head against her. He pressed and...

"Ahh," she breathed, loving this sensation of him sliding deeper into her on small, pulsing thrusts, stretching her flesh and sinking in, so hard and hot and implacable.

"Shhh," he reminded as he sucked her earlobe. "Fuck, you feel so nice."

The ropes beneath their mattress rubbed and groaned as they ground pelvis to pelvis. Her inner muscles clutched at his steely shape, and her sensations increased.

"I'm so ready," he panted against her ear. "Tell me when, love."

"Harder," she urged softly. "*Please*."

His exhale was everything—struggle and torture and laughter and acute pleasure.

The bed frame squeaked and protested as he moved with more power, withdrawing and returning, hitting all those delicious places so her sex felt as though it shivered and gathered and expanded. She hugged him tighter with her thighs, and joy suddenly burst within her, sending rippling sensations through her loins and stomach and into her nipples, pressing a cry into her throat that she fought to stifle.

His mouth stuck itself to the side of her neck. He sucked while his breath hissed and his body gathered. A jolt struck him, then he was shuddering above and around her. His cock throbbed within her, on and on, suffusing both of them in sweaty ecstasy.

Finally, they released their breaths and relaxed. He made a noise against her throat that was possessive and amused, satisfied and wistful.

She turned her head to kiss him, so lazy and filled with love, it put tears in her eyes.

Despite the half light of dawn, he saw the dampness. He frowned. "What's wrong?"

"Nothing. I'm happy." She touched her mouth to his again in reassurance, then drew back, still keeping her voice pitched very low. "Is it your day to be in the office?"

"Mmm. Everyone else is working on the bunkhouse."

"Should I drop by while I'm waiting for my baking at the cookhouse?"

"You don't have to leave the warmth of the oven."

"Virgil. I'm offering to deliver you a sweet roll."

"Ah." Laughter pulled a smile into his lips as he caught up. "I thought you just did. What a healthy appetite you have, Mrs. Gardner."

"Don't you want to make love again?"

"I want to make *noise*," he assured her, pressing his weight across her as he tickled her neck with his beard.

She squirmed, and they might have made all the telling noises they'd been trying to disguise, but they heard the children above them.

"Levi! Look. It's snowing."

Sharing a rueful look, they reluctantly pulled apart and dressed to start their day.

All he wants is peace and quiet…
instead, he got Mercy.

HITCHED TO THE
GUNSLINGER

MICHELLE
USA TODAY BESTSELLING AUTHOR
McLEAN

Gray "Quick Shot" Woodson is the fastest gun west of the Mississippi. Unfortunately, he's ready to hang up his hat. Sure, being notorious has its perks. But the nomadic lifestyle—and people always tryin' to kill you—gets old real fast.

Now he just wants to find a place to retire so he can spend his days the way the good Lord intended: staring at the sunset and napping.

When his stubborn horse drags him into a hole-in-the-wall town called Desolation, something about the place calls to Gray, and he figures he might actually have a shot at a sleepy retirement.

His optimism lasts about a minute and a half.

Soon he finds himself embroiled in a town vendetta and married to a woman named Mercy. Who, judging by her aggravating personality, doesn't know the meaning of her own name. In fact, she's downright impossible. But dang it if his wife isn't irresistible. If only she'd stop trying to steal his guns to go after the bad guys herself.

There goes his peace and quiet...

USA Today *bestselling author Eva Devon's bright, lively tale about daring to be more than just a lady…*

THE DUKE'S SECRET CINDERELLA

Charlotte Browne could just kick herself. What on earth possessed her to tell the Duke of Rockford that she is a lady? But something about the duke's handsomeness and kind intelligence makes Charlotte blurt out the teeniest, tiniest falsehood. Now, it's too late to admit she's just plain Charlotte of no particular importance—with cinder-stained hands, a wretched stepfather, and no prospects for marriage.

Rafe Dorchester, Duke of Rockford, has done what every self-respecting duke must do—avoid marriage at all costs. But the only thing stronger than the duke is his mother, and she lays down the highest ultimatum: he'll need to find a duchess. Immediately. Only, when he calls on a potential bride, he instead finds the pert, fresh-faced Lady Charlotte. Rafe was warned to never mix the business of marriage with pleasure, but when it comes to Lady Charlotte…oh, business would be a splendid pleasure.

Except, Charlotte knows that true life is nothing like the penny romances she reads. The duke can't actually end up with a maid. When her vile stepbrother catches her coming from the gardens with the duke close on her heels, Charlotte knows just what he'll do. And there's only one way to save them all from scandal…

*What a lady wants could
cost her everything...*

A
SCOUNDREL
OF HER OWN

USA TODAY BESTSELLING AUTHOR
STACY REID

Lady Ophelia Darby exists in two worlds. In one, she is the impudent, willful daughter of a powerful marquess and darling of the ton. In the other, she moves through the underworld's shadows as songstress Lady Starlight, protected only by the notoriously wealthy scoundrel Devlin Byrne. But when she stumbles upon her beloved father's darkest secrets, the line between her two worlds quickly blurs. Now she needs the help of the one man a lady should never trust.

Devlin Byrne stands on the edge of London society, knowing he will never be accepted. No one else knows that his obscene wealth and ruthlessness aren't without purpose. Or that his purpose has golden-brown eyes that shimmer with mischief, the palest of skin, and a lush mouth that beckons to be kissed, and deeply. But having Ophelia is only the beginning of Devlin's plans.

It's undeniable that Devlin Byrne is a dangerous temptation—but just as Ophelia begins to trust him, maybe even fall for him, she discovers she's not the only one with secrets. And his would lead her down more than just the path of scandal...

The Prospector's Only Prospect is a charming and heartwarming Western historical romance with a happy ending. However, the story includes some elements that might not be suitable for every reader. Divorce in character backstory; infidelity in character backstory; and dangerous survival situations are included in the novel. Readers who may be sensitive to these elements, please take note.